IGLOO HIGH

JACINTHE DESSUREAULT

Demiurge
Underground

Legal deposit – Bibliothèque et Archives nationales du Québec, 2019
Legal deposit – Library and Archives Canada, 2019

ISBN 978-1-9994431-0-8 (paperback)
ISBN 978-1-9994431-1-5 (ebook)

For Esmée—with love

PLEASE STATE YOUR EMERGENCY

Ella spent the first twelve minutes of the CPR presentation lost in thought, wondering how she could persuade her dad to get her a new cell phone, despite the contractual period not yet being over. The dang thing had been crapping out on her way too often lately, especially while texting, which was totally unacceptable. The auto-correct was also getting more senile than before, making her sound like a real dork as—she could swear—it would change words even after she hit *SEND*.

Today was September 7th. The school year had just begun, and the St. Mary's High School senior had scheduled in her new agenda book to badger her dad on Sunday, right after brunch, to get her a new cell phone. But if her silly and anti-quated two-year-old phone kept acting up like it had been doing all day, she might have to campaign sooner, despite the timing being less than ideal. To achieve maximum success in her endeavors, Ella liked to pace herself, and she hated the thought of having to pressure her dad again so soon after begging for last week's shopping spree.

A sudden jab underneath her ribcage brought Ella back to reality. Her friend Sandy, who was sitting next to her on the gym's rubbery floor, legs in a pretzel, had ceased chipping the flaking burgundy nail polish off her fingernails and was now elbowing Ella to get her attention. Ella turned to her friend. Sandy tilted her head and arched her eyebrows, trying to tell Ella to look at Mr. Moog, the gym teacher giving the CPR presentation. Ella looked up at the man, who was staring at her, along with every other student in the gym.

"Would you like me to repeat the question, Ms. Briggs?" asked the teacher in a monotone voice.

Mr. Moog was a controlled dude, who never lost his cool. He was tall and broad-shouldered, a real bodybuilder type. He could have been a martial arts star—or an assassin—you could easily picture him strangling someone with his bare hands. He inspired fear and respect in most students, who figured it was best to not mess with the guy. To Ella, however, he was just another boring old guy on the aging teaching staff.

Ella kept calm, trying to guess the question Mr. Moog had asked her. It had to be related to a medical act of some sort, from pounding on someone's chest to giving mouth-to-mouth to some disgusting stranger with revolting breath and who hadn't bathed in ages.

Ewww.

Seeing she was stalling, Mr. Moog added, "My question was, 'What do you do, Ms. Briggs?'"

What do I do? How very not helpful.

"That's a good question," Ella replied diplomatically, to buy herself some time. She pretended to think while leaning her head towards Sandy to give her friend a chance to whisper her a clue. Sandy mumbled something while hiding her mouth behind her hand, but—*dammit!*—Ella caught none of it. Today was going to be a long day.

Mr. Moog looked slightly annoyed. He cut to the chase.

"The full question was, 'Someone's lying on the ground in front of you, unconscious. What do you do?'"

Oh, *that*! She could answer that.

"I'd call 911. If I had a working phone, that is," replied Ella.

"Someone already called 911."

"Oh, right." *Fudge.* "But it never hurts to double check, no?"

"No. I mean, yes. You'd be wasting time. And we've already established that time is crucial when someone needs CPR. So, Ms. Briggs—focus—what would you do?"

Ella tried to focus and come up with a proper answer so that the gym teacher would get off her back and pick on another student. But since she hadn't been paying attention at all, this was difficult.

"I'd ask the person who called 911 to take over."

Some students chuckled. Mr. Moog took a deep breath.

"Let's say that person cannot take over."

"Why not?"

"Because . . . because that person is a ninety-two-year-old, little old lady who—"

"Who has a cell phone? Really?"

"YES, she has a cell phone!"

Mr. Moog's voice rose a notch, startling some of the students. "Can we agree that she has a goddamn cell phone, knows how to use it AND is too weak to give someone CPR? Can we just agree to that?"

"Okay."

"Good. So, what would you do?"

"I'd google how to do CPR on my phone."

The whole class erupted into laughter, the sound bouncing off the acoustic-enhancing walls of the gym, magnifying the hilarity. And making Mr. Moog's blood pressure go through the roof. His face was turning to a never-seen-before shade of red.

Noticing the teacher's face, Ella figured she had not only crossed the line, she had waaaaaayyyyyy crossed the line and was, in fact, so far over the wrong side of the line that she could never quite come back onto the right side of it. This was an unsettling situation, not only because no one had ever experienced the consequences of getting Mr. Moog angry—uncharted territory—but also because Ella remembered she was going to a birthday bash on Saturday and couldn't risk getting grounded. So, right now was a great time to step on her ego, backtrack and try to help the gym teacher save face.

"Sir, I'm so very sorry. I think I didn't express myself correctly."

Searching for the right thing to say to appeal to Mr. Moog, she stood up and put on her best face of contrition.

"Please hear me out, sir. What I meant is . . . I know what I'm capable of and that includes knowing my own limits. Believe me when I say I would be totally useless—and by that, I mean *actually dangerous*—in this kind of situation. I know that even if, under your excellent teachings, I were to learn this procedure by heart, I'm afraid I would only make things far worse for that poor victim by taking any kind of action. Actually, I'm so clumsy and clueless, I'd probably finish them off."

Mr. Moog considered Ella's plea with a skeptical eye.

Ella scanned the crowd of students. "In fact, my money would be much more on . . . someone like Tyler?" She was looking at Tyler Tremblay, one of Moog's biggest pets. The teacher surely had to agree that Tyler would most likely know what to do.

"Tyler, what would you do?" Ella asked him.

"May I answer, sir?" Tyler asked Mr. Moog in a brown-nosing tone. He seemed very happy to jump in and help Ella, on whom he had the biggest crush, and also show his mentor, once again, that he was great and reliable.

Frowning, Mr. Moog nevertheless took this opportunity to

put an end to Ella's circus and head in a different direction. "Of course, Tyler. What would you do?"

Ella sat back down, with an inward sigh of relief that her redirect did the trick and that she was off the hook. Sandy gave her a discreet little punch of victory on the arm.

It then occurred to Ella that she now had yet another life-saving argument in favor of a new cell phone: to reliably be able to google how to do CPR should she ever need to.

A NEW CATCH ON THE HORIZON

Turning the combination dial on her locker in a hurry, Ella went right past the correct numbers and had to do it all over again. The second time worked, but the crooked metal door of her locker was jammed, as always, and required an even harder pull on the handle than usual. Ella was convinced this set of lockers had come straight from the medieval era, handcrafted by a blind blacksmith hell-bent on cursing all humanity that would come after his time. He probably had a drinking problem, too.

The bell rang. Balancing her huge-ass physics book, a bunch of loose-leaf pages and her pencil case, all tucked underneath her left arm, Ella struggled to close the locker's temperamental door. She suspected Sandy was getting impatient. Zack was in their physics class, and the sooner Sandy got to class, the longer she'd be able to gaze at him.

Sure enough, Sandy tugged on Ella's sleeve to get her going just as the lock clicked shut.

"I know, Zack," muttered Ella.

"Shhhhh, not so loud!"

Ella knew all about Zack. And how Sandy would never dare to act on her crush, even with Ella's offer to help her hook up with him. Sandy was shy and, despite years spent under Ella's savvy social tutelage, just too nervous to jump off the boyfriend cliff. This was hard for Ella to understand, even with her friend's explanation that she couldn't bear rejection at this time. Or at any time, for that matter.

Instead, Sandy preferred to wait for Zack to make the first move. If he were interested at all, *he* would make the first move. Otherwise, she'd be fine to wait until college, next year, where rejection would be less noticeable in a sea of strangers. She could also reinvent herself then, at least a little. That was her plan.

For extroverted, go-getter Ella, things were all the opposite. She could have dated half, if not more, of the school's male student population if she wanted. But she was picky and getting pickier as she got older. She dated a lot of jocks, as it seemed like the natural thing to do. Not for the sports part—she couldn't care less about that—but because she liked tall, well-built and handsome. Some of them turned out to be total jerks, but a few of them had been pretty nice. Or interesting. But it was usually either-or.

Ella felt she was now ready for the next level: gorgeous, of course, but also nice *and* interesting. She didn't want to have to settle this time around. Ideally, she'd find the guy sometime over the school year and before the prom. She had almost a full school year to do so. This seemed feasible.

On the first day of this new school year, seeing all the old faces and her exes, she thought she might have to cast her net wider and fish outside the school's premises to find Mister Right. But then, miraculously, an excellent prospect appeared on her radar: a new student from Calgary named Ryan.

Ryan seemed a little quieter than your typical self-confident jock, perhaps because he was a swimmer. You didn't need to be ultra-sociable or big on team spirit to swim, Ella figured. You could do your own thing. He seemed at once friendly and at ease to be all by himself. He didn't seem desperate to find a posse. No doubt a freethinker. There was an aura of mystery around him, too. It was Ella's first time dealing with an aura of mystery, and there was something thrilling about it.

Ella was also not the only one attracted to the mysterious newcomer. In fact, there was a rumor Valerie Michaels, Ella's long-time main competitor on the dating front, had already tried to approach him, without success. This was at once scary and exciting as Valerie had never been turned down by a guy before. This meant that Ella would have to make all the right moves to have a shot with Ryan, to succeed where Valerie had failed, and she felt energized by the challenge.

Ella and Sandy made their way through the crowded halls as the students headed to class. A few feet ahead of the two girls, Ryan was talking with Julia, a first-class dweeb. Or rather, first-class dweeb Julia was no doubt talking *at* him, though he seemed cool with it. *He must be generous to put up with this, perhaps even go as far as listening to her for real,* Ella thought. Still, she couldn't help but feel a churning in her stomach. Surely Julia had no chance in hell to interest a guy like Ryan, a true water god. But since Ella hadn't had the time yet to figure out what made Ryan tick, she didn't dismiss any possibility.

Sandy noticed what was going on.

"Should we eliminate the competition?" Sandy suggested to Ella in a hushed voice. "Not that she's even *remotely* worthy of being called that." You could hear a major eye-roll in her tone.

Under normal circumstances, Ella would have jumped at the chance to eliminate—or at the very least discredit or humiliate—the competition right off the bat. She had never hesitated to "mark her territory," so to speak, when she was interested in a guy. She had pulled hair. She had bullied. She had started rumors. She had played dirty. Nothing had been beneath her.

But this time, it felt like these tactics wouldn't be appropriate. They'd even seem childish. Ryan was a guy in a different league, she could sense it. What if she did something nasty to Julia, and he heard about it, and it disappointed him? She still had no idea why he'd turned Valerie down. No, Ella would have to be smart about approaching him.

Ella and Sandy passed by Ryan and Julia, neither of whom paid them any attention. Ella wished he would turn around, even a little, to look at her. Just a bit? But he didn't. And this wasn't the first time. In fact, now that she was thinking back on it, he might never have looked at her. Was he ignoring her on purpose? Was she not pretty enough for him to notice her? Was she losing her touch?

What the hell was wrong with her?

Ella spent the whole physics class wondering why Ryan wasn't looking at her, why she hadn't caught his eye yet, and what he could possibly have been talking about with Julia that seemed so damn interesting. Perhaps he was just being kind. But that didn't solve the more important issue, the fact that he had never shown even a tiny little bit of interest in her. Even though she was almost directly in his line of sight in math class. Perhaps he happened to really like math (could there be such a thing?!) and loved to pay attention in class. Because the only thing that seemed to make him perk up was when Ms. Fielding asked the class a question, he was so keen to answer most of the time. But not in a nerd kind of way, of course.

Ella concluded that to get his attention, *she* would have to be more interesting than *math*.

She realized what she was thinking—her having to be more interesting than math—and couldn't believe she was actually thinking such a thought. *Wtf? How does this even make any sense?!*

She scoffed at the idea, and the students sitting around her all turned, eager to see what she was objecting to and what kind of sarcastic zinger she'd be sending the teacher's way. But all they got from Ella was a quizzical stare. What the hell was everyone's problem, looking at her? They all went back to what they were doing, mainly ignoring the lecture.

Math. Math. Math . . . How to handle math? In other similar conditions, Ella's advice to anyone would be to show Ryan a profound interest in math as a fast and easy way to bond with him. But there was absolutely no way she could fake loving math or being any good at it. Sandy could easily pull it off: she was such a good student in most subjects, except gym. Ella's late mother could have done it as well. She, too, had studied at St. Mary's—one of the reasons Ella attended the school—and had been top of her class and valedictorian. When Ella first started at St. Mary's, she'd wondered if she, too, would be top of her class and valedictorian. But it soon became undeniable that such honors were not in the cards for her. And so, for a while afterward, she'd also wondered if her mom would have been disappointed in her for not getting top grades, for not being up to par.

Ella's mom had passed away from cancer when Ella was only three. She didn't get to experience her daughter being in school. *And it might be just as well,* Ella had told herself on a few occasions, especially during her first year at St. Mary's. Because here she was, following in her mom's footsteps, but unable to keep the pace. She had felt bad about it for a while, unable to live up to some fictitious expectations from the great beyond. What if her mom was watching her in school from above, from a first-row seat?

These torturous thoughts had almost made a dent in Ella's

self-esteem. But thanks to all the positive attention she otherwise received—she was such a pretty, trendy, sociable girl—and with her father's support and paternal love, she eventually accepted the facts and focused on doing her best. Her dad often reminded her that life was short and encouraged her to make the most of it. Dan was a kind dad. Ryan was kind, too, she could sense it. He was perfect for her. If only it weren't for math . . . And then, it dawned on her. While she couldn't fake being *good* at math, the opposite was also true: she didn't have to fake being *bad* at math. She even had the marks to prove how much she sucked at it! And there was a test coming up at the end of the week. This was perfect. In fact, this couldn't be any more perfect.

For the first time in her life, Ella couldn't wait for math class to start, then to end. At last, the bell rang, and the students quickly filed out of the classroom. Ella took her sweet time putting away pens and paper and books and then stopped by the cork board near the door. She pretended to read an expired notice pinned on it, just so that she could leave the room half a moment before Ryan would, once he was done talking to the teacher.

Ella's timing was impeccable—she and Ryan bumped into each other without the collision feeling arranged.

"Oh, sorry! Hey, there," she said to him.

"No, I'm sorry. And hey back at you," Ryan replied as he crouched to pick up Ella's pencil case, which had fallen to the floor. He stood back up and handed it to her.

"Oh, thanks so much!"

"Don't mention it."

"So . . . You're the new guy, huh?"

"That would be me, yes. It's that obvious?"

Ella smiled. *Oh my God, he has a sense of humor, too!*

"Nah. You're doing well. And it's actually a good thing that you're new."

"Oh yeah? Why is that?"

"Well, for instance, you probably don't know all the good coffee shops around here yet."

"That's a safe assumption."

"So how about this? Take it or leave it, of course. I treat you to a great coffee—of your choice—at a coffee shop you don't already know, in exchange for some math tutoring. You seem really on top in that department. I mean, it seems like you could even teach the class." *That would no doubt be much more interesting than Mr. Atkinson doing the teaching. I might even pay attention.*

"I'm cheating a bit, though," Ryan said. "I took advanced math last year, and that covered a lot of what we're covering right now."

And he's modest! "Well, you have a great memory, then!"

A smile. Ella got a smile from him! A genuine smile.

"So . . . is that a yes?"

"When?"

"When is a good time for you? Tonight?"

"I got swim practice tonight. Tomorrow night?"

"That works!"

"Great!"

And that was it. They were on!

THE FATHER OF ALL ANNOUNCEMENTS

ELLA HAD TOLD Ryan she would text him the details. For two excellent reasons. First: she got his cell number—total win! Second: that would give her time to find the perfect place. Because she knew very little about coffee aside from making lattes at home and going to Starbucks with Sandy every once in a while. What kind of coffee shop would impress him the most? She wished she knew what he liked to drink so she could better tailor her search. Was he the latte-drinking type? Hopefully, he didn't drink drip coffee. Because—oh, God!—that was so *passé*. That was for people who didn't know any better, what real coffee was supposed to taste like. Yeah, hopefully, he didn't care for drip.

On the bus on her way home from school, Ella read reviews on her cell of the best coffee shops in downtown Montreal, soon finding out she should look for 3rd-wave coffee joints, which had the best baristas and were a big hit with coffee aficionados. She narrowed her list down to three sure-bet places, then looked at all the photos she could find to evaluate the decor and atmosphere. The right lighting was as important as the right roast, if not more.

She settled on a cute place named Pi Café. That was so perfect for math tutoring! She imagined Ryan would get a kick out of that. Perhaps he'd find Ella clever for suggesting the place. That would be sooooo great if he thought she was clever.

On top of that, the decor of Pi Café was modern, but it looked like it had super comfy chairs and sofas. None of those uncomfortable little plasticky chairs that had been all the rage in hipster places (and magazines) for way too long now and absolutely no rational reason whatsoever. They were ugly, to begin with, and no one could sit in them for more than five minutes without needing an appointment with a chiropractor. Whereas you could not possibly go wrong with comfy chairs—unless they were old and ratty, or stained or pierced with stuffing coming out—but here, this didn't seem to be the case.

Ella looked for other alternatives to make sure she was making the very best choice, but she kept going back to Pi Café. She looked at a few more reviews for good measure, but this was, without a doubt, the right place.

She couldn't wait to hang out there with Ryan.

Ella was still fantasizing about her trip to Pi Café with Ryan— mostly ignoring the math part—as she walked up the hill of Grey Avenue in Notre-Dame-de-Grâce, an old tree-lined neighborhood of Montreal.

As she approached her house, she was surprised to see her dad's car in the driveway. That was odd. Was he already home from work? And if so, why? Dan never came home early.

Ella looked around and saw no ambulances or police cars or anything to explain some sort of tragedy and the presence of the family car. That was a good sign. Still, she took those seven steps to the front porch with apprehension.

The front door was unlocked. She climbed the inside stairs leading to their second-floor dwelling. She was midway up when Dan poked his head out, at the top of the staircase. Why? This never happened before. On most nights, he was either working late at work or glued to his laptop at home working late. They would rarely have time to chat unless it was over dinner. And even then. But right now, Dan seemed very eager to engage with her. Not only did he unglue himself from his laptop to greet her, but his whole demeanor was slightly exaggerated. Enough to raise suspicion, at least.

"Who died?" inquired Ella as she was putting away her favorite fall jacket, the black trench coat that made her look awesome and adorable.

"No one! Why would you say that?"

Yeah, why would I say that?

Dan looked for words. It was clear he wanted to say something but didn't quite know how to say it. "How was your day?" he tried.

"Heavenly."

For once, Ella wasn't even being sarcastic. She would have loved to talk about her day—though, not right now and not with her dad. No, right now, she needed to know what the hell was going on, what was wrong. Her dad was never like this. Never big on surprises either. What was he hiding?

"What is it?" she asked bluntly.

"Let's go to the kitchen. Would you like some hot chocolate?"

Hot chocolate? Fudge . . . This was bound not to be good. Ella reluctantly followed him to the kitchen.

"Why don't you have a seat?"

"Should I be afraid to sit?" Ella wondered out loud as she sat. Was it something she had done? Did the school call? But over what? She couldn't see Mr. Moog still being upset with her for being fresh with him earlier today. It couldn't be that, because if it were, she'd already be in detention. Plus, Dan seemed oddly enthusiastic.

"Alright, Dad, just spit it out. You're freaking me out!"

"Alright. Well . . ."

Dan smiled broadly.

"We're moving to Iqaluit!" he blurted out.

Iqalu-what?

"What?"

"We are moving to Iqaluit."

"What do you mean?"

"I mean I've been offered the contract of a lifetime up North."

Ella's face darkened. A deafening silence ensued.

Dan's enthusiastic energy dropped. Ella wasn't usually this quiet. She had an opinion on everything. And now, her body language was nothing but shock and bad news. Dan wasn't used to seeing her stunned nor speechless.

"By 'North,' you mean, like, still on the island of Montreal, right? And the metro goes up there, right?" Ella ventured.

Dan reached for his laptop on the table and dragged it closer. He pointed to the territory of Nunavut, which happened to be way, way, waaaaay up North—closer to the North Pole than most other places on Earth.

"Right here."

Ella's ears started ringing. Surely, she didn't understand any of this correctly.

"What do you think? Isn't that exciting?" Dan asked carefully.

"Define 'moving'."

"Well . . . It's a one-year contract, but perhaps more. Anyway, we're keeping this house. We're just gonna pack some stuff and go there, and—"

"By 'we' you mean 'you,' and I'm staying here, right?"

Dan paused before answering.

"Both of us, Ella. We're both going. Together. It'll be great."

Ella stood up, overwhelmed by the distress of being unable to process the dreadful information that was coming out of her dad's mouth. If only he were joking. But Dan was not the type of guy to joke, let alone pull a cruel prank on anyone. So, he was being serious. He had to be serious, or he wouldn't be saying any of this right now.

"Look," Dan added, "I know this is a lot to process, and it's all very sudden—"

"Yeah, it is. You can go some other time."

"It's all very sudden because the guy who initially got the contract . . . he had a heart attack and—"

"Oh, so somebody did die!"

"What?"

"I asked you, 'Who died?' and you said—"

"That's not relevant—"

"What do you mean that's not relevant?! Some selfish dead jerk—"

"He didn't die."

"What? Whatever! Some jerk I don't even know is about to ruin my life, and that's not relevant?!"

"Ella . . ."

Ella had heard more than she could handle. She left the kitchen and headed to her room. Her sanctuary. With each step, she felt the rug being pulled from underneath her feet. Her whole world was crashing down.

How could a day possibly be the best one ever and the worst one ever, all within a matter of minutes? Ella was balled up on her bed, feeling numb. *This is not happening. This is not happening. This can't be happening. How could this be happening?*

Was the universe mad at her? What had she done? What the hell could she have done that was so . . . so . . . bad? This was supposed to be her year. HER year! Her senior year. And she had just found the perfect guy! Her reason to breathe and live, right now. This was the most important year in a teenage girl's life. It was her prom year. It was her EVERYTHING year. How could her dad do this to her?!

Dan knocked on Ella's door and opened it a crack.

"Can I come in?"

Before Ella could answer, he entered the room. Walking on eggshells. She didn't want to see him. For one thing, she hadn't had the time nor the clear-headedness to put together any killer counter-argument. And she had to come up with one to make sure that this nonsense was not going to happen.

"What are you thinking?" asked Dan as he sat at the edge of his daughter's bed.

Ella had to think fast. She took a deep breath and collected herself.

"I think you'll have a great time there," was the first thing that came out of her mouth. And that was a good start, she thought. Yeah, she might be on to something.

"I think we'll both have a great time there," he replied gently. "This is a dream come true for me."

"Dad . . . Look, that's great. I'm happy for you. But I can't go anywhere right now. This is the most important year of my life! I would totally miss you, but I'm fine to stay here by myself. And, you know, hold the fort."

Dan sighed. He knew this would be an uphill battle.

"Ella . . ."

"We could ask Mrs. Dunsmore to check on me from time to time, and—"

Mrs. Dunsmore was the downstairs neighbor of their duplex. She and her husband—and now two kids—had been renting the first floor for over ten years, and she was a very dependable and friendly mom working from home.

"Ella . . ."

"And I would keep all the doors locked, like you know I always do. And I promise I wouldn't go out—"

"Ella . . ."

"I swear, I wouldn't go out. So, you wouldn't have to worry!"

"I can't leave you here all by yourself."

"BUT I'M ALREADY HERE ALL BY MYSELF!"

While this was true, this had come out way stronger than intended. Ella realized how freaked out she was, how there was no way she could remain calm and collected in this conversation. This was a life or death situation. It would be the end of her life! The end of everything! The death of her!

Ella burst out crying.

"I'm sorry, Ella. This is how it has to be."

Dan stood up and left the room.

Ella kept crying. She didn't know how to make herself stop.

I OBJECT, YOUR HONOR

ELLA'S PHONE had been ringing and buzzing a lot, courtesy of Sandy. At first, Ella had buried it under her pillow to muffle the sounds, hoping it would eventually stop. She was so devastated, it only occurred to her later that she could put it on silent mode to stop the aggravation. She didn't want to talk to Sandy right now. She didn't want to talk to anyone.

Ella went to bed early but couldn't sleep. What could she do about her dad's completely unreasonable proposition? How could she convince him to reconsider? She woke up her phone to take notes, but seeing all of Sandy's notifications stressed her out, and she turned it off. Ella needed to think, not give in to the self-wallowing that Sandy would no doubt encourage. Now was the time to focus. Not to start spazzing.

She turned on the lamp on her bedside table and looked for a piece of paper on which to write. All she found was a clothing store receipt scrunched up in her trash can, but it was long enough to write a few thoughts and arguments on the back. So, she tried to brainstorm. She tried to concentrate, but nothing came to her. Her mind was drawing a blank from this unexpected stress. This overwhelming, paralyzing sensation that time stood still. And the impending doom that would ensue once the world started turning again.

Ella forced herself to think until a headache came on. The back of the store receipt was still blank. She sighed and thought she might as well try to have some sleep. At this point, there was no way she would manage to wake up refreshed in the morning, but if she could, at least, take some of the edge off, be a little less frazzled, perhaps she could be poised enough to have a convincing conversation with her father. He, too, would hopefully be more rested and, likely, more rational. He might even have come to his senses by then.

He was a reasonable guy.

But then again, the kid-in-a-candy-store kind of enthusiasm he had displayed earlier was so unlike him. Such a contrast with his usual taciturn self. A man who was so busy "adulting" and being serious, he wasn't the type to have a dream. This had to be just a hiccup, a temporary anomaly. And things would hopefully go back to normal before breakfast was even over.

"I'm on the social committee and, believe me, I play an essential role in it."

Dan had made blueberry pancakes—Ella's favorite—and she had made him a latte—his favorite. A subtle war of manipulation was on in the Briggs kitchen. Each party was well aware the other party was cranking up the charm.

Ella had woken up at the crack of dawn, with a bitter taste in her mouth and the resolve to argue her case without making a scene. If she wanted to be taken seriously, a tantrum was out of the question.

Upon waking up, she'd managed to jot down a few thoughts on why she was so upset, and these thoughts led her to formulate a bunch of arguments. She would express her feelings to her dad. One couldn't go wrong expressing feelings in a mediation.

Here she was, clutching her clothing receipt in her left hand, facing the moment of truth. She asked her dad to listen to everything she needed to say before interjecting. Being a good listener, he agreed to do just that.

"As you know, this is a very big year for me, and I have responsibilities to the school and the other students. And, also, I am building leadership skills, and that will be a great start for my résumé. 'Cause, like you often say yourself, it's never too early to start building a résumé."

Ella could see that Dan was listening, but was he getting convinced? She couldn't tell for sure. Perhaps she should bring up the heat just a bit, to be on the safe side.

"If I want to go to law school . . ."

This was the first time Ella ever showed any interest in going to law school. In fact, she wasn't even sure she cared to go to law school, but her mother had been a lawyer, and right now, she was trying to appeal to her dad's emotions—an approach that usually worked with him. But upon the mention of law school, Dan winced. And she caught that. A subtle wince, but enough to tell her this was not helping her case.

She corrected course.

"Also, there's a very good chance that I will be prom queen. And you know how much that would mean to me. Even if I'm not, I can't miss my prom. I can't miss my prom, Dad! I've been looking forward to this for so long! You know that! You know how much this means to me!"

For a moment, Dan looked like he was pondering her arguments. Perhaps he was about to admit how his plan didn't make any sense. At last.

"Tell you what. We'll fly back for your prom so that you don't miss it. I promise."

What?! Ella was not prepared for such a counter-proposal, for such a blow to her arguments. Why did her dad always have to be so damn practical?!

"Or . . . Why don't you go there *next* year?"

Ella promptly corrected herself, "Why don't *we* go there next year?" Not that she intended to go up North next year, but this offer would stall him for a while and give her plenty of time to come up with more and better excuses not to go.

Dan glanced at his watch—he had better get going.

"We can't go next year because the offer is for now. They really need someone. If I don't accept, they'll find someone else and won't ask me again. I know this for a fact. These kinds of openings are extremely rare. And I've been waiting for something like this my whole life."

"I could go live with Sandy. Her parents like me. And I'd make myself useful."

Useful at what? Hard to tell, but it didn't matter. It seemed like a convincing thing to say.

"I know that Isobel and Jerry like you very much, but taking care of an extra teenage girl—"

"We'll pay them!"

Dan cringed subtly.

"It wouldn't be a matter of money . . ."

"Then how about boarding school?"

"Boarding school?!" Dan's expression said it all, and he had a point. Though, right now to Ella, going to a boarding school seemed like a better option than moving to a dreadful place.

"Don't we have some kind of family around here? An estranged old aunt? Anyone?!"

Dan let out a weary sigh.

"I do have a distant uncle in Pointe-aux-Trembles, but he's in a retirement home and severely disabled and under constant care."

"Perfect! Would they—"

"No, they wouldn't."

Dan glanced at his watch again. He stood up, grabbed his dirty dishes and headed for the sink. "Come on, you're gonna be late," he added.

Ella didn't give a rat's ass about being late or on time or whatever. She reviewed her list of arguments. Did she forget anything good? Did she forget anything at all?

"But, Dad—"

"Honey, I'm sorry this will interfere with your social life, I really am. But this is very important to me, and I've never asked you for anything. This time, I'm needed over there, and I need to do this."

"But, Dad—"

"It's not always about you, El. I'm sure you can develop plenty of leadership skills in Iqaluit, just the same. And it'll be a great opportunity for you. For your résumé and many other things in life."

"But—"

"No more buts, Ella! At the end of the day, you're my child, and you're still a minor—"

"Not for long!"

"Doesn't matter. I would worry sick if I left you here, alone and unprepared, and it's gonna be a stressful enough job, I don't need to be worrying about you on top of it."

He reached for his briefcase, and as he walked out of the room, he mumbled, "I've already lost your mother."

Ella was quiet after that. Her dad had never played that card before, in their various negotiations. He was serious.

Ella's heart sank another level.

ONE LAST EMOTIONAL WEDGIE FOR THE ROAD

THE DAY at school was all a blur. At one point, Ella mumbled to Sandy what was happening to her, but it was all so surreal to Ella that her words sounded detached and barely coherent.

"And you're okay with that?" Sandy was confused. How could her friend possibly be okay with moving so far away and dropping out of civilization?

"How could you possibly think that I'm okay with that?" Ella found the strength to ask.

"You *sound* like you don't care. Your voice . . ."

Ella noticed how flat and detached she had been feeling and talking strangely.

"If I have to move there . . ." Ella started, but she couldn't finish the thought. There was no *if*, and she knew it. They were moving. Period. Her dad had never been so clear, so adamant, about anything. It was scary. She could deny reality or try to fool herself all she wanted, but that wouldn't change the fact they were moving.

There would be no way around this one. And that, alone, felt like a very strange thing to Ella. "He shot down all of my arguments." She was clearly still in a state of utter disbelief over that.

"Your dad?!" Sandy shared her friend's utter disbelief.

"I know, right? Makes no sense."

They stood in silence for a moment. The bell rang. But to Ella, it was just another layer of noise on top of all the white noise already sizzling in her head.

"So, what are you going to do?" asked Sandy.

"I have no idea."

"When are you moving?"

Ella didn't know either. She had not asked her dad for details.

Oh, God, what if they were moving soon?

Ella's thoughts got lost somewhere in the bowl of wobbly, cherry-flavored gelatin cubes in front of her, that she was merely poking at. She'd barely touched the rest of her lunch, either. Apparently, her appetite was another casualty.

A shooting pain in her upper arm made her let out a yelp. Sandy had given her yet another major elbow jab. What was wrong with her?!

Ella shot a look at Sandy, who replied by making big eyes at her. A throat-clearing sound made Ella aware that Ryan was standing right there in front of them with his tray.

"Is it alright if I join you two, Ella? Your friend seems okay with it."

Ella came back to reality.

"Oh, sure. I see you already met Sandy." Ella heard her own voice. Her tone was still flat, and she hoped she didn't sound bitchy. Even though she would never have a chance with Ryan now, she couldn't bear the thought of him remembering her as bitchy. She needed to watch her tone.

Ryan sat down in front of the two girls. He pointed to Ella's dessert.

"You'll have to introduce me to your pet blob. It seems fascinating."

"Yeah, we have a special connection."

He smiled at her, and she responded with a weak smile. The best she could do amidst all the fog and pain.

"It's comfort food, I guess. And that much can't be said of . . . whatever that's supposed to be," Ella said of the plate containing her main course from the cafeteria. She didn't even remember ordering it, let alone what it was. She turned to Sandy, who was eating a homemade sandwich.

"Don't ask me!"

"Fine."

Ella pushed her tray towards Ryan.

"It looks like it would go well with your salad," she quipped half-heartedly.

Ryan had taken a chicken salad. A very easily identifiable chicken salad. He made a face at Ella's so-called food.

"I already had the roadkill special yesterday, thanks. I have to rotate." Ryan seemed determined to get a real smile out of Ella. At least, it worked on Sandy—she snarfed apple juice out of her nose, and some got on Ella's tray.

"Thanks for the juice bits, Sandy. You just improved my plate by 100%," said Ella. With a sad smile, she added, "Everything keeps getting better at warp speed, doesn't it?"

"What's up?" Ryan looked genuinely concerned, which made Ella feel even sadder. When was the last time she had a potential boyfriend who was this caring?

Since Ella wasn't answering, Sandy jumped in.

"She just learned that she's moving. It's devastating."

"Oh. Really? Where?"

Ryan seemed interested to know, but Ella had been so busy denying reality, she didn't even remember what her dad had said.

"Long shot, but if it's near Calgary, I could give you some pointers," Ryan offered.

"No, it's not near Calgary. I don't think. It's more like Alaska or Antarctica or something. I'm not even sure."

Ella felt like an idiot. It was obvious she was both upset and so very uninformed, she felt like she was losing credibility. Thankfully, Ryan didn't seem to be judging her. Rather, he was studying her, trying to find the right thing to say. And you could tell he wasn't sure what that would be.

"Well, wherever that is, I'd be happy to buy you coffee if you ever want to talk about it. I know a thing or two about moving. And coffee too."

Ryan had said the very best thing he could have said. Why did he have to be so perfect right now?

"We can also postpone our math session if you'd like. I imagine your heart won't be into studying . . ."

Ella sighed. Ryan had no idea she would never have her heart into anything ever again.

"Iqaluit. That's where."

It was Friday—finally!—and Ella was spending the night over at Sandy's house. She was lying on her back on her friend's bed, eyes glued to the ceiling.

"Where's that?"

"In Nunavut."

"Oh . . ." Sandy had some notion of the Great White North and vaguely remembered such a place mentioned in history class a while back.

"What do they have there?"

"Nothing. Absolutely nothing. Nothing, nothing, nothing, and snow. And then, more of nothing."

Ella knew this not to be true. After her dad put his foot down, and she had to accept the fact they would be heading to Nunavut at the beginning of October—otherwise known as three long weeks of hell before a different kind of hell—she had reluctantly done some research on the Internet to be somewhat informed should Ryan ask her about it again. Even though she was likely to never, ever, ever see him again after that stupid move, she didn't want him to remember her as a supreme idiot.

But with Sandy, things were completely different. Ella wanted—she needed—to commiserate with her friend and let out as much sadness and frustration as possible. That's what BFFs were for. Sandy was the official punching bag and always very good at listening to Ella whine and rage, and she'd always agree that Ella's life was always so much more dramatic than hers. Woe was totally Ella: she'd been born a tragic figure, and she was about to start a new tragic chapter in her tragic life, a whole new level of suckiness. Suckiness to the power of crap, to be specific.

"You still gonna go to school over there, right?"

"Yeah. What else is there to do?"

"Okay, so, then, they have schools."

"Yeah. They have one. In the forest. And it's all made of wood and held together with blubber, and there can only be, like, ten students in it. Oh, and there's no washroom."

"Does it have Wi-Fi?"

"Electricity hasn't even been invented over there, so never mind Wi-Fi."

Sandy wasn't sure whether to believe Ella. "You're pulling my leg."

Ella felt around the bed to locate her cell and dramatically handed it over to Sandy.

"Here. I want you to have it."

"How are we gonna stay in touch?" What the hell would Sandy do if Ella didn't have a phone?

"Smoke signals."

Sandy didn't know what to reply to that.

"Do you guys have chips?" inquired Ella.

"What?"

"Are there chips in this house?"

"Oh. Yeah. Probably."

Ella dragged herself off the bed.

"My dad stopped buying food. He wants us to use up what we have in the house, and every day feels like a bad episode of Chopped. I could use some chips right now."

Ella grabbed her phone back from Sandy and headed out of the room.

"He's cute."

Sandy shoved her tablet in front of Ella's face. She had been googling "Iqaluit" to see if they indeed didn't have electricity. It turned out, they had way more than electricity, and it actually seemed like an interesting place to visit. People looked like regular people over there. And they did not live in igloos at all like Ella had tried to make her believe.

Sandy was a pretty bright girl overall, but a tad easy to fool at times, especially when it came to what her friend would say. In the past, Ella had said the weirdest things that turned out to be true. She had the most eventful, colorful life. Things happened to her! Sometimes, Sandy wished things would happen to her, too.

Ella was watching a rerun of some generic urban cop TV show. She wasn't really watching it, more like mindlessly absorbing content. So that she'd have memories to remember later when she'd be bored out of her skull in a dark, TV-less living room. She liked to dwell on the worst-case scenarios that were surely going to happen. She was trying to make herself believe the lies she was telling herself, to keep feeding the pain and the brooding.

Sandy's tablet was obscuring her view of some forgotten B-actor. It was on a web page showing a group of Inuit teenagers in a classroom setting. There were a few boys their age in the picture. Sandy pointed to one of them.

"Come on. He's cute."

Ella shrugged.

"Perhaps he'll be in your class," Sandy added.

"That's probably my whole class right there," Ella muttered.

"Perhaps you'll find a kick-ass boyfriend there."

Ella didn't answer. She had decided she would be dragged there kicking and screaming, sulk the whole time there and only do the very bare minimum not to land herself in trouble at school or have any kind of fun, so the odds of her finding a boyfriend—or even of her caring to look at boys—were less than nil.

"I take it back. He's not cute, he's gorgeous! Look at those eyes." Sandy was still staring at the guy in the picture. "I bet he's even more gorgeous in person. Will you tell me if you see him? He's totally your type."

"I won't see him."

"You don't know that."

"I *do* know that, 'cause I won't be looking. In fact, I don't plan on actually *being* there. I'm gonna spend my time with myself, just trying to survive."

And my dad will realize how much he ruined my life. And there would be no turning back from ruination because she'd be scarred for life. She'd make damn sure of that!

"Why don't you look at the whole thing as, like, a science experiment then? Or a business project?"

Ella shot Sandy a *wtf?* look.

"I mean, since your goal is to survive anyway, you might as well try to make your life as easy as possible, no? Like, make friends with the right people, in case you have problems. Hell, buy their friendship if you have to—"

"I don't think I'll be talking to anyone, Sandy."

Sandy was running out of advice. And patience.

"Alright. Suit yourself."

Sandy hated it when Ella wrapped herself up in bad faith like this. Once the bad faith protocol had been engaged, it was nearly impossible to shake her out of it. And it was getting pretty late right now, and she was too tired to battle with Ella.

"Turn off the TV when you're done, 'kay?"

Sandy stood up and left to go to bed. Ella pretended not to care, keeping her eyes on the TV screen, but she felt like her friend was giving up on her, abandoning her. And she had no more room left in her to welcome more hurt.

Her eyes started watering. She felt like the whole world was now officially against her.

That night, Ella didn't sleep very well, nor very much. She kept rehashing the latest clash she had with her father the day before. Playing all or nothing, she had made one last attempt to sway him. She had told him about Ryan and how she thought he might be the one for her.

"Remember how you and Mom met in your last year of high school?" she had tried.

She thought this would bring back sweet memories for her dad and he would finally understand how much this all meant to her. But her father's expression became awash with grief. He looked at his daughter and told her, very softly, that this was a new low, even for her. That he'd had enough of her trying to manipulate him, that there had to be a limit to her selfishness. They were going to Iqaluit, and that was that.

Ella couldn't recall ever seeing her dad so deeply upset. She had gone too far, she could clearly see that now. But so had he. How dare he treat her like that? And make such a huge life-changing decision without her even having a say? She was hurt and pissed off, too!

She had gone to her room and quickly decided it would be best for both of them if she spent the night at Sandy's. And so, she wrote a note and left.

As Ella's anger slowly receded, she realized how nasty she had been to Sandy—her one friend and ally. Who didn't deserve her wrath. She would apologize in the morning and make sure never to put her in her crosshairs again.

"We'll find a way to stay in touch," was the first thing Ella said to Sandy when her friend woke up the next morning. "I'm not sure how, but I know that I can't survive without you. Your support. Your friendship."

Sandy thought Ella must have had a good night of sleep to be this apologetic despite her looking like hell.

"I'm sorry I was a real bitch to you last night," Ella added.

"No prob, dude. I know you're going through a lot."

Ella looked so despondent, so different from her usual confident self.

"I don't know that I'll be able to make it there, Sandy. What if it's unbearable?" Ella's voice was meek, and she looked terrified.

"You're strong. And you're a survivor. If anyone can make it up there, it's you. People like you, Ella. When you're not being a first-class bitch, that is."

Ella snorted a laugh.

"Right."

"So, if you skip the bitch part, people—at least some of them —should be nice to you. And that's all you need, right?"

Ella wanted to believe Sandy.

"I have no doubt that you'll make friends. Or allies, if you don't care for friends. And you better see and do all sorts of weird things, 'cause I can't wait to hear all about them. Okay?"

Ella nodded despite not being convinced. In fact, she didn't want to be convinced. She just wanted to be on good terms with Sandy again. She didn't have to let on how dark her thoughts still were.

Sandy perked up.

"How about we go shopping this afternoon? We could get you new outfits to wear up in Iaqui— Iqui— that place."

Ella pondered the proposition and sighed. "But what's the point? I'm sure I'll be wearing a snowsuit around the clock."

OH, HENRY

Iqaluit was Eastern Standard Time, the same time zone as Montreal. So, when Ella found herself glancing at her alarm clock at 5:30 a.m. on this fine Monday morning, cursing the world for having hardly slept—yet another crappy night—1,275 miles away, high school senior Sera Kalluk was also wide-awake and cursing. However, the reason why Sera was up at this ungodly hour was not insomnia, but rather, a guy named Henry.

Sera had known Henry for as long as she could remember. They grew up on the same street, and both still lived in their same places on that same street. Being of the same age, they used to play with the same group of friends when they were young. In school, being in the same grade, they were often in the same classes. They had never been close friends or anything like that, but they still knew each other. Or, at the very least, they knew *of* each other.

For the longest time, Henry was a timid, scrawny boy known for giving the shirt off his back to anyone in need, a very honorable trait in the eyes of most people, but an oh-so-very-boring quality for Sera, who would never have dreamed of giving him the time of day during their early teenage years. She always considered Henry blander than beige. That is, until very recently.

At the beginning of this past summer, Henry had left town and gone to Salluit, an Inuit community in Northern Quebec, to help his uncle Sam on a renovation project. Henry was quite handy and wanted to learn some carpentry skills.

When he returned to Iqaluit at the end of summer, he had clearly gone through an amazing growth spurt while away, pushing six feet five, making him tower over just about everyone else around him. He had also gained for himself a glowing kind of confidence, which affected his demeanor and highlighted his good looks. When he talked to people now, it no longer looked like he wished to hide underneath the floorboards. Now, he always looked so at ease with himself, to the point of being hard even to recognize. He still came across as the nice guy he had always been. Except now, he was a *really* nice, and major, hottie. And Sera—like all the other girls around him—had noticed his surprising, even jarring transformation.

Who is this guy? Sera mused. Where had he been all her life?

The new Henry had come out of his shell at a great time for Sera. She had pretty much dated all the guys in town in whom she'd been interested and had quickly run out of love interests. She worried about the limited dating pool of Iqaluit. It wasn't like she could just travel to the next town over to check out its dating scene—there was no neighboring town to go to!

Mere days after Henry's return, the wheels in Sera's head spun nonstop to find a way to get close to him. And pronto! Before any other girl got to him!

Remembering how timid he used to be, she suspected that just pouncing on him would only make him run for the hills, far away from her. A subtler approach would be paramount.

On the subject of running, Sera had noticed that Henry had

taken up running at the crack of dawn before school. Early one morning, as she lifted the Roman shade covering her bedroom's window, she saw a guy running in front of her house. A split second before she recognized him, she wondered what kind of an idiot would wake up at stupid o'clock to go run this early. And now, she herself was about to become such an idiot, too.

Taking up running would be a great way to show Henry they had at least one interest in common and, should she be able to run alongside him, she'd have him all to herself in a quiet and intimate context.

But for her plan to work, Sera first had to figure out at what time Henry left home for his run. She had no idea for how long he'd go running, and she didn't want to take forever to find out. So, she set her alarm early enough to catch him for sure—4:30 a.m.—cursing a blue streak as she forced herself out of bed. Was this really worth it? She couldn't help wondering. It was so tempting to slide back underneath the warm blankets of her cozy bed. But Sera was getting more and more obsessed with Henry, and when she had something in mind, the word "tenacious" only just began to describe her.

At first, she parked herself next to her bedroom window, lifting the shade slightly from one side to spy on the street without being seen. But this awkward position fast grew uncomfortable. So, she swiftly tiptoed to the living room and plopped herself down on a recliner. From there, she had a good view of Henry's house, which was kitty-corner from her own. And since the living room was dark, there was no chance she could be seen from outside. The one danger, though, was that she might fall asleep in this oh-so comfortable environment. So, Sera imagined herself poking tiny imaginary toothpicks underneath her eyelids to keep them open. The imagery made her shudder. And kept her awake despite absolutely nothing happening.

5:30 a.m. was the time Henry left his house, an hour after

Sera had begun her watch. One hour of staring at an empty street had made her bleary-eyed. If a loud pickup truck with a roaring muffler hadn't driven past her house a few seconds before Henry headed out—jolting her from her zoned-out state —she might have missed him easily. Thank God, she didn't.

So, 5:30. *5 effing 30. Ugh.*

Sera headed back to bed and reset her alarm for 6 a.m. *Friggin' school.*

The next morning, Sera's alarm went off at 5:20 a.m. Dazed, she still managed to drag herself out of bed. She gathered her hair in a ponytail as she headed to the bathroom to splash handfuls of cold water on her face. That never failed to force her awake, though this time, it was beyond brutal. As she brushed her teeth, she felt some jitters. How ridiculous it was for her to feel nervous!

Anticipating chilly weather outside, she put on her thickest pair of curve-hugging yoga pants, a windbreaker over a light but warm sweater, and her lavender running shoes. Once outside, she did a few stretches—picked up from YouTube the night before—in the middle of her driveway. To appear credible as someone who had a true interest in running, she'd have to play the part and play it right.

Every twenty seconds or so, she glanced at her Fitbit watch. It was 5:32 a.m., and there was no sign of Henry yet. She kept stretching, shooting sideways glances at his house, looking for movement.

5:32:24.

Stretch.

Look at Henry's house.

Stretch.

5:32:44.

Stretch.

Owww. Stiff leg.

Sera had always been quite athletic, especially during the school year, involved in various sports and teams. But over summer and for the first time in years, she had taken things easy sportswise. Instead, she put her time and energy into the internship she had at the bank where her mom was the branch manager. She was determined to show the bank staff that she was indeed her mother's daughter and, so, also blessed with the overachieving gene. And she had pulled it off beautifully. But she realized the downside now: her body felt totally rusty. She had not anticipated this. Perhaps taking up running was not such a bad idea after all, aside from her Henri-related motivation, since she wanted to outperform in sports, once again, during the school year.

Movement caught the corner of her eye—Henry was stretching in his driveway. Sera immediately set out running towards the street and took a left, heading in the same direction Henry had the day before. She hoped he would have the same itinerary. Her pace was slow, more like jogging than running, in part so that he would easily catch up to her before the intersection ahead, but also because her heart was already beating faster and she didn't know how far she would last.

"Hey!" hailed a male voice behind her. Sera smiled to herself before looking over her shoulder and acting surprised.

"Henry!"

"You're running, too? I don't think I've seen you—"

"It's my first time in the morning." Sera could hear herself being out of breath between her words. *Crud.* She might as well own it. "As you can probably tell, I'm out of shape."

Henry smiled. "I know the feeling. You're doing the right thing."

"I think so."

Henry had slowed down to match Sera's pace, but even then, this was more than she could handle.

"I *hope* so," Sera added. *Crap.* With each word she spoke, she felt she was getting tired twice as fast. How did she not see this coming?

"Don't push yourself too much, eh? I'm sure you'll rebuild your endurance in no time. I'll see you at school."

Henry waved her goodbye with a smile and went back to his much faster pace. Sera slowed and stopped, gasping for air. It felt like her lungs were on fire, her heart pounding like crazy—partly from the effort of running and partly from a feeling of exhilaration at this first real exchange with the "new and improved" Henry.

Henry . . .

She pictured him again, as he was running away, just now, and nearly swooned. He was taking her breath away in every sense.

DEATH MARCH

Ella yanked herself out of bed at the very last minute. The house was quiet. Her dad had just left. She had heard him leave and had, in fact, waited for him to leave before getting out of her room. She didn't want to interact with him. She didn't need time to eat breakfast, she was soooooo not hungry. She didn't care to make herself a latte either.

She dragged her feet to her closet and picked the first outfit she came across. She didn't even notice what it was or if it matched. What did it matter?

Ella later realized she was standing at her bus stop. She had no recollection of getting there—she just had. And it looked like she had brought her school bag with her, too, which was a very good thing since she had zero energy for getting herself into trouble at school, let alone dealing with trouble. Life, in general, was just too much right now.

The days and weeks leading to the move all felt like a slow, agonizing death march. Ella was in a constant daze, feeling numb, barely eating. She had already slipped into survival mode, trying to remain indifferent so that she'd stop the exhausting feelings of being punched in the gut every time she remembered what was going to happen. She felt like she was treading water in the middle of an ocean while knowing full well that no one would be coming to fish her out of it. She had lost interest in pretty much everything—including shopping and Ryan—because what was the point of caring about anything at all? She was losing everything she had anyway.

At school, she tried not to be too morose since she no longer wanted anyone's sympathy or attention. She just wanted to be left alone. It was easier to hurt quietly when no one was around, when no one was talking to you. Or trying to cheer you up. Or telling you how amazingly lucky you were. When you isolated yourself, you could concentrate on the pain. Hang out with it. It would be your best friend from now on.

At home, Ella also tried to conceal her pain from her dad. She was still mad at him and was giving him the silent treatment, but he was so busy preparing for the move that he barely noticed her giving him the cold shoulder. Perhaps that was for the best. She didn't have the strength to fight with him. But deep down, she was hoping he would notice her pain and take her into his arms like when she was little and tell her everything would be fine. And she would believe him. And feel safe.

And she'd be blissfully oblivious of what lay ahead.

DIRECT FLIGHT TO HELL

"Would you like a snack?" asked a lanky male flight attendant. Ella, who was scrunched up in her window seat, rolled an eyeball his way.

"Only if you have moose jerky. Or raw fish pudding."

Ella was aiming for an all-time high as far as being unpleasant was concerned.

"Please excuse my toddler. She clearly needs a nap." Dan jumped in with a cheerful tone to apologize for Ella's rudeness. Fortunately, the flight attendant had seen it all before on his many flights and was unfazed.

"We're out of moose jerky, raw fish pudding, smoked seal, *and* Eskimo pies, but I have these," he retorted, offering Ella a bag of Snyder's pretzels.

Ella didn't know how to react. On the one hand, she was being mocked, and she knew she deserved it. On the other, she loved those pretzels! They were so addictive . . . She timidly reached for the bag.

"Can I sweeten the deal with a Cherry Coke?" the attendant added, already reaching for a can.

A Cherry Coke. That sweetened *and* sealed the deal,

alright. Ella grabbed the can, managing to mumble "thank you" with pursed lips as he moved on up the aisle. She was annoyed at herself for being bribed so easily. What a sell-out!

She sighed as she struggled to open the bag of pretzels. Dammit, being miserable full-time took a lot of energy! And she was getting sick and tired of it. For real.

Ella managed to fall asleep during the rest of the flight, and for the first time in a long time, she reached a deep, deep sleep. Like her body was finally starting to let go of some stress and giving her a break.

The landing announcement woke her. It took her a few seconds to realize where she was before all the bitterness came rushing back inside her. Dan touched her arm and pointed, urging her to look out of the plane's window.

The sun was setting, and its golden hour glow gave the endless, white landscape a tint of gold. The land all around was sparkling. Ella was struck by the sheer vastness of it and the absence of trees. The horizon seemed like it was going on forever. There was something kind of impressive about all of this. Not that Ella would admit to thinking it.

She felt her dad looking over her shoulder. Probably trying to gauge her reaction.

"Oh, look, a Starbucks!" she said with as much snark as she could muster.

"You're hilarious, dear," Dan replied.

At least, she had bothered to give the landscape a chance, even if it had been ever so briefly.

It took a while for any kind of man-made structure to appear. Eventually, little houses and small buildings came into view. Many were colorful. Blue, red, green. Probably an attempt to cheer up an otherwise very white and very grey backdrop.

The deep-red Iqaluit Airport could be seen in the distance as the plane was nearing the ground. It looked so cheery and surreal. Everything looked and felt so surreal to Ella.

She braced herself for impact.

A ROUGH LANDING

"Welcome to hell frozen over," Ella muttered to herself as she struggled to enter an ugly and old burgundy minivan that pretended to be a taxi. *Is this trash can on wheels even safe to be on the road?* she wondered.

The wind was sharp and cold. She rushed to close the door before her dad had a chance to get in. For all she cared, he could go around and get in from the other side. But Dan, excited to be here and busy trying to take in everything at once, was in no hurry to get in the cab. And when he did, he sat in front, on the passenger side, right next to the driver. *How dorky of him.*

"We're new here!" Dan said to the driver as the man climbed behind the wheel.

"Way to state the obvious, Dad."

"Welcome to Iqaluit. I'm Mike."

"Dan."

The two men shook hands.

"And that's Ella."

Mike smiled at Ella in the rear-view mirror. Put on the spot and trying not to appear impolite, she forced a smile back.

"We're happy to be here," Dan added.

You're happy to be here.

"Where to?"

"Frobisher Inn, please," Dan said and then explained to Mike how they would sleep at the hotel tonight because the house they were renting would be ready only tomorrow morning, but that was all fine because that way they could have a lazy breakfast in the morning without having to worry about anything.

Ella tuned out her dad, looking out the window at the scenery, which was at once familiar and bizarre. There were low buildings that could be houses, but perhaps they were commercial buildings? She wasn't sure. They differed greatly from the old two-story brick houses of her old Montreal neighborhood. Everything was different, yet not. She was surprised to see this much civilization. In the previous weeks, she had pictured herself getting picked up at the airport in a dog-sled and fully expected to see streets lined with igloos. She really could be such a moron sometimes, she thought to herself.

A brightly lit area ahead caught her attention.

"Look, Ella, your Starbucks!" teased Dan.

"What?! Where!?"

Ella craned her neck even though she suspected her dad was joking. And he was. But only in part: it was a Tim Hortons donut shop. Ella wasn't sure she had seen right.

"Was that a Tim Hortons? Like, a real Tim Hortons?"

"Yup," Mike confirmed.

"They have, like, real coffee?" Ella was still not sure this was real. Everything was making her brain hurt.

"Hmm, yes. They have real coffee. And real donuts too, I hear," added Mike facetiously.

"Not bad, eh?" Dan contorted himself to look at Ella, waiting for her reaction. But Ella wasn't ready to concede that there was at least one thing here that was "not bad." She went back to staring out the window.

The Frobisher Inn was a beautiful hotel with a gym and free Wi-Fi. The room on the 7th floor that Ella was sharing with her dad had a kitchenette, a fireplace, and a big screen TV. It was, at least, as luxurious as any hotel one might find just about anywhere else on the continent, whether in a much bigger city or next to a well-traveled highway, if not more. This same room could have been near Trudeau airport or in Vancouver, or New York, even.

Dan noticed how stunned Ella seemed to be.

"This is awesome, right?"

Ella took a moment to answer.

"This is . . . boring."

This was definitely not an igloo. Not that she would have liked to sleep in an igloo. It was just that she felt like the universe was playing a major prank on her, making sure to debunk every single one of her expectations. *So what* if she had relied on every cliché in the book? Couldn't she at least be right about a few things? Making it worth it for her to have wasted so much time and effort on concocting apocalyptic scenarios?

Ella walked to the corner window of the room and discovered a stunning view of the softly illuminated town that would be her new home, at least for a while.

She stared at the lights of Iqaluit until they went out of focus.

HOME IS WHERE YOUR STUFF IS

ELLA NOW WISHED they had never left their boring hotel room. It was only 10:30 a.m., and she had already lost count of all the things that made her go "ugh."

Her dad had called taxi driver Mike to pick them up and drive them to their new house. At least, Mike seemed like a nice guy, and he even offered to give them a hand if they needed anything. He was born here, knew just about everything there was to know about Iqaluit and most people in the community, too. And he was just a phone call away. That was reassuring.

Mike had volunteered to give Ella and Dan a free tour around town, so they went up and down the small streets. Culture shock reached a new height for Ella as she saw ATVs and snowmobiles drive by. This was so *not* urban.

They drove past a street called "Road to Nowhere," which made Ella scoff. She was in too foul a mood to appreciate the self-deprecating humor of the street sign and thought that perhaps the locals were just being realistic.

The cab turned into yet another residential street. Most of the houses were modest. One of them had Arctic char drying on a porch rack in front of the house. Ella tried to make out what these "decorations" were until she realized it was real fish. No way! That was so gross. She let out a fairly loud "ugh." Mike heard her and guessed what she was reacting to.

"Don't knock it till you try it, Ella!"

"I think I'll take your word for it." She added, "No offense."

"None taken. I understand it takes a while to adjust. Take your time. You might find some interesting things."

Ella kept any future reactions to herself. She didn't want to appear rude and bitchy, now that she was in an isolated town where everyone knew each other. And Mike didn't deserve her grumpiness. But she was not officially done sulking yet, either. And the drying fish was not helping.

"You want to see something else that's gross, Ella?" asked Dan.

"Not really, no."

"You see those pipes running aboveground over there? You know what that is?"

"A gas pipeline?"

"The sewer system."

"UGH!" Her dad had succeeded in grossing Ella out big time. "But . . . why?"

"Because of the permafrost layer," explained Mike. "The ground is permanently frozen. We can't have pipes under the ground. Mind you, lately, the ground has been thawing a bit with climate change. That's gonna cause major problems before long. Everything's built assuming the ground would remain hard. The RCMP station even started sinking into the ground."

"The whole building?" asked Ella.

"Can you believe it?"

Great, thought Ella. They just got here, and things were already heading south. She hoped this was not a sign of things to come.

The Iqaluit housing market was exorbitant. Dan had found a furnished rental, a small red house that would meet all their needs—that was how he was putting it anyway. But Ella didn't want her needs to be just *met*. She was accustomed to things being grand or dazzling or . . . something more. Just more. She had no need for the word "modest" to even enter her vocabulary. But right now, "MODEST" was staring her in the face, all in uppercase, and she apparently would have no choice but to learn to live with it.

"Could we look at other places?" she sheepishly asked her dad, just in case.

"This house is by far the best option. What's wrong with it?"

What isn't wrong with it? she thought as she rolled her eyes. "Seriously?"

Dan gave her a thin smile.

"I guess I'll have to adjust to this much *luxury*," she couldn't help but quip with a snarky tone.

"I know. This place might even have running water."

Ella's eyes widened. Noooooooooo. She went straight for the kitchen tap, lifted it in a hurry—thank God, it worked! She tested the hot water too. And then it dawned on her: what about the bathroom? Was there even an indoor bathroom, connected to one of those hideous aboveground sewer pipes? Or not even? Were we talking outhouse in the backyard?

Ella ran down the hall and was extremely relieved to see an indoor toilet *and* a bath/shower combo. Once again, modest, but, at least, they were there. Indoors.

"Don't give yourself a heart attack!" shouted Dan.

"I might. I can barely contain my excitement."

Ella poked her head out of the bathroom.

"Is the water safe to drink? Or do we have to boil it over a campfire?"

"Ella, dear, we moved to Iqaluit, not the 1800s."

Ella came out of the bathroom and looked around. A small room across the hall caught her eye. It must be her bedroom. She walked in. The walls were pale beige like the rest of the house. It had a twin bed with a down comforter that looked cozy. A bedside table. A small closet. All very plain.

She walked to the window and saw that the view was, at least, interesting. Nowhere near as spectacular as the one from the hotel room, but still. They were slightly uphill, and she would see the lights from the houses below at night. As well as the vastness of the frozen waters of Frobisher Bay. The landscape had a soothing effect.

Ella kept going with her tour of the place, checking out her dad's bedroom, which was just as plain as hers. She looked out his window, which was facing the street. Movement on the right side of the blue house right across the street attracted her attention. It was a side door that opened, letting out a gorgeous husky. The dog went down a small set of stairs with dignified steps. It went down the driveway then stopped and sat. It looked around, surveying the street.

Ella observed the dog for a while—she had always wanted a dog, but with her dad working odd hours and them traveling, it was never a practical choice. That was the official reason anyway.

The dog spotted Ella and studied her with a calm gaze. Ella couldn't help but smile.

A FIRST TIME FOR EVERYTHING

The kitchen was modern enough, and Ella was grateful that her dad had thought of bringing their espresso machine to Iqaluit. It was shiny metallic, and it gave the kitchen a nice modern touch. Ella was willing to cling to anything that would remotely make her feel at home.

The kitchen came equipped with various pots and pans, cooking utensils, dishes, and mugs. While rather basic, this was greatly useful as it had prevented the Briggses from needing to move such items in a container on a sealift ship, a way to ship goods to Iqaluit during the warmer months. Dan and Ella had brought the bare minimum with them on the plane, in suitcases and a few boxes. Dan had allowed Ella to bring a good amount of clothes as he knew this would make a difference to her. They would also be traveling back to Montreal for Christmas and would be able to bring back more things with them then, should they need to adjust.

In the afternoon, Dan called Mike once again, this time to get a ride to the PolarMart, a big-box store, which happened to sell groceries. It was near the Tim Hortons. As Ella hopped out of the cab, she couldn't help but spy through the window of the donut shop, curious to see if it was a bona fide Timmy's or a knock-off—its presence still felt so incongruous to her. But, sure enough, it looked like a Tim Hortons.

"You're not dreaming, Ella. It's the real thing," Dan said.

"Actually, I wouldn't mind dreaming. That would take away the awful feeling that I'm stuck in a never-ending nightmare."

Dan took a deep breath and headed to the PolarMart. Ella followed him, realizing how annoying she was being. *Oh, well. That's what you get for dragging me here!*

The PolarMart looked like your typical big-box store. Back in Montreal, Ella mostly shopped in boutiques and at the downtown malls, but she had been to the likes of Walmart, of course, and here she was in familiar territory. Still, two things struck her. The first one was, as this was her first time seeing a good-sized crowd, how diverse the local people were. She somehow thought she would stick out as the only white girl for miles, but this was definitely not the case, and these other white folks didn't all seem to be tourists either. Oddly, she felt disappointed —it would have made her feel unique to be different. But then again, since she planned on keeping to herself, not being in the spotlight could only be a good thing.

The second thing that struck her was how extremely expensive food was.

"Twenty bucks for a brick of regular cheese!? This is highway robbery," she whispered to her dad.

Dan nodded but didn't seem surprised.

"It's outrageous, isn't it?"

"Good thing we won't be here long."

"Right. But think about the ones who live here permanently and have to put up with that."

She looked at her dad. His point sank in.

"And the majority, who might not have a high salary, like I'm very fortunate to have," he added, pushing the cart forward.

Ella looked around to see what the other shoppers had in their carts. Her dad was right. Several Inuit families were planning to buy much fewer and cheaper staple articles than the *Qallunaat*—the non-Inuit folk—who were more likely to be temporary workers with higher salaries, like Dan. Ella stopped being selfish for a moment and could appreciate the clear advantage they were having over the local families. This was awful.

The thought still lingered in her mind later on as she helped unpack their precious groceries. She had never really given much thought to the price of food before, but here, now, for the price of this jar of peanut butter and this pack of ground beef, she could buy a brand-new outfit. This was totally crazy.

For dinner, Dan made a huge batch of spaghetti sauce so that he could freeze most of it. Cooking in large batches seemed like the best thing to do from now on.

The kitchen smelled like it always did when he made his terrific sauce, and the homey smell of it crept up on Ella, providing a calming effect. So much so was the power of smell and taste that at dinner time, as they started to eat, things felt somewhat normal. Ella let her guard down, welcoming the feeling. It felt so good to feel at peace for a moment. They ate in silence, but a serene kind, not the tense one they'd been so familiar with lately.

It was unfortunate that, eventually, all bliss must come to an end.

"You'll be walking to school."

Dan was washing the dishes, and Ella was drying. The mention of school reopened the gates to the pit of acid in her stomach—she had repressed all thoughts of it so far.

"That's because we live too close to the school for you to take the bus," added Dan. "Plus, you know, fresh air!"

"Yeah, I can't wait to get fresh air."

Ella sounded resigned this time. *That's a new one*, she thought. She ought to look up the 12 steps of mourning or whatever number of steps it was. Perhaps she could find tips or instructions on how to cope. If she was to go through different shades of being miserable, at least if she knew what to expect, what was ahead, perhaps she could either brace herself ahead of time or even skip some of the steps. And not be such a slave to her feelings and whatnot.

"Let's take a walk tonight. I'll show you where it is."

Ella didn't respond. She just kept drying the same plate already dried, over and over.

"That alright, El?"

"Whatev."

They finished drying the dishes in silence. And before Ella knew it, she was heading outside with Dan, in the darkness of the evening, dragging all the dread in the world along with her, like cans on a string attached to the back bumper of a newlywed couple's car. The dread was just as loud but on the inside.

The neighbor's husky was outside in the driveway and provided a nice distraction. Its eyes were on Ella and her dad the moment they opened their front door. Knowing the dog was loose, she wondered: what if it was mean? What if it went after them? But they were approaching the bottom of their driveway, and the dog still hadn't moved one bit, with the exception of its stare, trained on Ella. She made sure to stay close to her dad, who didn't even seem aware of the dog.

The road was covered with a fresh layer of snow. Some of the homes along the street were in the dark while others bustled with life. Smoke came out of several chimneys. The air was crisp, with a cozy smell of wood burning.

"I'm going there next Monday?" asked Ella flatly.

"Yeah. First day of school for you. First day of work for me."

Dan sounded very eager to start his new contract. In contrast, Ella could barely hide her anxiety about facing her own unknown.

"Would you like me to go with you, Monday morning?" Dan offered.

"Oh, God, NO! I'll already have a target on my back. You want to give everyone a box of bullets to go with that?"

Dan gave her a sympathetic smile.

"I just thought that might help. But clearly not. I don't think you'll have a target on your back. Why would you even think that?"

Ella shrugged. But deep inside, she thought that since she had no intention whatsoever of being sociable, it was a given that the other students wouldn't react too well to her. She had never been unsociable or rejected before. And she was not looking forward to finding out how that felt.

"Of course, if you keep up the Little Miss Sunshine thing you've had going these past weeks . . ."

Dan was looking at her knowingly. She hated it when he read her mind.

"I think it's worth it to make a tiny effort, El. It'll be easier for you. Give people a chance. You might be surprised. Otherwise, you'll just end up hurting yourself and no one else. And that would suck."

Ella let out a sigh. Perhaps her dad was right. Actually, she knew that he was right.

"I know this is not easy for you, luv," he added. "Thank you for being here with me." He gave her a side hug before she could mumble anything unpleasant.

They turned into a street, and there it was, right in front of them: Agloolik High.

"Oh . . . my."

Those were the only words Ella found to express her surprise. The building was quite different—pretty much in every way—from the St. Mary's brownstone exterior that breathed of tradition and centuries of academic excellence. Agloolik High was kind of like a rectangular purple blob and looked to Ella more like, say, a museum of modern art than any high school.

"Do you know what *Agloolik* means?" Dan asked her.

"It means 'looks like a bunch of Legos slapped together'?" Ella tried.

Dan chuckled. The very colorful building was indeed reminiscent of a giant Lego project.

"It's the name of a spirit. A spirit that lives underneath the ice and helps fishermen."

"Of course. That would have been my seventeenth guess."

Dan gave Ella another squeeze.

"They named the school after a spirit? That's not creepy at all."

Ella sounded sarcastic for Dan's benefit when, in fact, she was amused and intrigued. She couldn't wait to tell Sandy she'd be going to a place called, in essence, "Haunted High."

That evening, in the middle of unpacking her suitcases, Ella stopped and surveyed her room. It was so bare and bland, it reminded her of a room in a convent as seen in movies, such a contrast to her old glittery, fashionable digs. This was all so drab, so depressing. Discouraging, even. She almost felt like crying.

She hung a haute-couture-themed wall calendar—with illustrations of cute dresses—on the wall by her bed and looked at the day's date . . . at all the months ahead . . . With a pen, she made a big, fat X on today's date.

This was going to be a long year.

Suddenly, on the wall next to the calendar, Ella noticed fluctuating, colorful bits of light appear. She turned around to see what was going on. She walked up to the window and gasped. There was a bizarre light show in the sky.

"Oh my God, aliens! DAD!"

Dan came running into the room. Ella was ducked underneath the window, as if trying to avoid a sniper from outside.

"What's wrong?"

Ella was speechless. She pointed to the sky. Recognizing the northern lights, Dan hit the light switch, killing the lights in the room.

"Don't leave me!" Ella was on the verge of freaking out.

"Calm down, El. Don't you know what this is?"

How was she supposed to know, and why was her dad not panicking, too?!

"Is that a spirit? Like at the school? I think we should go hide in the basement." It dawned on her that their new home didn't have a basement. Where could they possibly hide?

"It's the northern lights, Ella. The beautiful northern lights."

Ella had heard of the northern lights before, but she never thought she would ever get to see them with her own eyes. She instantly felt silly for first thinking aliens and spirits. It was her general nervous state, she reasoned—there were only so many emotions she could juggle all at once.

She lifted her head and saw Dan so moved and enthralled

by what he was seeing. She stood up to look too. And what she saw was of spectacular beauty, powerful beyond words.

The distant sky danced with colorful candle flames. Ella felt at once so small and so uplifted.

For a moment, she forgot to feel miserable.

CRACK OF DAWN

Henry managed to keep an even running pace as he spoke. By now, Sera was matching his pace almost effortlessly. After her first failed run, she had tripled her efforts and started to run after school and on some evenings after homework to be able to keep up with Henry in the mornings. And, sure enough, she was able to join him for a full run in a matter of days, without slowing him down. He looked impressed at her progress too, which was a lovely and encouraging bonus. As was the fact that he simply welcomed her to tag along, without any fuss or questions.

"It hurt for a long time . . ." Henry started. "But things eventually went back to normal. You don't really notice it. But it happens. Or that's what happened to me. Perhaps it's not the same for everyone."

There was a tinge of nostalgia in Henry's voice as he opened up to Sera about his parents' divorce when he was ten. Some nostalgia, but no judgment.

"So . . . whose fault was it?"

Sera was curious to know. Not just for gossip, but also because this hit close to home. Her own parents' relationship had been rocky for as long as she could remember, and the thought of them divorcing often crossed her mind. In the past, she would worry about what would happen to her if they split, and the prospect was stress-inducing. But now that she was old enough to take care of herself, the practical challenges of them eventually splitting were less a part of her worries. However, emotionally, there was still a pinch of pain whenever she thought about the possibility of her family coming apart. Or whenever a silent—or not so silent—war was being waged at home. What would happen if they broke up? Would one of them feel forced to leave town? To go where?

Sometimes, Sera wished they would just get over with it— once and for all—and move on so they could put an end to this uncomfortable state of affairs.

Sera had never brought this up to anyone until now. Henry turned out to be so easy to talk to and such a good listener. One conversation led to another, and the next thing she knew, she was spilling her guts and her angst to him about her family's situation.

And she felt such a relief. Being with Henry was a soothing experience.

"Were you too young to know?" ventured Sera. Henry had not answered her question, and she was curious to know whether he blamed his dad or his mom.

"Both? Neither?" Henry finally answered. "Does it matter?"

That was a good point. Or, at least, not an answer Sera was expecting. Henry seemed at peace with what he was saying. Sera wished she could say the same about herself.

After three weeks of running together, Sera pushed her luck. They were arriving in front of her house and were in mid-conversation about the Cory Doctorow book *Little Brother* they had been assigned to read in English class. While Sera hadn't cared for the book, Henry seemed passionate about all the techno-geek stuff and questions on civil liberties. She asked him if he'd like to finish the discussion later, over coffee perhaps?

But the question seemed to take him aback a little.

"How about we finish it next Monday morning? That'll give me time to build a better argument to convince you of its brilliance," he proposed with a smile.

Sera tried to hide her disappointment. "Sure."

"I'm sorry. It's just that I have so many commitments right now. I got tons of work this weekend, and I'm coaching the peewees. And then my mom—"

"Oh, it's okay!" she jumped in. "I completely understand. It's all good! Really!"

Sera started heading towards her house so that Henry wouldn't have to keep justifying himself. *Crap-on-a-Popsicle-stick.* She should have known it was too early.

"See ya in school!" she added with a chirp in her voice to convince him that all was well in the world, and nothing at all had changed. Nothing at all.

While this bummed Sera out, this was also no reason to give up. This was a mere wrinkle in her plan. It did occur to her that Henry might be gay—a plausible explanation as to why he didn't enthusiastically accept her invite—but she didn't think it was the case, and unless she ever got concrete proof of that, she chose to ignore this hypothesis for the time being. For now, she would keep at it. She had a feeling that patience and dedication would pay off. She would take all the time needed to make this happen. To make Henry fall in love with her.

And then, Ella had to arrive in town.

ONCE YOU ENTERED the front doors of funky purple Agloolik High, you could see it was a typical high school. Long beige corridors with the mandatory cork boards to either side, on which a variety of announcements were pinned. Doors leading to typical classrooms, typical washrooms, a typical gym. However, on that very Monday morning, as Ella walked down one corridor, clutching her backpack, she didn't feel like she was in a typical high school. She was too busy searching for her locker and trying to lay low and not get noticed.

As she made her way through a crowd of students, most heads turned to check her out. Her. The new kid. She gave most of them a timid smile and avoided making too much eye contact. She was feeling too intimidated to carry out her previous plan of giving everyone attitude. And right now, she was even kind of hoping some zealous welcoming committee would spring up, out of the woodwork, to break the ice and help her stop feeling so uncomfortable.

Her wish came true, though in a much different way than wished for. As Ella was desperately trying to find her locker, some shrimpy, pimply white boy with a black turtleneck and a baritone voice came to her rescue. Of all the kids in the entire school, there was no doubt he had to be the absolute most awkward-looking of them all. *Really?!*

"Can I help you with something?" he volunteered.

Ella looked at the weird kid, unsure he was talking to her. She looked around. *Ugh.* He *was* talking to *her.*

"Looking for a classroom?"

"My locker."

She reluctantly showed him a piece of paper on which she had scribbled her locker number, hoping that no one would see her—let alone remember seeing her—interact with him. She suspected she'd get branded early enough, but not minutes out of the gates!

"This way."

The kid started walking, expecting Ella to follow him. But she didn't move.

"You can just tell me where it is . . ." she tried.

"I'm heading that way."

Fine. Ella started to follow.

"I'm Tim," he said.

"Nice to meet you, Tim," Ella forced out a hushed reply.

"And you are?"

I'm none of your business . . .

"Ella."

"Nice to meet you, Ella. Where are you from?"

"Montreal."

"Ah, Montreal. I'd love to go there."

"Me too." She couldn't help letting those words slip out of her mouth and regretted saying them just as fast as they came. "Sorry, I'm not trying to have an attitude," she quickly added.

You're such a wimp! she scolded herself. What the hell was she doing apologizing to this kid? And where was that damn locker?! This was excruciating.

"Montreal . . . Some of the greats come from there."

Oh, good, small talk. Ugh.

"Dolan, Villeneuve . . ."

Villeneuve . . . That was the street near the bagel place. Dolan, though, didn't ring a bell.

"Do you like their films?"

Films? Oh. These must be . . . actors?

"I . . . They're on my list."

"Good stuff."

"Where are you from?" Ella asked politely. She figured if she got him to talk about himself, she wouldn't have to feel like an idiot answering obscure questions.

"I was born here."

"Oh?"

"My mom is an Inuk from here, and my dad's a white dude from Toronto."

Ella thought this was kind of interesting. Too bad he seemed like such a dweeb. She couldn't afford to associate with a dweeb at a brand-new school.

"We live here, but we often travel down South to see family."

As Ella was going down a seemingly never-ending hallway with Tim, a pack of senior jocks—*some things just never change*—appeared ahead, headed their way. *These* guys should be her peeps! But that was not going to happen, now that she was seen with this turtleneck shrimp loser.

Ella tried to distance herself from her guide. But with every inch she moved to the right, he followed her lead and moved to the right. There was no hope of ditching this guy.

"Hey, hey, hey, Tim!" one jock teased.

Ella braced herself for the worst. The jock started swinging his arm towards Tim, as if to smack him. But this presumed incoming slap turned into a high five, then a fist bump. This guy

—probably one of the biggest guys in the school—was now bro-hugging a guy who could easily fit in a small trash can. What the hell?! Was this opposite day?

"Yo, guys!" said Tim. "Say hi to Ella. She's new. Be nice, alright?"

Ella had to admit that Tim had some class.

"Elllllllllllllla," the jocks said in a chorus.

"Hey," she told them with a little wave. She felt grateful to Tim. What he just did was pretty awesome.

"Welcome here!" added one of the guys.

"Nice to meet ya," said another.

"Tell us if you need anything." That was the buffest one of the gang. "Tim, you be nice too."

"Always!" said Tim. Ella was beginning to like this guy, despite being unable to figure him out. Oh, well, he was not the first person or thing that puzzled her in Iqaluit.

Ella felt relieved that the ice was starting to break. Perhaps it was the workings of the Agloolik spirit, she thought, finding herself witty.

The pack of jocks continued on in the opposite direction as Tim pointed to a set of lockers.

"This is where our paths go their separate ways."

"Thank you, Tim."

"Don't mention it."

Tim kept walking, and Ella went to her new locker. She was pleasantly surprised to see that its door opened and closed without a fight. The edges of the door were straight as an arrow. It felt good not to have to battle for a change.

Ella wanted to get to her first class ahead of time to be able to survey her new classmates and figure out where to sit—preferably near at least one student who seemed popular or to have some kind of influence. She could usually spot such people pretty easily on a regular day, but today was anything but regular.

Having been delayed first by the locker search, then by trying to find the English room, when she finally arrived at room 207, all the other students had already taken a seat. Her future was sealed, Ella thought. And on top of it, she'd have no choice but to take the only free desk in the room, and that bugger happened to be in the front row, smack in front of the teacher.

Ella had never before chosen nor been forced to sit in the front row—that zone was reserved for nerds and teacher suck-ups—and she felt supremely exposed, sensing that all eyes in the room were on her. Now, she felt her face and neck turning red. Even worse than feeling exposed was the feeling that everyone knew how uncomfortable she was.

Ella knew she wasn't meant to be vulnerable in public. She'd have to find ways to cope with this and pronto, before she got pegged as something she wasn't, like a shy dork. Because once you made that first impression, you couldn't take it back, and it was nearly impossible to change it. No matter who you were, no matter how popular you used to be.

For now, she thought that her best bet was to attract some sympathy or, at the very least, appear sympathetic. She would have to seem friendly. And modest. So, she started to look around her, smiling timidly. While this was the absolute oppo-site of her earlier plan, she decided she would not, under any circumstances, let herself be made into a target.

Miss Wilson, the teacher, introduced Ella as the new student at Agloolik and asked her to tell the class a bit about herself.

Ella was a quick study, and after the eye-opening trip to PolarMart and her awareness of how privileged she was, she wanted to avoid antagonizing anyone by coming across as a self-entitled rich snob. Thinking on her feet, she needed to find a way to not really say anything at all about herself, the best way to avoid people hating her from the get-go. She'd have to stay on neutral ground or, better yet, find common ground. Or praise, or bribe. Okay, she had options. She stood up and turned around.

"As Miss Wilson said, my name is Ella . . . I'm from Montreal. I was born there, and this is the very first time that I've ever moved, so please bear with me—I have a lot to learn. I'm still a little dazed and confused."

She smiled wide, playing a little dumb (but not too much) and trying to appear endearing. Yeah, endearing would work if she managed to pull it off. It was a threat to no one. She made eye contact with her fellow students and could see most of them were attentive, some even smiling back to make her feel more at ease. She was on the right path.

"Can you tell us a bit about your interests?" asked the teacher.

Fudge. Shopping was probably not the best answer. And besides shopping, what were her interests? Seriously, what did she care about? How could she spin this?

"Hmmm . . . I like clothes . . . I noticed there are so many amazing artisans around here that . . . uh . . . I'd love to learn more about the craft."

Thank you, airport gift shop, for exhibiting and selling the handiwork of local garment artists and giving me an out, here.

Several students nodded, as if she had really opened up about herself. On top of studying law as an option, Ella might also have a bright future as a politician or marketer.

"Like sewing?" the teacher asked.

Sewing, really? She was all thumbs! But only *she* knew that.

"Yeah, things like sewing."

A mousy girl named Justine raised her hand eagerly.

"There's a sewing and needlepoint club at lunch! I can bring you!"

Great. Ella struggled to keep her smile from turning sour. Add painter to that list of career options—painting herself into corners.

She skated to remain non-committal. "That . . . might be . . . great. After I settle in, maybe?" She managed to say this cheerily.

"Okay." Justine's answer was just as cheery, on top of being genuine.

"Thanks for offering." Ella turned to the teacher. "How about I don't further hijack your lesson, Miss Wilson."

And on those words, Ella saved herself from making a bad impression and becoming the center of negative attention. For the time being.

When the bell rang, Justine made a beeline for Ella. But just as she was about to talk to her, Sera—who looked super confident and dazzling—cut right in front of Justine, physically dismissing her.

Ella recognized the bitchy move and thought *queen bee at 4 o'clock.* And she was right. Sera was the school's number one ice queen.

"Is that cashmere?" Sera asked, pointing at the periwinkle-colored sweater Ella was wearing.

"It is! You could spot cashmere from that distance?"

"Of course."

"I'm impressed!"

Two cute girls, Olive and Brianna, showed up behind Sera. Her posse. Sera didn't bother to introduce them. Instead, she turned to them and pointed at Ella's sweater. "See? That's the real deal." And they all started oohing and aaahing over Ella.

Ella's cashmere sweater turned out to be her ticket to the school's top clique. Just like that, she was in. And the days ahead would surely be marvelous.

One should never underestimate the rallying power of fashion and expensive garments.

THE HOMELESS ARTIST

ELLA WAS OVER THE MOON. Going to school was no longer a dreaded affair. She started to sleep better too, which made her feel a lot less like crap. She no longer had to make gigantic efforts not to look miserable because she *was* no longer miserable. She had found her peeps!

Sera's occasional entourage—Olive and Brianna—were fun girls. And Sera, of course. Ella felt like she had never before had so many affinities with someone else as she had now with Sera. Not even with long-time best friend Sandy. Ella and Sera were like two peas in a pod, and it was exhilarating. Ella started missing Montreal a little less.

The great thing about Sera was that she understood Ella, who she was. And Ella didn't have to pretend with her or explain herself. Sera was born in Iqaluit. Her dad was an RCMP officer, which acted as the local police (Ella found this bit at once exciting AND intimidating), and her mom was an executive. As an only child (just like Ella!) and as the little princess of a well-off family, Sera could afford to have expensive tastes and a terrific sense of style. She also happened to love Ella's clothes and, before long, they were swapping garments.

Ella even gave Sera a black velvet choker with a peach-colored faux stone pendant that Sera kept eyeing.

"Call it a friendship necklace," Ella told Sera, who was thrilled to get the necklace.

Sera also wanted to hear all about Ella's past shopping adventures. And how it was at St. Mary's High. Was it like those American high schools depicted on Netflix? What was it like to live in Montreal? Sera had always dreamed of going to a big city. Perhaps someday her dad would be transferred. And if that ever happened, she would move in a heartbeat. Wouldn't it be fun if they both ended up in Montreal together? They could be roommates! And Ella would bring her to all the right stores and all the right places.

One night, as they were bonding over makeup tips at Sera's place—a nice and thoughtfully decorated home—Sera noticed that Ella seemed a bit down as she talked about shopping at the downtown Montreal Sephora store, and how much she missed going there. To cheer her friend up, Sera brought Ella to a small green building called The Snack, a snack bar with poutine on the menu.

"I wanted you to know that if you ever feel homesick, you can always get poutine here. And from other places too."

That was so perfect! Ella had been craving the beloved Quebec dish of French fries and cheese curds drenched in a brown gravy. This was terrific news! But more importantly, this made Ella feel taken care of and appreciated.

"Just like home." Ella smiled wide before diving into her poutine. She savored the first bite—it was great. The warm cheese curds had melted a bit and were just squeaky enough.

The gravy was well seasoned, and the fries just the right balance of crispy and mushy.

"Actually, better than home!" she added.

"Oh my God! That makes me so happy!" Sera was pleased to have shown her friend this place and to know that her little town could compete with the best of them.

From then on, they began to hang out at The Snack on a regular basis.

On a fine Saturday afternoon, as the two girls were chilling in one of The Snack's cherry-red lacquered booths, Ella spotted an elderly woman going from table to table and assumed that she must be a homeless person begging for change.

"We have those at home too," she said, pointing at the woman.

Sera turned to see what Ella was talking about.

"Wait a minute . . ." Ella started whispering. "She's not homeless! She has a house! She lives across the street from us!" Ella had just recognized the lady as her neighbor with the husky.

"Well, yeah, she's not homeless. She's an artist."

"What is she doing begging?"

"She's not begging. She's selling her crafts to tourists."

"Oh. Good. I was afraid we'd have to go hide in the bathroom to avoid her, or something."

Sera's face turned serious. She leaned over and whispered to Ella, "You should still hide away from her."

"What?! Why?"

"You've seen horror movies, right?"

"Some. Why?"

"That's all I need to say."

Sera went back to sipping her Pepsi.

"Well, what!? What do you mean by that?"

Ella didn't want to have to fear and avoid her neighbor. At the same time, this mysterious revelation piqued her curiosity, and the sense of danger was somewhat titillating. And, of course, she couldn't pass on good gossip.

But Sera took her sweet time slurping through her chewed-up straw.

"Is she a murderer?" Ella ventured in a hushed tone.

Sera shook her head no.

"Is she . . . a witch?"

Sera shook her head again. Negative.

"Then, what!?"

Sera cracked a smile. "She's just really annoying. She'll talk your ear off if you ever let her."

Ella let out a laugh of relief.

"I had you going, eh?" Sera gloated.

"That was not funny!" laughed Ella. "Okay, fine, that was kind of funny."

"Well, it's funny now. But don't forget. You've been warned."

Ella couldn't believe she had fallen for this prank. Sera was good—she kept her cards close to her chest.

Sera whipped her cell phone out and, using the front-facing camera, checked to make sure she had nothing caught in her teeth. She noticed the senior artist a few tables back behind her, getting closer.

"Oh, God, she's coming our way. Let's split."

Sera stood up, grabbed her jacket and was already out the door before Ella could even voice an opinion. She imitated her friend and made a run for the exit, feeling bad about leaving her tray behind at the table, for someone else to clean up. She knew that was not very nice of her to leave her garbage, but she was too giddy not to follow her friend's lead.

Ella pushed the door to exit the snack bar and found Sera waiting outside, giggling her head off, ready to move on to the next thing.

THE AVENGING TYPE

"So, which one's your type?" Sera asked Ella on their way out of the Astro, Iqaluit's movie theater, after seeing the latest Avengers movie.

"What d'you mean?" Ella put her mittens on. It was a nice day outside, but chilly.

"I mean, which Avenger is your type? Who would you go out with?"

Ella made a face—what a bizarre question.

"Why would I care to go out with a superhero? What part of me says 'nerd' to you?" Ella pretended to be offended.

"Oh, come on! Don't tell me you were watching that film for the plot!" Sera playfully elbowed Ella. "Would you swear on a polygraph that you weren't checking out Thor or Captain America?"

Ella held back a smirk, but it quickly spread across her face. A matching smirk appeared on Sera's face.

"That's what I thought. So?" Sera asked as they started walking downhill on Queen Elizabeth Road.

"I dunno. What about you?"

"Okay, well . . . When I was younger, my cousins dragged

me to see the Iron Man movies, and I had the biggest crush on him. On Tony Stark."

"Right. Cute and rich. I can totally see that."

"And smart and inventive. Geez! You make it sound like I'm a superficial gold digger."

"I would sooooo not say that. But then, you mean that even if he were dirt poor?"

"I didn't say that. The fortune part is important, 'cause it's practical."

"Fair enough. So, for you, Tony Stark is boyfriend material?"

"*Was*. He's an old geezer, now."

"Right. So, you'd rather stay single than date an old crouton?"

"Who says I'd have to stay single? I could marry Tony Stark and go for Thor on the side."

"Oh, you can pick more than one?"

"Why not? We're talking about flying grown men in tights with magical powers. There are no rules!"

Ella chuckled.

"So, who would you pick?" Sera asked again.

"Hmmm . . . It's hard to tell. Like, I think Dr. Strange is really cute, and he's a high-income earner—see, you don't have the monopoly on practicality—but he's a bit of an asshole."

"Yeah . . ."

"And believe me, I've already dated that guy. Several times, in fact. Different guys, same type. I'm not sure I'd care to do that again."

"Interesting. Who else, then?"

"Captain America, I guess. He's cute and nice."

"And boring."

"I think I'm willing to risk boring over asshole, quite frankly."

"Right."

They walked in silence for a moment. Sera was pleased that Ella was playing along. She once asked her friends Brianna and Olive the same question, and they had both answered "Thor" because he's buff and gorgeous, and they quickly went back to talking about Carl and Silla, their moronic boyfriends, without even asking Sera who she would choose.

Sera had been friends with Brianna and Olive since middle school, when they all discovered a shared interest in fashion and boys. They still shared these interests, but Sera often wished that there was more to their friendship. That they could discuss other things than just clothes and boyfriends who go fishing and hunting. In that regard, Ella was a godsend as she had so many fun things to talk about, so many experiences to share. She had been to New York and had shopped in the best boutiques on Fifth Avenue. Sera's mind was still being blown from hearing about her friend's trips.

"You did notice that Thor is dumb as a post, right?" Ella remarked.

"Yeah."

"And that wouldn't bother you?"

"Well—"

"Oh, how about this? What if none of them had any powers at all and were just regular joes? Would you choose differently? 'Cause I mean, Thor, for instance, what would he be without his magical hammer thingy? He'd be like, what, a blacksmith?"

"A blacksmith? They still have those?"

"I think so. Or a mechanic, then. A very sexy, but not too bright mechanic. Would you go for a not too bright mechanic?"

Sera let out a fake scoff.

"God! And I thought you were fun. Way to shit on my dreams!" she said, holding back a grin.

Ella giggled. "I wouldn't dream of shitting on your dreams."

"Right. But don't laugh so quickly! Your Captain Boring would still be a Goody Two-shoes. And your Dr. Weird would be on disability. An asshole on disability. So, not only would you be broke, but you'd also have to put up with his assholeness—"

"But I wouldn't put up with that! I'm done putting up with that!"

"Okay, so then you're stuck with Captain Milquetoast. Who'd work for social services. And bring home sob stories. And sing Kumbaya at karaoke on weekends. You know, for a little excitement."

Ella laughed again. Sera loved to make her laugh. This sophisticated girl from the city found her funny, and it made her feel special.

"I always thought you'd do better, Ella. Quite frankly, I'm disappointed in you," Sera teased her.

Ella made a sad face.

"Disappointing you is the last thing I'd want to do. You know that!"

Sera gave her a side hug. "There's still hope, Ella. Don't give up. There's still hope."

"Oh, yeah?"

"Yeah. Like, perhaps Olive and Brianna will break up with Carl and Silla, and we'll have some choice bachelors before us."

"Oh, God, gag me with a spoon! That's so depressing."

"It is. Hey, let's go grab a bite!"

"Okay."

"The Snack or Timmy's?"

"Hmmm. Timmy's? I'm gonna be digesting popcorn until Thursday."

Sera chuckled. "Yeah. Never mind, then."

"Nah, it's fine. I'll just have coffee or something. And for the record, Dr. Strange wouldn't be on disability. His fingers are still kinda working. He's smart and educated. There are so many jobs he could get. He could, like, teach surgery, at the very least."

"Oh, and where would he do that?"

"A med school?"

"I know, but where do you see a med school around here?"

Ella let out an amused scoff. "Oh, now it has to be in Iqaluit?"

"Well, yeah!"

"You can't just change the rules to suit yourself!"

"It's my damn game!"

Sera was smiling wide. This kind of silly repartee had been missing from her life.

"Fine! Then, you think that sugar daddy Stark would move all of his high-tech shit over here? For you? No way in hell! The weather sucks snowballs!"

"Oh, yes way, he would. He'd drop everything the moment he saw my stunning beauty."

"And your stunning modesty. Don't forget that one."

"Very much, yes. And powers or no powers, money's no object for him. And he'd still invent that flying suit, 'cause that's based on technology, not on magic or some other superpower dorky crap. And he would make me a suit, too. And I could go shopping wherever I want around the world and not have to worry about obscene delivery fees. So, I win."

"Oh, clearly. You totally win. But what you're saying is that in the end—correct me if I'm wrong—that guy rocks your boat because of delivery fees?" Ella teased.

Sera laughed. "Is that so wrong?"

"I dunno. But you're weird."

"Thank you."

"You're welcome."

ALL IS CHILL

When Ella first arrived in Iqaluit, she texted and phoned Sandy so many times that her friend could have considered getting a restraining order against her. Sandy was her security blanket, and Ella was clinging to her for dear life via her phone like she had never clung to anyone before.

But now that Ella was friends with Sera, it took her a whole week to get back to Sandy. Her old bestie had tried reaching her through texts and social media, voice mail even. But Ella had become too busy, really, to follow up with Sandy, and she kept postponing getting in touch. *I'll reply to her in an hour*, she'd think, but then, she'd get busy and forget. Until this Friday night, that is.

Ella was home alone. Dan was still at work. Sera was busy celebrating one of her cousins' birthday. Ella found herself all alone in front of the TV, which barely had any channels, surfing between nothing, nothing and a rerun of nothing. She had seen everything she cared for on Netflix and didn't feel like poking around YouTube.

For dinner, she made herself yet another peanut butter sandwich. It turned out that Dan was working much longer hours than originally planned, and Ella didn't want to cook. Or rather, Ella knew how to make lattes and peanut butter sandwiches. She didn't even dare to grab something from the freezer. She hated having to deal with thawing stuff out in the microwave. Nothing good ever came of that. And that would be too much trouble anyway, and she felt way too lazy to deal with too much trouble.

Ella looked at the time—it was 8:30 p.m. When would her dad be home? She was bored out of her skull. In the past, she would have been all over social media. But ever since she'd moved to Iqaluit, she had drastically cut down on Instagram and the like since any glimpse into the "real world out there", her old life back in Montreal, would highlight everything she was missing back home, everything that was now out of reach for her, and it never failed to drag her down. As a result, she had quit cold turkey and had stayed away ever since. For the time being anyway.

Ella remembered she hadn't gotten back to Sandy, and now would be the perfect time to do it. She texted her friend—*Yo!*—and waited for an answer.

Five minutes later, still no reply from Sandy. Ella was tired of staring into space and decided to make herself busy while she waited. In an unprecedented move—for a Friday night, that is—Ella reached for her school bag to fish out the math homework due on Monday. She was dreading doing it—she might as well get it out of the way now and be able to enjoy the weekend.

As she cracked the workbook open, she surprised herself thinking: *This is probably Ryan's idea of a kick-ass Friday night.* The thought made her chuckle.

Ryan . . .

Whatever happened to him? Who was he seeing now? Surely, he was seeing someone. So, who was the lucky girl?

A girl like her?

If the two of them had gone out, would they still be together?

She should ask Sandy about him.

Thinking about Ryan made Ella feel strange. This former crush felt like such a thing of the past. So unimportant now. How could she have obsessed over him so badly and, mere weeks later, no longer think of him?

Out of sight, out of mind. Wow, for real.

Ella's phone rang. It was Dan picking up some fried chicken on his way home. Would she like some?

Hell, yes!

As Ella was finishing a small crinkled paper cup of coleslaw, her phone chimed. She quickly wiped her greasy fingers on a napkin and reached for her cell.

It was a text from Sandy. *OMG ur alive! I'll cancel the search party!* Ella smiled, so happy to get a note from her friend, as if Sandy had totally forgotten about her and was finally reaching out for her. Ella was about to text her back but decided a phone call was a much better idea. She yearned to hear her friend's voice.

She headed to her room for some privacy.

"Ella?" Sandy answered, as if not believing she was hearing from Ella for real.

"The one and only." Ella smiled again. This was weird. It felt as though she had grown so much in so little time, as if she was a different person than the one who had last talked to Sandy.

"Oh my God, you're alive! What's up? How come you never got back—"

"It's just been totally crazy!"

"Too crazy to text?"

"Hmmm . . . yeah! Actually, yeah. So crazy and, gee, I don't even know where to start."

"Start anywhere. I wanna hear every detail!"

And so, Ella told Sandy about the town, and the Tim Hortons and the price of milk, and her time at school, and the poutine, and the fact she had met some tolerable people. She mentioned Sera but tried to minimize her impact on her life. She didn't want Sandy to think she had been replaced so fast and so easily, especially since Ella had given her total radio silence. So, she made it sound like Sera and her clique were mostly helping her with her transition, which made Sandy react favorably to them. She sounded truly happy to know that Ella would be fine, despite the previous odds.

"So . . . have you seen him?" Sandy asked eagerly.

"Seen who?"

"The guy from the website! Geez! You know, when you were over at my house?"

It took a moment for Ella to remember, and when she did, she let out a good laugh.

"Geez, Sandy! I don't know. I really haven't been paying attention."

"But you have to!"

"Fine. I'll try. But that won't be easy."

"Why not?"

"First, there are a lot of cute guys around here . . ."

Ella was only saying this to tease Sandy since she hadn't given much thought to the local guys. But now that she said this out loud and was much more relaxed than she had been the weeks before, there indeed seemed to be a few interesting specimens at her school, a good handful of contenders.

"Oh, there's a school dance next Friday!" added Ella. That would be the perfect time to take a good peek. For fun. Even though, a few weeks earlier, she had vowed to Sandy not to make friends with anyone and avoid any kind of romantic interest at all cost, things had changed so much since that silly pledge. Things had evolved.

Perhaps Ella was ready for a fling. At the very least, it wouldn't hurt to keep an eye open.

One thing for sure, though: she forgot to ask Sandy about Ryan.

<h1 style="text-align:center">OH, MY</h1>

Despite being in a few classes together, Ella hadn't noticed Henry, even though he was tall and handsome and totally her type. Henry hadn't noticed Ella either, other than knowing she was a newcomer from the South, and as the welcoming kind of guy he was, he said "hey" to her whenever appropriate to make her feel welcome. But that was pretty much it. So far, their paths had not crossed all that much, and sitting on opposite ends of the classrooms in which they both were hadn't helped either, nor the fact that they both kept to themselves during lessons.

The first time they interacted for more than ten seconds was in the cafeteria. Ella was despondently staring at the unidentified food choices before her. Henry happened to be in line behind her. Unable to choose, she was starting to panic, aware she was slowing everyone down. She turned to him and mumbled, "I'm sorry. You go ahead."

"You should have the brown stuff," he said to her, jokingly.

"Everything's brown."

"Then you can't go wrong."

She looked at him and noticed the smile. A kindly teasing smile. And a lively spark in his eyes. She giggled.

Henry turned to the cafeteria lady behind the counter, who was getting impatient. "Could you please give her a bit of everything so that she can have a taste?" He whispered to Ella, "That way, you can be sure to eat the bits that suck less, and you won't go hungry."

Ella laughed again.

"You can't argue with that kind of logic. Thank you."

"Happy to be of service."

Ella paid, said a quick "bye" to Henry and surveyed the room to find Sera. She located her friend, who happened to be staring at her. Sera waved. Ella headed to her table, looking happy.

Sera had witnessed the interaction between Ella and Henry and tried to hide her unhappiness. She had noticed a chemistry between them. How he had leaned towards Ella to whisper something to her. He never leaned that way towards her. And what was so important that he'd be whispering to her? Did they already share secrets?

Despite the smile she was offering Ella, Sera was forcing herself to act normal—on the inside, she was screaming with rage.

From then on, Ella would glance at Henry whenever she got the chance. Sometimes their gazes would cross. He would smile at her. She would smile back, wondering whether he was simply being nice or if he might be interested in her.

"Do you know if Henry is going to the dance?" Ella asked Sera, one day, on their way to gym class.

"He said he might." Sera tried to sound detached, uninterested.

On a recent run with Henry, Sera had asked him if he was

going to the upcoming fund-raising dance at the school, and he replied that he might pass by for a donation, but probably wouldn't stick around since dancing wasn't his thing. She countered that there were things other than dancing that could be done, like just hanging out and eating cupcakes. Who didn't like eating cupcakes? He should come! That'd be fun! His friends would be there. Henry conceded that it was indeed hard not to like eating cupcakes, and he'd see what he could do.

"Do you know if he's seeing anyone?" Ella asked.

Sera wished Ella hadn't asked but suspected the question was inevitable, Henry being such a catch. She weighed her answer carefully. On the one hand, she and Henry weren't an item, but she didn't want to give Ella the impression she could have a shot at him either. This was delicate. She wasn't sure yet how dirty Ella could play.

"He and I have been hanging out quite a bit lately." Sera's tone had a hint of a warning in it. Ella got the message.

"Oh. Cool. He seems nice."

"He is."

And that was that. Sera quickly changed the subject.

Since Sera was her best bud, Ella stayed away from Henry, though she couldn't help stealing a glance at him, discreetly, whenever he was around. Now was not the time to rock the boat. She would have plenty of time to see how serious this Sera and Henry relationship could be, and should her friend turn out no longer interested, Ella would consider making a move. She'd have to see.

Later on that week, while Ella was walking home after school, a snowmobile caught up to her.

"Hey, Ella!"

It was Henry, on his way to run errands.

"Hey!"

Henry killed the snowmobile's motor. "Want a lift home?"

Ella would have loved a lift home, but that'd be playing with fire if she accepted, and she knew it.

"I'm alright. But thanks for offering."

"Is it the snowmobile? Are you afraid of riding on one?"

Ella made a face. She wasn't afraid of riding on a snowmobile! She was afraid of riding on a snowmobile with the guy on it!

"Nothing to be afraid of," he added.

You'd be surprised.

"It's freezing! I can't believe anyone would turn down a lift!" He beamed her a knee-weakening smile.

"I guess I better start walking again, then. I'll see you at school tomorrow!" This felt like the right thing to say. Not what she would have *liked* to say, but the *right* thing, nonetheless.

Ella resumed walking. It *was* freaking cold! Still, she wished she could have made the moment with Henry last longer.

She heard the snowmobile starting behind her. The noise became louder as Henry caught up to her again, riding slowly next to her as she walked with a determined pace.

"How about I ride next to you until you feel frostbite coming on?" he shouted over the engine.

"You just don't take no for an answer, do you?" she shouted back.

"At this point, I guess not. Now, I'm worried you're not gonna make it home safely. You need to dress warmer."

Henry had a point. Since fashion was paramount to Ella, she had been favoring her nice slate blue jacket, which made her look great, but which was indeed not at all made for this kind of weather. She was used to suffering occasionally to look good and, as a general rule, would rather be cold and delay putting on a snowsuit than suffer for looking bad.

"How about I pick up the pace and get home faster? Perhaps I'll run," Ella volunteered.

"Wow, you're stubborn!"

While still going forward, Henry shifted his position on the snowmobile and lifted the back seat to access a storage compartment. He took out a helmet and offered it to Ella.

"I'm the stubborn one?" Ella asked with a smirk.

Henry answered with another killer smile.

Ella realized that neither of them would back down and, at this pace, they'd be arguing with one another until the baby seals came home and all her limbs fell off from frostbite. No matter how warm this Henry guy was making her feel, the bone-chilling wind was starting to seep through her thin jacket. And she still had several blocks to walk! She was doomed.

Ella looked around her. The street was empty. She grabbed the helmet Henry was still brandishing and put it on, thinking that, at least, with that hair-unfriendly monstrosity over her head, she'd be harder to recognize.

If only she had not underestimated how tightly knit the community was . . .

Henry slowed down as they neared the red house Ella was frantically pointing at, to make sure he wouldn't go past it. She jumped off the snowmobile before it came to a full stop, struggling to take the helmet off.

"Let me help you with—" Henry tried, but Ella yanked on the helmet like a wildcat trying to escape a bag of fleas, and the helmet was off before he even finished his sentence.

"I must have the best hair ever," she quipped self-consciously, suspecting how disheveled she looked. Henry let out a laugh and assessed Ella's hair.

"Yeah, I doubt that'll ever be in style."

"Hey! You're not supposed to say that!" Ella giggled. She couldn't help giving him a little punch on the arm in fake protest. It dawned on her they were fast approaching flirting territory. And that could only lead to no good. She quickly added, "Thank you, Henry. I appreciate it, but I gotta go. See you around."

"See ya," he replied, and just like that, he was gone. A bit faster than Ella would have liked. This gave her the sense that perhaps he had, indeed, just been looking out for her welfare after all. And nothing more. Perhaps he had not come on to her. She felt at once relieved and disappointed.

A few streets over, before Ella even had her key in the lock of her front door, Sera was receiving a text with a photo of Ella on Henry's snowmobile, clinging to him. Her blue jacket and a lock of her long, honey-blond hair, sticking out from underneath the helmet, gave her away. The photo came from the cousin of a friend. Since Sera had been seen running with Henry, folks suspected her interest in him.

Sera fumed when she saw the picture. She couldn't believe Ella would dare do this to her, especially after she had warned her. She thought they had understood each other.

Apparently not.

That two-timing bitch!

THEY SAY: "Keep your friends close and your enemies closer."
Sera had long understood that notion. And the very first time
she had laid eyes on Ella, she had instantly recognized the city
girl as a potential foe. Ella's shy, helpless, adorable girl shtick to
gain everyone's sympathy had not fooled her. She had that very
same trick in her own repertoire. And now, she was glad she had
befriended the newcomer right away. To know Ella and her
weaknesses might come in handy sooner or later. It turned out
that "sooner" came much sooner than anticipated.

Ella's popularity had grown like crazy, practically overnight.
So much so that Sera couldn't help but feeling a bit threatened
by that reality, even before the Henry wrinkle. She enjoyed
Ella's companionship very much but never lost sight of the fact
she was a likely competitor. And she never had this much
competition before! Olive and Brianna were cute but in such a
different league. Until now, no one other than Ella had come
even close to Sera as far as popularity and pure hotness were
concerned.

But even worse than the possibility of being outshone was

the very real possibility of losing Henry—the one and only guy she wanted—to Ella. And the thought was torturous.

The next day was Friday, the day of the much-anticipated school dance.

As Sera had done the night before, she spent all morning ruminating on Ella's betrayal, trying to see how she could put her former, so-called friend in her place before it was too late. A part of her was hurting with disappointment and bitter sadness —she was angry at Ella for ruining the best friendship she'd had in ages. She and Ella had truly hit it off, and now everything had gone to hell because of her.

Even though Sera would miss that friendship terribly, she was used to cutting her losses promptly and taking care of business wherever necessary, to avoid getting hurt any further, to avoid making herself vulnerable. The sad fact was that her friendship with Ella really *had* to go, as painful as this was. The bitch had betrayed her, and as far as she was concerned, there was no coming back from a betrayal.

So, Sera mulled over how she could make Ella understand— clearly, this time—that no one messes with her. The Montreal girl obviously had no code of ethics nor any moral qualms or otherwise. Sera had no choice but to strike the first blow. And strike hard. To make Ella lose credibility. To make her take a social fall so high that she couldn't get up and recover from it.

And Sera would have to make it all look innocent.

But how?

Walking down the corridor at lunchtime, Sera spotted Ella at her locker down the hall. Henry was hanging out with a friend a few lockers away. From Sera's perspective, he might have been looking at Ella. She was too far to tell for sure, but it was a possibility, and that was good enough for her. From the picture she had seen of the two of them, she would have bet money on it.

Sera felt her blood pressure rise. Her face turned red. She whipped around and ducked inside the girls' bathroom. There was no way she would lose her composure now. There was no way she would lose her chances with Henry so damn easily. They were meant for each other, and Ella was a loser. The sooner he would see this, the better. She would help him see what tainted goods Ella truly was. That sweet, conniving little tart.

SIMON SAYS

"Hey! Pass by my house after school?" Sera whispered, all smiles, craning her neck towards Ella. The physics class was about to start.

"Sure. Why?" Ella leaned forward and whispered too.

"To help you get ready for tonight."

" . . . Um. Okay. Do I need help?"

Sera shrugged.

"D'you wanna be queen of the ball?"

Ella let out a muffled laugh. "Sure. Why not."

"Great."

And that was it. Nothing more. No details, no fine print. Just a vague notion that it was the right thing to do for Ella.

She felt so relieved to have been playing nice since day one. *It's paying off*, she thought to herself. And being nice had been so much easier than being on the warpath with everyone and watching your back all the time.

In Sera's room, Ella stood by her friend's desk, going through several wicker baskets filled with random makeup products, checking them out. She and Sera shared similar tastes in color schemes—lots of plums and corals—and favorite brands, like Urban Decay.

"Must cost you a bundle in shipping," Ella mused. "Too bad Tony Stark hasn't shown up yet."

"Hmm?" Sera was busy going through the drawer of a shelving system in her very large closet, otherwise filled to the brim with beautiful clothes and a wide selection of footwear.

Sera's bedroom was pretty and felt a bit like Ella's old bedroom, full of electronics, books, and stuff. It was nice and cozy, and it made Ella feel at home. This was the third time she had come over to Sera's house. It was always quiet since her friend's parents also worked long hours and no one else was home.

"Okay, first . . ." Sera mumbled to herself.

Ella wondered what her friend was up to. It wasn't like *she*, Ella, was a party amateur. If there was one girl in town who knew how to look her best, aside from Sera, that was her. What could there possibly be for her to improve?

From the closet, Sera retrieved a stunning, shiny, electric-blue, low-cut dress. A garment fit for a New Year's Eve party in Ibiza.

"I'm gonna wear this."

"Wow! Really? I assumed it'd be more of a jeans and a cute top kinda thing—"

"It's a fundraiser. I can lend you something if you don't have anything."

Ella actually did have something. More out of nostalgia than practicality, she had brought a sexy, bright-red party dress with her to Iqaluit, mostly to have something to look at once in a while, whenever she needed a tangible dose of glamor. But she never thought she'd have an opportunity to actually wear it while here.

"Thanks so much, but I think I'm good," she replied, giddy at the thought of getting to wear her red dress. *Am I ever good!*

"Oh, okay. Great!" Sera almost looked disappointed. She whipped around and, from a drawer, took out a few sheets of temporary tattoos, several of which were shimmery, colorful rhinestone gem stickers to put on one's face and other body parts.

"You familiar with these?" Sera asked. "They're all the rage."

Ella looked at the tattoos. She might have come across them online, but the trend had not hit her previous school while she was there.

"I reserve this one for tonight." Sera put aside a sheet that featured a large blue tiara design for the forehead. It had little glimmer dots in darker and lighter shades to go underneath the eyes and on the cheeks.

"Oh, that's pretty! That'll go great with your dress!"

"I know, right? You can pick any of the other ones."

Ella studied the other sets. One featured feathers. Another had sequins and looked like an elaborate Mardi Gras mask. Some were just plain stickers like the ones she used to get in elementary school on a test or homework.

Ella settled on a set of random colorful gems. She'd be able to create the design herself.

"I'll take that one. What about makeup? Are the tats enough?"

"Oh, God, I wouldn't go without makeup! I'm gonna go with, like, extra-smoky eyes. And a dark lipstick. It's the best night for a dramatic effect."

Ella nodded. "Dramatic. Got it."

"Would you like me to braid your hair?"

"What?" That was an incongruous proposal.

"Braids are a must," Sera added in all seriousness.

"Braids? Really?"

"Yeah. On each side of your face. Or pigtails. Pigtails are hot too."

Ella was looking at Sera like she was crazy.

"Of course, you don't *have* to. It's just that, you know, when in Rome . . . Just telling you how it's done around here. You do what you want with the info."

Right. Sera had lived here all her life. Who was Ella to question her on local mores? Sera had been a great guide so far. Ella trusted her decisions.

"Alright, I'll braid my hair." Ella shrugged.

"Good. You're all set! Go home, eat, get ready. I'll see you there."

Ella gave her friend a big hug.

"Thanks for being there for me. I don't know what I'd do without you."

A NIGHT TO TOTALLY NOT REMEMBER, EVEN IF THAT MEANS GETTING A LOBOTOMY

Despite wearing high heel ankle boots, there was a spring in Ella's step as she headed to the school dance.

It had snowed earlier, and the snowplow had compacted the snow just right along the road, making her boots sound like they were crunching potato chips as she walked. She usually noticed that sound because she found it amusing. But right now, she was too absorbed in memories of past parties to pay attention to the snow chip soundtrack accompanying her.

Ella had mostly good memories of parties. She loved to dance and was pretty good at it too. She never failed to own the dance floor, attracting the perfect amount of attention from her fellow students. Sandy would always be by her side, along with a few other girls—on-and-off pals—who were happy to hang out and bask in Ella's cool.

One thing for sure: Ella had never been a wallflower, one to awkwardly observe from the sidelines, a bellyache brewing, yearning at once to join the crowd and run home to hide.

Tonight, Ella was also on a high from wearing her gorgeous red dress and looking forward to seeing what this intriguing party would be like. She had followed Sera's advice to a T.

Unsure of the face gems at first, Ella had stuck a few dark-red, star-shaped ones on a cheekbone, then decided to recreate a gem tiara on her forehead, much like the one Sera said she'd be wearing. She then moved on to creating the smoky eye look that her friend would also be sporting and, lastly, she added deep-red lipstick to her lips.

Glancing at the results, she found this was quite different from her usual approach but in a fun way. She added more gem stickers—because why not?—some underneath her eyes, some down her neck and below her shoulder blades. Glitter too.

She started to braid her hair but stopped. She felt like trying the pigtails. *Oh my God!* She kinda looked like Harley Quinn from Suicide Squad!

Ella laughed. This was crazy. And yet so dope. People up North sure knew how to party!

As Ella entered the school, she could hear music blaring from the gym. There were still some palpitations in her gut, but she was confident that she would have a great time.

She hung her winter jacket in her locker and headed towards the gym. She walked past a group of guys, who were staring at her. They were wearing heavy metal t-shirts and looked as plain as they did every day. *They're just younger boys,* she thought to herself. *They probably don't care whether they fit in or not.*

"Oh, look, the stripper has arrived!"

Olive snickered at Ella. Behind the girl, Brianna, Carl, and Silla stood like idiots, staring at Ella with mocking expressions on their faces.

"What?" Ella wasn't sure she had heard Olive's crass remark correctly. The music was so loud in the gym. The place was plunged in darkness, lit mostly by colorful strobe lights. But still, Ella could see very clearly that everyone else was dressed casually, including Sera, who was wearing jeans and a cute black top, tasteful makeup, and loose hair.

With her fire-red, very short, tight-fitting dress, matching lipstick, pigtails, raccoon eyes, and gem tattoos glimmering on a fair amount of exposed skin, Ella had never looked—and felt—so out of place as she did right now. Sera was also staring at her with an expression of surprise. Henry was nearby, chatting with his friend Wallace and oblivious of Ella's awkward presence.

"I SAID—" Olive was too happy to humor Ella. "YOU LOOK LIKE A LAP DANCER AT A KIDS' BIRTHDAY PARTY!"

Perfect timing. The music had segued to a slower, quieter song, and Olive's shouting got the attention of Henry and a handful of other students gathered nearby.

"Oh, hey there, Ella!" Henry said in a very casual way, as if there was nothing different nor weird about Ella's over-the-top attire. He even leaned towards her to add, "I hear there are cupcakes!"

Sera looked taken aback by Henry's reaction or absence thereof.

"Good to know," Ella managed to reply to Henry, still struggling to figure out what the hell was going on. Was Sera pulling her leg, like she had in the past? Was this a playful trick? Inuit humor? Some kind of hazing? Would everyone shout "surprise!" at her in a few seconds?

This seemed very unlikely since the people staring at her were staring aghast at her. Not at all as if they were a part of some big, harmless prank. If this was some kind of joke, she didn't find it funny.

But even worse: this didn't seem like a joke at all.

"Is that a Montreal thing?" Ella turned towards the voice. It was Tim, the black turtleneck-wearing shrimp guy. He was scrutinizing her makeup and gem stickers, genuinely intrigued, as if he wanted to understand what kind of statement she was trying to make.

"Yeah, Ella, is that a Montreal thing?" Sera asked all innocently, getting Ella's attention back.

"What happened to your dress?" Ella tried.

"What dress?" Sera gave her a confused look. "Are you okay?" she added. Her expression morphed into a look of concern.

Definitely not a playful trick, Ella told herself. *A setup.* Sera was clearly setting her up. But why?

Sera shot Henry a quick, sideways glance to make sure he was watching. Ella noticed.

"I'm just dandy, thanks for asking," she replied to Sera with an even tone.

Ella had to keep calm. She didn't want to show how freaked out she truly was. The crowd of spectators around them was growing. Word of Ella's weird look had spread like wildfire, and everyone wanted to see for themselves. She could feel every last pair of eyes on her, sharp gazes piercing through her skin, stabbing her ego, her soul. Some students, feeling awkward for her— pity perhaps—stifled shy laughs, while others had huge grins plastered across their faces.

All would probably agree that Ella looked off her rocker. All would remember this moment for years to come. No one would ever take her seriously ever again. She was used to being admired, for her good looks and great taste—not to be laughed at now, for both.

It was excruciating for Ella to keep a cool expression. To pretend that none of this mattered to her and that she looked like that on purpose. Especially since she had spent most of her life crafting and controlling the image of herself she projected to others.

Sera would pay for this!

"Oh. You don't seem dandy." Sera got closer to her, still faking concern. "Did you forget to take your meds?"

Ugh!

A series of nasty expletives ran through Ella's mind. She came very close to outright screaming obscenities in Sera's face, but she caught herself in time. This was *exactly* what Sera wanted. To get Ella to look crazy . . . that is, even crazier than she already looked right now. She was trying to rile her up, trying to make her react. Make her lose control and go ballistic in front of everyone. In front of Henry. She was having so much fun screwing with her right now, and Ella was totally helpless.

Ella knew the kind of game Sera was playing. She herself had played versions of it in the past, either to get back at someone or to cripple them preemptively. Like the time she flushed Jacqueline Weber's clothes down the toilet after gym class, while the girl was in the shower. Jacqueline had started some nasty rumor about Ella —she couldn't even remember now what it had been—and Ella had seen fit to get back at her. She only managed to clog the toilet, but she knew that Jacqueline—being the last one out—would have to wander around school wrapped in a towel one way or another. Which was pretty much what happened. "Your face is a little red. You get *flushed* pretty easily," Ella had taunted Jacqueline afterward to make sure that her nemesis would know she was the one who had done it, but without being able to prove it.

Which was also what Sera was doing to her at this very moment.

The gaslighting bitch.

"You know, it's nothing to be ashamed of, being different," Sera added.

Ella could tell that some of the students were enjoying this passive-aggressive little cat fight, while others were questioning her sanity. She was trying very hard not to stare bullets at Sera, or beat her up, for that matter.

The little shit.

"Perhaps you should go home," Sera suggested to her with a defiant stare. "You know—change?"

What was Ella to do? Sera had her *exactly* where she wanted her. Her next move had to be smart if she didn't want to become the town's number one pariah or the butt of everyone's jokes for as long as she lived here. If she left the gym, she would admit defeat. If she stayed, Sera would make the rest of the evening unbearable, and Ella would look worse by the minute. Who knew how much damage Sera would be capable of doing in any given amount of time?

Cutting her losses and containing the damage already done was probably Ella's best bet. By now, everyone in the gym was looking at her. Anything she would say or do could be held against her.

"Well, that was fun, and I think I will call it a night. You know, before things stop being fun," Ella managed to say with a smile and started to walk away.

"Hey, Ella, you need a ride?" Henry jumped in.

Sera's face dropped. Henry couldn't be serious! Ella turned around. Sera shot her a murderous look. *Don't you dare . . .* Ella leveled her stare. She was tempted to accept Henry's offer, just to rub Sera's nose in it. Really tempted. But she suspected that move would cost her dearly in the long run.

"I'll be good, Henry. Thanks. Why don't you go raid the cupcakes before they're all gone?" Ella replied, walking away for good. She'd had enough for the night, and downhill was the only way to go from here anyway.

Henry made a move to catch up to her, but Sera threw herself in front of him, blocking him.

"Cupcakes. Great idea!" Sera slid her arm underneath Henry's, guiding him in the opposite direction.

Ella left the gym at an even pace, as if none of this had affected her. A stroll in the park. She knew that if she rushed out, she would show how upset she was, and she didn't want that. She had made enough of a spectacle out of herself as it was.

PARKING LOT BLUES

CROSSING the side parking lot of the school, Ella made her way around a few older cars and snowmobiles. She let out a scream of frustration.

"CONNIVING, BACK-STABBING BIIIIIIIIIITCH!"

Now that she was out of the gym, out of the school, she wanted to run, but her legs felt at once heavy and like they were made of cotton. She felt dizzy with anger.

This was totally crazy and unreal. This could NOT be happening!

She paced around before whipping out her cell. She dialed Sandy.

The line rang.

And rang. Sandy used to always pick up. Why wasn't she picking up? She needed to talk to her!

Ella got her voice mail. *Dammit!* She wanted to scream again. But she heard the tone to leave a message and decided to do that instead.

"Hey, it's me. You won't believe what just happened. I got set up by a total bee-atch! Can you believe this? Me?! I don't even know why! That nasty, skanky piece of—"

Ella turned as she was pacing and venting, and she noticed a tall, imposing silhouette standing nearby.

"I'll call you back," Ella whispered and hung up. Unsure whether or not to feel threatened, she started backing away slowly as the silhouette approached, brandishing something. A weapon?

"This is why," said a soft female voice.

Ella stopped and saw it was a female student coming at her with a cell phone.

"Take a look," the girl added.

Ella looked at the girl's cell, at the picture displayed on it. It was a pic of her with Henry on his snowmobile, when she had reluctantly agreed to a lift.

Well, that figured. Sera was declaring war on her over a boy. Dammit, she knew she shouldn't have accepted that lift!

"I'm Bobbie. And I swear I'm not trying to make things worse."

Bobbie was a well-built Inuit girl Ella's age and twice her size. They were in a few classes together, but Ella had never really paid attention to Bobbie, who seemed like the polar opposite of her, with her shabby, rough-around-the-edges look. She had no idea that Bobbie had been quietly observing her ever since her arrival at Agloolik High.

"Sera can be toxic. I'm sorry you had to learn this the hard way." Bobbie's tone was peaceful. Soothing.

"Nobody's learning anything," Ella snapped. "This is just the beginning. She wants war? I'll show her war!"

Ella was no longer concerned about hiding her ugly side. Everything had gone to hell for her, and there was no turning back.

"I wouldn't recommend doing that," Bobbie replied calmly.

"Sure, I'll just let her walk all over me! In front of everyone! Like hell, I will! I know how to handle this."

"I understand you're upset. But how about you sleep on it, at least?"

"I'll never be able to sleep ever again if I let this slide!"

Bobbie sighed.

Ella rudely reached for Bobbie's phone so that she could see the incriminating picture again.

Sure enough, there she was, holding on to Henry, tightly. To not fall off, of course.

Ella shook her head. This was so unfair.

"I don't even care for the guy!"

"Okay. Then why don't you just offer her—"

"I'M NOT GONNA APOLOGIZE TO HER!"

"—an explanation. Tell her you're not interested in Henry. Tell her what happened." This seemed simple and logical enough.

"Oh, 'cause she's gonna believe me?! I look like his Siamese twin! Which part of this picture says 'I know you wanted me to stay away from him, but—oops!—I didn't think that resting my head on his shoulder and holding onto him like a barnacle in heat was off limits?' Which part of the picture says 'I'm innocent' to you? Tell me! I'm all ears!"

Ella had a point.

"I see what you mean," Bobbie conceded. "But isn't it worth it to at least try—"

"You really think she'd believe *anything* I would say at this point?! I know her type. As far as I know, she couldn't *wait* for something like this to happen! Just so she'd have a reason to—"

"Alright . . . Alright." Bobbie seemed all out of reasonable answers. "Suit yourself. But watch out."

"I'm not afraid of her."

"I don't think you are. But here's the thing. After what just happened in there, if you go after her and play her game, no one here will want to touch you with a ten-foot pole, let alone be on your side. They'll be afraid to associate with you."

Ella scoffed. "So, you're saying no one has a spine around here? No one is smart enough to see what happened?"

"It's more a matter of . . . experience. Sera can be nasty. No one wants to be on her shit list. And her dad's an RCMP—"

"Officer! Yeah, I know! Good for her!"

Ella's angry behavior didn't faze Bobbie. Her tone remained even and calm.

"Yeah, well, it's a nice little deterrent for a lot of people. It helps her get away with more than she should. How about I walk you home?"

"Who the hell are you?!"

Ella didn't need some kind of Inuit Yoda to walk her home. She was so beside herself and full of adrenaline, she could have taken down just about anyone with just her nails right now, and screw the manicure.

Ella turned and walked away, swinging her arms in the air to make it clear that she just wanted to be left alone.

Bobbie didn't insist otherwise and let her leave.

RACCOON CLOWN PARTY OF ONE

Ella spent most of the way home stomping as she walked, trying to empty her anger with every footstep. But the rage driving her soon evolved into practical concerns, and she started to feel fear. Why did that strange girl offer to walk her home? Was she in any kind of physical danger now that she'd had a fallout with Sera? What did that girl know that Ella should know? She seemed insistent. Perhaps she should have listened to her.

Ella started looking over her shoulder to see if she was being followed. The good news: there was no one in sight. The bad news: there was no one in sight. If someone wanted to attack her —right here, right now—would anyone even hear her scream?

Ella picked up her pace. She would soon turn into her street. Each step was getting her closer to home, and her dad would be there for her. Perhaps he could help her make sense of this nightmare.

But as Ella approached her house, to her horror, it became clear that Dan was having another late night at work, despite it being Friday night. Their red house was plunged in darkness, meaning that—again—her dad was not home.

"For crap's sake!" she muttered to herself.

She was usually okay with being home by herself—aside from eating the same stupid peanut butter sandwiches all the time (expensive as they were!)—but tonight, of all nights, she could really, *really* have used him being there.

It was so unfair! She had just been the victim of one gigantic injustice, that she didn't even provoke—at least not on purpose—and she felt all alone in the world, because she was. And here she was, literally in the middle of nowhere, where she couldn't even hide, let alone escape from this Arctic desert. There was nowhere for her to go. This was unfair *and* scary.

Ella got inside the house and turned on some lights. Seeing her reflection in the entrance mirror, it struck her how much she looked like some sad raccoon clown, if there ever was such a thing. But even worse than that, seeing her reflection under this light—crowned with the stupid sticker-made tiara—it struck her how ridiculous she looked, too.

How could she look this grotesque? How did she let this happen? How did she let Sera do this to her? She had been such an idiot! Which part of this had made any sense to her? How could she have so easily fallen for it? Like an amateur! A total friggin' amateur! She would NOT let this slide. That nasty bitch from hell would NOT get away with this!

Desperate to blow off steam, Ella stomped in place, arms flailing. She let out an ear-piercing scream with all her might and for as long as her lungs could keep up. And then, she let out another scream. And another, until her throat started hurting, and she burst into tears. Crying tears of sadness and anger and hopelessness. With some banshee-quality wailing thrown into the mix, as it seemed to help with the pain.

The doorbell rang.

Startled, Ella stopped dead in her tracks. And came partly to her senses. Who the hell could this be?

What should she do?

Nothing. She should do nothing. Whoever was there would eventually leave.

Or perhaps they wouldn't, given there was light inside the house. *Crap.* Why didn't she think of killing the lights before allowing herself to fly off the handle like this?

The doorbell rang a second time.

Go away. Go away. Go away.

But the person at the door didn't go away. The person at the door started to knock instead.

And then the most horrible thought crossed Ella's mind: what if it was Sera and her posse, coming to hunt her down and finish her off? Whatever that might mean in their psycho little minds.

Another knock. Louder, more insistent.

Ohgodohgodohgod.

In her glorious pissed-off-ness, did she even remember to lock the door? Should she go hide in the bathroom? Where the hell was her dad?!

"I know you're in there," said a muffled voice. An adult voice. Did Sera hire a goon? Was there such a thing, here, way up North, as goons for hire? Like a local Hells Angels equivalent, riding through town on souped-up snowmobiles? Ella's mind was racing and making her freak out even more.

"Are you okay?" the voice at the door asked.

Okay, what kind of hitman would ask his target if she was okay? Ella realized the voice didn't sound threatening.

She grabbed a tissue to wipe her eyes and blow her nose, and lying as low as she could, she sneaked up to one of the curtain panels framing the living room's bay window to see who was there. She was beyond relieved to see it was her elderly female neighbor with the husky. The same one Sera said was beyond annoying, the one to avoid at all costs.

The neighbor spotted Ella in the window and waved to her. Oh, good. She was totally screwed. Now, she had no choice but to go open the door.

Ella reluctantly opened the door.

"Are you in distress or practicing for a talent show?" asked the neighbor with a twinkle of mischief in her eyes.

"Are you spying on me?" Ella couldn't help but feel indignant.

"No. It just so happened that I was gazing outside my window . . ."

"Figures. Like there's so much else to do around here." Ella bit her tongue. Dammit, she hated it when she couldn't help being nasty—and to a senior, no less.

The elderly woman smiled at her, unfazed by Ella's attitude. Ella wondered if it was a local trait to remain unfazed.

Pointing to her dog, the neighbor added, "Frank thought we should come say hello. Just in case."

Ella looked down at Frank, who was looking at her intently with his deep-blue eyes. *What a beautiful dog.*

"Look, I'm sorry, it's been a very long evening," said Ella, softening her tone as she knelt down closer to the dog. He gave her a friendly nudge, and she started to pet him. Some of her stress and anger subsided.

"Why's he named Frank? Because of ol' blue eyes Sinatra?"

"Sinatra? Nahhh. That'd be too fancy. He just happened to like hot dogs as a pup. So, it was either Frank or Wiener."

Ella looked at the old lady. Was she for real?

"Frank or Wiener? Really?"

"Frank seemed like a better fit."

The neighbor let out a laugh. It was deep and a little hoarse —you could hear a coughing fit in it, coming soon. But it was also a kind-hearted laugh. "You're right. He was indeed named after Sinatra."

Ella let out her own laugh of relief. "I'm glad you were joking!"

"So am I. He's such a noble animal."

Ella couldn't agree more. There was something noble about this dog. And the fact that she herself was named after Ella Fitzgerald, who had sung *with* Sinatra, it just made things more special for her at this very moment.

"He likes you," the old lady pointed out.

Ella smiled a sad smile. "That probably makes him the only one around here, right about now." Her voice began to quaver, her eyes to well up again. Fortunately, she managed to stop the tears.

"Why don't you come over for tea and tell me all about it?" the neighbor suggested.

Ella didn't know what to answer. On the one hand, she didn't want to be alone right now. On the other, what if this lady was as weird as she was told? Did she want to open up to her? And risk getting stranded in her house? Or worse?

"That's a very generous offer, but—"

"You don't have to tell me anything if you don't want to. And I'm a little old to kidnap you."

Was she a mind reader? This was getting creepy.

"I don't think I can be very good company right now."

"I wouldn't expect you to be."

What the hell did she mean by that?

As if on cue, Frank pressed his face against Ella's leg. Her hand brushed against the beautiful fur on the top of his head. This loving canine gesture took her by surprise and melted her heart again. She started crying. Again.

"You can bawl your eyes out at my place over tea and tissues. Come hang out with Frank. He'd like that."

Ella sniffed. The thought of hanging out with Frank actually sounded very pleasant right now.

What did she have to lose?

"Alright."

The elderly neighbor turned and motioned for Ella to follow her.

"The name's Inuuja, by the way."

THE BLUE HAVEN ACROSS THE STREET

Inuuja's house was even more modest and much less modern than Ella's. But there was something warm and welcoming about the place. The walls and shelves were adorned with a variety of Inuit art.

Ella was calmer now, though on her guard—she didn't know what to expect from this strange old lady. Would she be yakking her ear off until Christmas? It seemed unlikely, so far, as the only noise Inuuja was making was her humming while preparing the tea. She finally said something when she saw that Ella seemed interested in her artwork, noticing the girl was also too polite and hesitant to move around to look at it.

"You can look, dear. Look at whatever you like."

Ella took a few steps closer, to get a better look at a colorful painting. Frank, who hadn't left her side since they entered the house, moved as well, remaining by her side. Inuuja wasn't kidding when she said Frank would love to hang out with her. Perhaps he was like one of those service dogs that could feel epilepsy coming on or a heart attack. Perhaps he sensed how angry and sad she was. She gave him a scratch behind the ear. This had a soothing effect on both of them.

Ella smiled at the dog, and she could swear he was smiling back at her.

Turning her attention back to the painting, it didn't take long for Ella to become aware of its intricacy. Not that she understood what it meant, it being rather abstract. But the brush strokes, the textures, the overall effect . . . She imagined one needed real talent to produce this kind of imagery.

"Did you make this?" Ella asked.

"Indeed."

Ella glanced around the room at the other pieces of art.

"All of it?"

Inuuja nodded.

"Impressive." Ella meant it. Inuuja's artwork was inspired. And inspiring.

The kettle whistled. Inuuja took it off the stove top and poured hot water into a handmade ceramic teapot. Ella kept browsing the room. She came across a photograph of a much younger Inuuja—in her twenties, perhaps?—with a black man, taken in what seemed to be Old Montreal, circa the 1960s.

"This is me, landing on a different planet," volunteered Inuuja.

"That looks like Montreal."

"It is."

"Oh, so, you've been there?"

"Yes, I have. I even lived there for a while."

Inuuja brought the teapot to her little round kitchen table. She went back to fetch two mugs from the cupboard.

"Would you like some cookies?"

"Sure."

Ella realized that perhaps she shouldn't have agreed so fast to cookies. What if Inuuja had made them herself, with seal blubber or whatnot? Oh, God, what did she get herself into?

The sound of a cardboard box being cracked open gave her

hope. She turned to see Inuuja put some Oreo cookies on a plate.

"The Queen of England would shudder at the thought of dunking Oreos in her approved brand of Earl Grey tea. But she's not here," Inuuja joked.

"Sucks to be her. But it's for the best. I'm in no state to put up with any more royals tonight," Ella retorted. And then the irony hit her as she remembered her gem tiara tattoo. She touched her forehead. *Dammit.*

"How bad does it look?"

"Original. And temporary."

Inuuja's words were kind and comforting.

"Tea's ready. You may come sit at the table with me, or you can keep looking."

Intrigued, Ella had gone back to the photograph of young Inuuja in Old Montreal. "If I come sit, would you tell me about your time in Montreal?"

Inuuja considered Ella's request as she poured tea for them. From the look on her face, Ella guessed that her time in Montreal was heavy with memories, perhaps not all good.

"The man in the picture—Marvin—I was madly in love with him. He was an art dealer who came here in the sixties and *discovered* me—as an artist, but also as a young woman. I moved to Montreal to be with him."

"And experience city life?"

Inuuja took a moment to answer.

"Mostly so that my parents didn't find out about him."

"What happened?"

Ella wanted to know more, but Inuuja didn't seem ready to say more. After a brief moment of silence, she changed the subject.

"So, what's the story behind your facial artistry?"

Ella took a deep breath. The being-punched-in-the-gut

feeling came back. Thankfully, Frank came to sit next to her and laid his head down on her lap.

When Ella had reluctantly agreed to tea at her neighbor's house, she thought she would go over to Inuuja's place only for tea. This would take her mind off things, and when her dad came home, she would simply excuse herself. But having Frank rest his head on her lap, coupled with Inuuja's warm hospitality, Ella found herself opening up and telling her neighbor everything. From her neat, perfect life in Montreal to her becoming a piece of work to make her dad regret bringing her here against her will, to being friends with Sera, then being set up with this foolish look and not deserving this and how her life was now officially over.

Inuuja listened to all of it, sympathetically.

"But I guess I don't expect you to believe me," Ella concluded.

"Why is that, dear?"

"Because . . . because that sounds over-the-top and paranoid. And I'm accusing someone you're possibly related to."

"You think I would automatically dismiss what a white girl says about an Inuit girl?"

It turned out that Inuuja was neither a witch nor a murderer like Ella and Sera had joked. But perhaps she was psychic.

"Well, at the very least, you don't know me. I could be lying through my teeth."

"You seem too sincerely upset to be making this up." Inuuja looked at her dog, still busy comforting Ella. "And Frank believes you."

Ella smiled and petted Frank's head.

"If Frank believes me, then everything will be right with the world . . . eh, puppy?" She smiled at the dog as he looked up at her. But her smile vanished. "Except that it won't be."

She let out a heavy sigh.

"How do you ever come back from something like this? *Can you ever come back?* I have a hundred mocking faces burned into my memory. I'll have to go to school on Monday and face every single one of them. How the hell am I supposed to go to school ever again? Or even show my face outside in daylight?!"

"I bet many shared in your discomfort."

Ella had felt that and knew that was probably true.

"Perhaps. But they've moved on with their life the moment I left. Whereas I'll have to live with that. And face Sera, too."

Just as despair was creeping back inside Ella, her phone chimed—social media alert. Her name had been tagged next to a picture someone had snapped of her glorious moment in the school gym.

Shit! Of course it had to be immortalized in pixel form! Because the whole thing hadn't been humiliating enough. Humiliation now had to last for all eternity.

Seeing the picture made Ella cry again.

"May I see?"

Ella turned her cell phone towards Inuuja. The elderly woman took in the picture, nodding.

"See?" Ella wailed. "I can't come back from this! What am I gonna do?"

Inuuja thought for a moment.

"Own it. Go bold."

"What?"

Confused, Ella looked at Inuuja. She stopped sobbing for a moment to hear her out.

"You have nothing to lose, right?"

"Unless there's a level underneath the bottom of the damn barrel I just hit."

Inuuja took Ella's hands into her own and gave them a little squeeze.

"Trust me. You have nothing to lose."

The teenager nodded, albeit carefully. "All right."

"And you strike me as someone who's not afraid."

Why would she say that?

"I'm a mess! And I'm scared shitless!"

"Yes, you are a mess and scared, right now. And rightfully so. But I've seen the way you walk. With your head up high. You're an independent spirit."

No one had ever told Ella such a thing. That she was stubborn, yes. And that she always did whatever the hell she wanted to, yes, that too. Often. But being called an independent spirit? That sounded so . . . positive.

"What do you have in mind?"

"Fight fire with fire."

"Okay. But what do you have in mind, aside from spitting out clichés?"

Ella had done it again, that acerbic tone. She was about to apologize, but Inuuja burst out laughing. They were clearly on the same wavelength.

"Make light of it! Destabilize them all," Inuuja suggested.

"But they'll think I'm crazy!"

"They already do."

TRIPLE FUDGE WITH FUDGE ON TOP

SERA COULDN'T WAIT until her Monday morning run with Henry to find out what he thought of Ella's crazy appearance at the high school dance. She had tried to read him at the party, clinging to him and his friends, but not long after Ella's spectacle and her leaving, he said he had to go and left. This had been a rather unexpected and anticlimactic ending for Sera, who had anticipated a much better and more triumphant evening.

Soon after Henry left, she, too, found a pretext—the ever-so-convenient headache—to leave her friends behind in the gym and head home. It had snowed while they were inside, and she had hoped to find Henry shoveling his mom's driveway or something, but that was not the case. And despite being on the lookout for him all weekend long, she didn't catch a glimpse of him then, either.

"I wonder what possessed Ella to show up like that at the dance."

Sera and Henry were running, and she was fishing for a reaction from him. He hadn't seemed to mind Ella one bit at the party, and that gave Sera cause for concern. *He should think she's a weirdo by now!* If not, then things were even worse than she had imagined. All weekend long, she had ruminated over the fact that Ella had not suffered a nervous breakdown in front of everyone as she had hoped. Ella had proved much stronger than planned given the embarrassing situation in which she had found herself.

Sure, some kids at school would be teasing her from now on. She had made a royal idiot out of herself in front of the whole school, and that fact wouldn't go away anytime soon. But Sera got the feeling that she had failed to intimidate her properly and now expected Ella to turn on her, to retaliate, the logical next step. And she had no idea what Ella could do. She would now have to watch her back, and the thought was tiring.

Sera looked at Henry, still running at a steady pace without taking her bait.

"I don't think she's well," Sera added with a layer of fake concern.

"Hmm?"

Henry glanced over at her, not at all interested in gossiping.

"Ella. There's something wrong with her."

Henry shrugged. "Is there?"

Aaaaaaaaaaaaaaaaaaaargh.

"Didn't she look a little 'out there' to you at the party?"

"She looked like someone who came from somewhere else. Who might be used to other things. She just has to learn how things are, here."

"Okay. Perhaps, but . . ."

"But she can also keep doing her own thing. That'd be cool too."

Disappointment and agony started to overwhelm Sera when Henry added some killing words: "She is a cool girl."

Five words. Five simple words. *She is a cool girl.*

This. Was. Unbelievable.

How could he possibly think that Ella was cool?! He never said that *she*, Sera, was cool when *she* was *so much cooler* than Ella could ever be! How could the party's embarrassment of the century not even make a dent in his opinion? He thought Ella was cool!? How could her perfect plan have backfired this badly? It was so wrong! So unacceptable!

"She takes pills, you know!" Sera blurted out.

This was not true. Or, rather, not to Sera's knowledge anyway. But the party had already set the table regarding Ella's mental health, so hinting some more at it could only help Sera's cause. Right?

But Henry seemed deaf to what she was saying.

Sera started to slow down. "I think I'm getting a cramp." Her voice was quavering.

Henry slowed down and came to a halt when Sera stopped. She massaged her left calf, but it was on the inside that she was aching the most. She hoped he would say something to comfort her.

But he didn't. He just stood there.

"I think I better head back home," she finally said.

"That's probably a good idea." He nodded. It looked like he was about to resume running, but he refrained and asked, "Are you gonna be okay to go back by yourself?"

This should have been music to Sera's ears, that Henry was expressing concern for her well-being, but she could read between the lines: he didn't really mean it. He was only being nice because that's who he was, and he couldn't help himself.

"Yeah, I'll be alright."

"Great. Take care, then. I'll see you at school."

Henry went back to running.

Sera headed home. Devastated.

Early on that same morning, Ella went to Inuuja's home before heading to school, armed with a box of Oreo cookies. Her elderly neighbor responded with a delighted laugh upon seeing the box.

"You don't need to bribe me, child!" She laughed some more, clearly happy and touched by Ella's present and presence.

"It's not a bribe. It's to give you enough energy to do the whole thing. There's no way I'm going to school with a work in progress around my neck." Ella grinned.

Inuuja's plan involved putting out the fire, first. Her theory was that rebuilding Ella's reputation and credibility might take time, but if she showed a sense of humor and some dignity, she might get back some positive attention from her fellow students. And she would no longer live with the paralyzing fear that the entire world would be against her forever.

A concrete part of the plan consisted of Inuuja painting a band of delicate, beautiful Arctic animal tattoos around Ella's neck, much like an artsy necklace. They would be hidden underneath the collar of a black turtleneck sweater, and Ella would make them visible only if and when she wished to. This would also be discreet enough to not get Ella in trouble or detention. The idea was that if anyone mocked her about her tattoos from the party, she could show them Inuuja's art and make it look like the tattoos were a very deliberate choice on her part.

"That's a weird-ass idea," Ella had told Inuuja when she first proposed it.

"More like bat-shit crazy, I think," Inuuja had replied.

At first, Ella was reluctant to go along with the plan. She had just been laughed at enough—for more than a lifetime, as far as she was concerned—and she was in no hurry for another round of mockery. But Ella also suspected and recognized that trying something out of left field might be the one thing to work in her favor. Surprise people and redirect their attention. Plus, Inuuja's art was so beautiful, who would dare laugh at it?

She also liked the idea of being seen as audacious and artsy. They already thought she was weird and crazy. She might as well embrace her new reality now and act the part too. So, she agreed to Inuuja's plan.

"Since I'm gonna crash and burn anyway, I might as well do it in style."

Inuuja gave her a high-five.

Ella thought she would also braid her hair into two braids as an extra layer of "go to hell" for Sera's benefit.

She was going to own the whole shebang, alright.

Ella walked to school with a mixture of pride and nervousness. On the one hand, she thought the painted tattoos looked great and was happy to be embracing this newfound originality. On the other hand, the thought of what was awaiting her, the hardship ahead, made her queasy. But she kept her head up high all the way to school.

An independent spirit, she was. Damn straight. And screw the naysayers.

Bobbie's Friday night predictions in the school's parking lot turned out to be mostly right. Ella could feel a chill in the air at school as she walked in, the students parting like the Red Sea around her. Girls who had been friendly with her so far ignored her or scurried away as she approached to avoid her. Several students were staring at her. Some held back a grin or a snicker. Others whispered something funny to other students, with their eyes glued on Ella.

Ella did her best to keep a dignified expression while her stomach was tied in an intricate knot even a Marine couldn't untie.

As she took books out of her locker, a male voice called out to her.

"Digging the look, girl!" That was Tim, who was wearing a similar black turtleneck.

Ella couldn't help cracking a smile. Thank God for people like Tim.

"That's because you have style, Tim."

"Thank you, ma'am. That means a lot." Tim walked away.

"Hey, Ella! D'you forget something?" asked another male voice behind her.

A choir of chuckles erupted. Ella took a deep breath and put on a brave smile. This was thoroughly unpleasant and potentially even more embarrassing, but she could do this.

She turned around to face the jeering voice. It was a guy named Hunter who was heckling her. Hunter was a class clown, and the good thing about him was that his ribbing was usually more good-natured than gratuitously mean.

"You mean this?" Ella's voice cracked a bit but remained controlled. She came closer to Hunter and lowered the neck of her sweater to expose the band of animal tattoos. "It's Monday morning. I thought I'd go for something a little more discreet."

Please work. Please work. Please work.

Hunter leaned in to take a look.

"Whoa!" he said, impressed. He went all around Ella to see the entire band of drawings around her neck. Other students came forward to look as well, all too intrigued to think of taunting Ella any further.

Appreciating her good fortune, Ella began to breathe more easily. A timid smile appeared on her face.

"That looks like something Inuuja would do." Ella hadn't seen discreet Justine make her way to see her tattoos. She couldn't believe the crafts-loving girl had recognized Inuuja's style.

"Wow, you're good! You're right. Inuuja made these."

"They're beautiful. All the details. That's so cool," Justine added. "It must have taken her a while."

"Actually, she was pretty efficient. She's really good."

Behind Justine, across the hall, Ella spotted Olive and Brianna looking on, arms crossed, snickering. A reminder that while the day was looking up, the battle was far from won, let alone over.

"May I take a picture?" Justine asked, rescuing Ella from the negative vibe of Sera's posse.

"Of course."

Justine took out her cell phone. Hunter and a few other students followed suit. Ella found herself swarmed with cell phones in her face. It was physically overbearing but completely worth it.

Hunter put his head next to Ella's, brandishing his phone before them for a selfie.

"Smile!"

Ella was happy to smile. Other kids squeezed in close for a group shot.

"Please take one of all of us, Hunter! Your arm is longer than mine," Justine said.

Hunter snapped a few pictures of the handful of students piled up around him, Ella and Justine.

"Can you please send me those pics? I think Inuuja would get a kick," Ella realized.

"Sure thing."

The bell rang. The students dispersed and headed to class.

Ella caught up to Justine and asked her if there was a sewing club at lunch. She figured it would be a good place to lay low.

By the time Ella entered her classroom, the word had already gotten around, and all eyes were on her—including Sera's, who was barely able to hide a sneer. Thankfully, the number of students who looked at Ella in a non-negative way outnumbered the hostile ones.

It dawned on Ella that she could deal with this, focus on the positive, and ignore anyone who cared to look at her funny or in a mean way. This was their problem after all and so immature anyway. So, whatever. She was just so happy that Inuuja's crazy plan had given her a second chance at making a better impression.

Heading to her desk, she passed Bobbie, the first time she noticed her in a classroom setting.

"Well played," Bobbie said to her softly.

Ella acknowledged her with a nod. "Thanks."

THE CAVALRY

THE REST of the day went pretty well. Ella managed to keep a relatively low profile. She did look a bit silly in the sewing room, as it was obvious she knew less than nothing about crafts and sewing, but there was no cruelty towards her in the room, and she took everything in stride. She asked Justine if she could shadow her for a while, and her classmate was only too happy to oblige. Looking at her lack of dexterity, Ella thought it might be good for her to learn a thing or two while hiding in there.

After school, things went south again. First, Henry casually said "Hi" to her in the middle of a busy hallway. It was immensely kind of him not to ostracize her, but he was clueless as to how much of a lightning rod he was making her into, just by interacting with her.

And then, as Ella walked home, she got the impression she was being followed. It was already dark outside, and the street lights were few and far between. She looked over her shoulder, and sure enough, a figure dressed all in black, wearing a balaclava, was walking behind her. Ella did a double take. Was she *really* being followed? For real?

What the f . . . ?

The thought of Sera hiring someone to take her out crossed her mind again. It felt so absurd and bizarre.

Ella tried to keep her composure and her pace steady, but she felt the heavy gaze of this mysterious stalker on her. She had no idea what his plan was, what he might do to her. She had already laid low in the library for over an hour after class to avoid any kind of trouble, but she forgot that the sun would have set by the time she came out.

She scanned her surroundings. Aside from her and her new fan, the street was empty, and most of the houses were in the dark, their inhabitants not yet home from work. There was no one around to help.

Ella picked up her pace, wondering if the sinister figure was still after her. She glanced over her shoulder again.

Not only was he still there, but he was also picking up his pace. *Dammit!* Ella prepared herself for a sudden sprint.

The jackass was getting closer.

Ella started to run, despite being in no shape to outrun anyone.

A tug on her scarf slowed her down.

The stalker had caught up and was staring at her in silence through the eye-slits of his headgear.

No, not creepy at all. Bullying at its finest.

Despite her panic, Ella was able to size up her bizarre opponent: slightly taller than her and, judging by the figure . . .

Of course! Her first guess was Sera herself, and what she was seeing matched her hated ex-friend. It had to be her!

"Look. If you're mad about the picture, I can explain. It was totally unintentional," Ella tried.

"Really?!" It sure sounded like Sera's voice and a very pissed-off Sera at that.

Sera tripped Ella, who face-planted into the road's dirty mix of snow and sand.

"My bad, totally unintentional," Sera added with disdain.

Ella was too stunned to get back up. She instinctively bunched herself up, bracing herself for more abuse—a kick, a punch, hair-pulling? It seemed like nothing was beneath Sera at the moment.

Ella had gotten a mouthful of sand-laced dirty street snow when she landed flat on her face. She spat out as much as she could but felt little bits of grit still left inside her mouth. This was soooooo gross! She'd have to avoid swallowing until she could rinse her mouth at home, even if that meant going around drooling. Good thing she was only a few houses away from home. But only God knew how long before Sera's fury would subside or whether she would feel satisfied enough with the results of her assault to let her go.

A string of menacing barks echoed in the bitter air.

"Shit!" Sera whistled between her teeth and ran away.

Ella lifted her head and was overjoyed to see Frank barreling like a mad dog towards her, the reason Sera split so fast.

The dog stopped right by Ella, in a protective stance. She hugged him and realized how shook-up she was.

"Looks like the gates of hell have opened again," said Bobbie, appearing out of thin air, it seemed. She scooped up a handful of fresh snow from the top of a nearby snowbank and offered it to a confused Ella.

"For your mouth."

Ella took the snow and nodded a thank-you.

"Hey, Frank," said Bobbie to Frank. He acknowledged her with a nudge, and she gave him a good petting in return.

"How's the palate cleanser?" Bobbie asked Ella.

Palate cleanser. Ella snorted. She often heard that term on the Food Network when she was bored and channel surfing. She doubted this was what they meant by it.

Bobbie offered Ella a hand up. "Are you hurting anywhere?"

"Beside my pride?"

"That's a good sign."

Ella wiped the snow off her jacket. Her pants were already soaking wet from the melting snow seeping through the fabric. Bobbie rummaged through her pockets and found a clean tissue.

"You got a bit of a nosebleed."

"Oh, God! My face!"

Ella started to freak out, so Bobbie shoved the tissue under Ella's nose to plug the leak.

"Is it bad? Am I gonna have scars?"

"You'll be fine."

Ella came back to her senses and took hold of the tissue under her nose.

"You live near?" inquired Bobbie.

"Yeah. Just over there."

The two girls began walking towards Ella's place, accompanied by Frank, still on high alert. Ella turned to look behind them. Sera was long gone.

"What the hell is her problem anyway!?"

"You are."

"I know, but she already made me look bad! Really bad. What more does she want?"

"You stood up to her and managed to gain back some sympathy from people at school. She wants you to suffer. And you haven't yet."

"You'd think she'd have better things to do with her life."

They took a few steps in silence.

"Are you okay?" asked Bobbie.

Ella was about to say yes, but she felt tears rolling down her cheeks. Her anger, sadness, and stress levels were off the charts.

"I thought I'd only have to put up with being humiliated.

But now, I also have to worry about getting beaten up on my way home? This is insane!"

Bobbie nodded.

"Yup."

"So, what now? Hire a goddamn bodyguard?"

They walked in silence for another moment. Bobbie didn't seem to mind the silence. And Ella found it awkward to talk with her nose stuffed with blood.

"I can help," Bobbie volunteered.

"I can't afford to pay you. Or anyone else for that matter." Ugh, she sounded so nasal and whiny.

"I don't need your money. Just your advice."

"Okay . . . What do you have in mind?" After Inuuja's crazy tattoo plan, which had actually worked out great, Ella was open to just about anything.

"How about I walk you home on school days until she comes to her senses or moves on to her next prey? And in return, you . . ." Bobbie hesitated. "You teach me how to be a . . . an urbanite."

Ella gave her a blank stare. Now she had heard it all.

"I'm sure you already own jeans and t-shirts. What more do you want?"

"I want to be more refined."

For what? Ella thought Bobbie was meant to be more of a woodsy type—despite the total absence of woods in Iqaluit—than she would ever be the latte-sipping type.

"What for?" she finally said out loud.

Bobbie stopped walking. "Can you keep a secret?"

"Yeah."

"Can you swear not to tell anyone?"

"Yeah, yeah, whatever. Spill it!"

Judging by the face Bobbie was making, this looked very important to her.

"No one knows . . . I want to move to Toronto for college, but I'm afraid I won't be accepted."

"Well, that would all depend on your marks, no?"

"Not *that* kind of acceptance. I mean, not getting accepted by people there. You know, not fit in. I worry that I'll be a social outcast."

"Oh, so you're asking the social outcast for advice? I can see how that would work out well."

Bobbie got the irony and let out a smile.

"And besides, ever heard of the Internet?" added Ella.

"It's not the same. Come on, I'll be your bodyguard. I'll walk you to and from school. In return, you give me some cultural insights and behavioral tips. Nothing complicated."

"Complicated is using words like 'cultural insights' and 'behavioral tips'."

Ella hesitated—the task seemed peculiar and impossible to her.

"No more eating tainted snow for you . . ." Bobbie gently teased.

"Ugh, don't make me gag!"

"You can't deny it's a powerful argument."

Bobbie had a point.

"Even if you can't or don't want to help me, I can still walk with you. It's just that I'd appreciate any help you *can* give me."

"I wouldn't have to guarantee any results?"

"Is that a diplomatic way to call me a lost cause?" Bobbie retorted, amused.

"Well . . ."

"Come on. You have nothing to lose."

"Funny, I hear that a lot these days."

"Look, I have a cousin who went to study down South, and she couldn't take it. She came back after a few months. She's so bright, but she missed home so much, our culture, nature. And she couldn't help feeling like an outsider most of the time. So, I'd like to acclimate myself as much as I can beforehand. So that I can give it a good, solid try."

Ella pondered, petting Frank at the same time. " . . . Alright. I already got two miracles today. Let's see if we can make a third one happen."

Ella offered Bobbie her mitten-covered hand to shake. And Bobbie shook it.

Bobbie ended up staying at Ella's place until Dan came home. Ella found it a little weird, at first, looking for small talk to fill the silence. She could usually yak on and on about anything, but she was so overwhelmed right now, she just wanted to be left alone. But not really alone. Who knew what Sera would try next? She appreciated that Bobbie was there with her, but she was also hoping that her dad would come home soon so she could go lick her wounds alone in her bedroom.

Bobbie suggested they do their homework, putting an end to the awkwardness. They ended up working side by side at the kitchen table. Ella wondered what she would say to her dad, how she would explain the small scrapes on her face. But if she said anything, he might well phone Sera's parents, and nothing good could come out of that. It was probably best if she didn't say anything and dealt with Sera's moronic crusade herself.

With Bobbie's help.

"I don't think I should say anything to my dad. At least not yet," said Ella. Bobbie looked up from her math homework.

"Okay."

And it was that simple. There was something about Bobbie's laid-back demeanor that told Ella she could trust this girl, regardless of her being peculiar and so utterly different from her.

When Dan came home, Bobbie said hello and left, without saying much more. Ella was free to tell her dad that she had slipped on an icy patch and fallen. And that was that.

That night, Ella watched the northern lights from the bathroom window. She also caught Inuuja moving around in her house—the spry senior seemed to be dancing happily . . . all by herself. Ella imagined Frank watching her too, perhaps even dancing with her. But, certainly—dancing or not—he was watching over his artistic master.

This made Ella smile. Perhaps all was not lost in the world after all.

Bobbie was true to her word. The next morning, there she was, waiting in the driveway when Ella came out of her house.

At first, they walked in silence. Ella's mind was racing, but not over dealing with Sera at school. She had gone over just about every scenario in her head the night before, as she tried to fall asleep, and she imagined Inuuja telling her to keep owning it. That she was strong. That she'd find a way, a smart way, to overcome this unwanted conflict for good and recover from it.

Rather, right now, Ella's mind was revving about what she could do to help Bobbie. Should she prepare, like, a class with an outline and tests? How did one teach someone else to feel sophisticated and at home in an urban environment?

Ella had no idea. It all came naturally to her. Of course, living in a big city sure helped. But here, that wasn't an option. What was? What options did they have?

"Perhaps we should go to PolarMart after school, and I'll teach you how to spot a bargain," Ella offered after some thought. Bobbie gave her a sarcastic look, and it dawned on Ella, again, that Iqaluit was not exactly the mecca of hot deals.

"Right. Never mind."

At school, it was inevitable that Ella and Bobbie would eventually cross paths with Sera. They had just walked into the building when they spotted her down the hall. Upon seeing them, Sera looked away, pretending they were not even there. As Bobbie and Ella walked past, Ella tensed up and couldn't help throwing a sideways glance at Sera.

"Just ignore her," Bobbie whispered to Ella.

"She's hard to ignore," Ella replied.

"I know. But . . ."

Bobbie was looking for something to say. She started to grin. "Okay. Here's a theory . . . Some people—actually, *many* people—exist in the gaze of others, right? Needing other people's constant approval. Validation. Obsessing over being seen and getting endless likes and attention on social media, for instance."

Ella gave her a blank look.

Bobbie went on, "They *need* to be seen. It's all about what others see of them. What *you* see of *her*."

"What I see of her is a conniving, backstabbing b—"

"Not quite where I'm going with this."

"Okaaayyyyy . . ."

"What if she exists because you are *looking* at her? Paying attention to her?"

"Feeding the troll?"

"Kinda, yeah. And therefore, if you ignore her . . . If you stop feeding her . . ."

Ella shook her head, amused.

"She'll no longer exist?"

"Logically."

"Yeah, obviously. Did you smoke your breakfast?"

"No." Bobbie laughed. "I think that came from Sartre. Or

one of his friends. Or someone on the Internet. Whatever. Isn't it worth a try?"

"Oh, totally. I'm always looking for new ways to fool myself!"

"That's the spirit!"

Surprisingly, the day turned out pretty good.

At lunchtime, since Bobbie had a previous tutoring engagement, Ella hid in the crafts room again, where she picked up tricks from Justine. She even volunteered to cut a pattern for her.

It took her forever to carefully scissor her way around the printed forms on the ever so thin, bible-like paper of the pattern, but she did it. Yes, she did it! And a pretty good job at that!

Justine was making a skirt. A very simple one, but she had chosen a stunning burgundy velvet fabric, and Ella could picture how the garment would turn out and was pretty psyched to see it come to life.

Justine showed Ella how to place the pattern pieces over the fabric—respecting its grain—and how to pin them down. Ella pricked herself several times, jumping every time and letting out a well-felt "Dammit!" It made Justine and the other students laugh.

"Don't worry. You'll eventually stop pricking yourself. That, or you'll grow a very thick skin at the end of your fingers," teased Justine.

"And then I can play the guitar," added Ella.

"There you go!" replied Justine.

A girl named Sophie patted Ella on the back.

"You're learning fast. You'll get there."

Ella was touched by the encouragement these girls were offering her. Sometimes, a little kindness goes a long way.

Later on, Ella had a similar thought about Bobbie, someone else in her life who was being kind to her. Who was being generous to a fault. She, herself, would have to be up to the task and be nice, too, in return. She must try to be helpful. That was the least she could do.

Ella invited Bobbie to hang out with her at her house after school. Since she was already walking her home, she might as well stay a bit. Ella would make her a latte or whatever she'd like. Better than that, she would teach her how to make a latte. That was probably one good way to start "city life."

Bobbie was mostly used to making instant and drip coffee, but she was up for it. And so, Ella played barista in her kitchen, teaching Bobbie how to make the perfect froth. The Inuit girl was pretty dexterous and turned out to be a natural at surfing the surface of the cold milk, producing the *shhhhuk shhhuk shhhuk* noise that would froth the milk nicely.

"Instant coffee, really? You've done this before! My first attempts, it sounded like I was strangling a truck full of pigs!" whined Ella.

"I'm just a good study."

"Or your teacher—"

"Yeah, it must be my teacher."

Ella smiled. She liked the idea that she might have something to do with Bobbie picking things up so fast.

Bobbie finished making the second latte.

"Okay, so . . . what next?" she asked enthusiastically.

Ella wasn't sure. "We do homework?" She grimaced. "You're learning too fast for me."

The next day, over lunch at the cafeteria, Ella suggested they go to PolarMart after school and give Bobbie a makeover with the testers.

"That would be so much fun!" Ella was becoming more and more enthused with her idea.

"So much fun for you, you mean?" Bobbie retorted. "Which part of me looks like a Barbie doll to you?"

"It's not about being a Barbie."

"Look, I want to be comfortable being who I am. Not be uncomfortable being someone I'm not."

"But . . ." Ella was miffed that Bobbie was shooting down her best idea. "But that's the way they do it on TV. And in films . . ."

Makeovers were the way to go if you wanted to change for the better. How else would she class Bobbie up to Toronto standards?

"You mean, like, when they use a gorgeous actress and put glasses on her because that's supposed to make her ugly? And then they give her contact lenses and style her hair differently and stuff her in a tight strapless dress and the whole world starts to view and treat her differently?"

"Yeah?" What was wrong with that perfectly good plan?

"That won't work. If you stuff me in a tight strapless dress, I can assure you the world will look at me differently, but not for the right reasons."

Fudge. Bobbie had a knack for making sense.

"And the last time *you* were stuffed in a tight strapless dress, how did that work out?"

Ella understood Bobbie didn't say this to be mean but to illustrate a point. "Right."

"I rest my case."

Dammit. Ella was scrambling for other options.

"What about your hair?"

"What about it?"

Bobbie's hair was long, straight, and of the deepest, darkest black with natural highlights of blue. "Never mind. I'd love to have hair like yours," admitted Ella.

The girls picked at their plates for a moment. Ella was not ready to give up.

"How about we try a light, non-aggressive version of a makeover at my place? Using my own makeup and all?"

Bobbie didn't look convinced.

"I dunno. I don't want to show the whole world that I'm trying hard to look more feminine. That'd be so embarrassing."

"What do you mean?"

"If I can't pull it off . . . I don't have a delicate build like you."

"We'll lock the doors. No one has to see you if you don't want them to. And you get to choose." She could see Bobbie's hesitation. "I'm not trying to make you into someone you're not. But if you don't try something, how do you know it won't work?"

Just then, Ella caught Sera staring at her from a few tables over, shooting her a nasty look.

Noticing Ella's expression change, Bobbie guessed what was wrong without even turning to see.

"I know it's hard, but ignore her. Just let it go."

Ella sighed. Why was she the only one who had to make efforts and be out of her comfort zone?

And then it struck her that she didn't have to be alone in her struggle. Misery loves company, right?

"How about this? I'll let it go about Sera. I'll let my fears go if you also let yours go," she suggested with an impish grin.

Bobbie suspected she wouldn't have the last word and Ella would hound her until she gave in.

"Fine. Let's try a tiny—and I do mean tiny—makeup makeover whatever at your house."

Ella gave her a big smile.

The makeup makeover session went better than expected. Not that Bobbie was sold on everything Ella did to her face—they did go through half a pack of makeup removal wipes. But Bobbie learned tons from watching Ella disinfect her brushes and products before putting anything on her and studying the techniques she was using. Ella was quite knowledgeable about it all, and while Bobbie thought eye shadow and foundation were too much, she kind of liked what a little mascara did to her eyes. Ella cracked open a new bottle just for her and gave it to her.

In the end, Bobbie didn't look like she was wearing much makeup, yet it did make her face look a little different. Stylish. That was interesting. And not intimidating at all. She might very well start wearing some makeup occasionally from now on.

The following weeks, Ella and Bobbie followed a routine. Every morning before school started, Bobbie would show up at Ella's place, and it wasn't long before Ella invited her to just let herself in upon arriving—no point in her freezing outside. By now, Ella prepared two lattes to go, every day, for them to drink on their way to school. She also gave Bobbie a swanky pair of sunglasses that matched hers, and the two of them soon looked like they owned the place. And, to their surprise and utmost delight, Frank started to join them in the morning and even waited for them outside of school on most afternoons.

Once at school, Bobbie tried her best to escort Ella, waiting for her outside her classroom if they didn't happen to be in the same class, but it quickly became unnecessary since Sera seemed to be laying low anyway. Still, for good measure, Ella would spend her lunchtime in the crafts room when she was by herself. But more and more, she went there for fun more than just to keep safe. The sewing students had started working on making parkas for themselves and, while Ella doubted she could pull it off, she still decided to try. Once again, she had nothing to lose. Plus, with Justine's guidance, she was learning tons and, surprisingly, getting pretty decent at working with her hands.

As time passed, Ella learned to truly ignore Sera, and it started to work. She no longer felt nervous and uncomfortable at school. She still watched her back since she didn't expect Sera to ever like her again and suspected, from experience, she could easily set her off again. Just like she herself was previously known to be an expert at holding a grudge and making other people's lives miserable.

Through trial and error, Ella and Bobbie found a Q&A approach—chatting about various topics and experiences that Ella had living in Montreal—worked much better than trying to get Bobbie to wear high heels, which even Ella admitted to finding pointless in making her city-savvy, especially in winter.

But they also recognized there was only so much Bobbie could learn about being comfortable with living in a big city, short of actually living in one. Still, Bobbie would often joke that she was learning by osmosis, just by hanging out with Ella.

LETTING GO

For a while, life was good. Ella felt at ease with Bobbie—a bit like when she used to hang out with Sandy—and grew to enjoy her presence and humor. She felt safe and, overall, she could even say . . . happy.

At school, the pretty teal-blue parka Ella was making for herself at lunchtime with Justine's help was, slowly but surely, taking form. Sure, some stitches were uneven, and some bits looked awkward, but Ella felt impressed with herself, which hadn't happened in a long time.

In other words, Ella was too busy feeling awesome to obsess over Sera. So, life was pretty good.

Until it all came crashing down again.

One Friday afternoon at the end of November, Ella went to the bathroom at school before heading home with Bobbie. It was bitterly cold outside, and they had planned to spend their Friday night binge-watching a new series on Netflix, with popcorn.

As Ella exited her stall, Sera came out of the other one at the very same time. This was the first time the two of them had been alone in a confined space since that dreadful day all hell had first broken loose.

The bad timing took both of them by surprise. But Sera recovered faster than Ella and wasted no time getting in her face.

"If I were you, I wouldn't get too comfortable just yet . . ." Sera spat out with contempt.

"Oh yeah?" Ella shot back and kicked herself for not coming up with a more menacing or clever reply. However, old bullying reflexes kicked in, and she got in Sera's face, leveling a stare at her. She wasn't going to back down either.

Ella's attitude spurred Sera, and the Inuit girl made it clear, in her stance and her hateful gaze, that she was far from being done.

"Watch your back, bitch!" She shoved Ella out of her way and stormed out of the bathroom.

Ella stood there, seeing red.

"You . . . DIDN'T EVEN WASH YOUR HANDS! THAT'S SO GROSS!"

This was all Ella, fuming, managed to retort.

Ignoring Sera from then on proved much easier said than done, especially now that she seemed actively on the warpath again. She took every opportunity to antagonize Ella as much as possible.

In the crowded halls of the school, she'd find ways to sneak near Ella and, more than once, tripped her—discreetely, of course, and without making it look like she was to blame.

At first, the other students thought Ella just happened to be particularly clumsy as she'd stumble, her books and papers flying all over the place. Or when the hot contents of her traveling mug landed on unfortunate fellow students.

Thankfully, these incidents didn't last. Before long, most students started swerving away from Ella whenever she got too close to them, making it harder for Sera to trip her without being noticed, putting an end to this particular flavor of assault.

But Sera redoubled her efforts in gym class. When they played badminton, Ella was repeatedly whacked over the head, arms and legs with the badminton bird, courtesy of her nemesis. And each one of those whacks stung! Soccer was just as bad, if not worse—the soccer balls flying at Ella, from Sera, would rarely fail to pull a yelp of pain from Ella or raise bluish bruises on various parts of her body.

"It's downright abuse!" Ella told Bobbie with clenched teeth after one particularly aggressive gym class. "I don't know how long I can let this slide."

Bobbie sighed heavily. "Technically, yeah. But if you retaliate in any way, if you even point a finger at her, she'll escalate things."

"But I don't do anything, and she's escalating just the same!"

"I know. But in the long term, you'll beat her by taking the high road."

"Maybe. But it sucks eggs through a bent straw in the meantime. I'm serious! I don't know how long I'll be able to put up with this!"

Bobbie patted Ella on the back.

"Hang in there. You can do this."

Ella kept doing her best to "hang in there." But she suspected that one day soon—very soon—there might be a last straw.

❋

"I'm all out of straws! I've tried very, very hard, but I swear, I can't let her keep doing this to me. I can't just move on. I can't just let it go. Actually, I don't even *want* to let it go!"

Ella had woken up on the wrong side of the bed that day, and everything had gone wrong ever since.

It started with her favorite toothbrush falling in the toilet as she was trying to rush out the door for school. It went downhill from there, class after class, as Ella tried to concentrate on school work while fearing Sera's next assault. It proved to be a surprise food attack at lunch in the cafeteria. Sera knocked Ella's food tray from her hands, sending the contents of the tray flying all over the place. Not only did Ella lose her beef curry, but she was also still wearing it on her once cream-colored top— one of her favorites!—despite all her efforts to wash it clean in the bathroom.

The hellish school day had mercifully come to its end, and Ella—still in a raw mood—was now walking home with Bobbie and Frank.

"You've been doing great for weeks. Things are better now. Why rock the boat?" Bobbie asked.

"First, it's not a boat. We're talking effin' battleships. And I'm gonna sink hers."

"But why? I thought things were starting to blow over."

"Were they, really? Because they're not! And letting things go won't right a wrong. She needs to learn that she can't do nasty shit like that to people and get away with it."

"So . . . you're gonna do some nasty shit back to her to teach her that she can't do nasty shit to others?"

Ella walked in silence, frustrated that Bobbie wasn't on her side. Sensing her turmoil, Frank got closer to her, touching her leg as he kept pace, as if to calm her down.

"I thought you'd moved on. You seemed happy lately," Bobbie added.

"Yeah, well. It keeps being there at the back of my mind and in front of my face. Right there, in front of my goddamn face. What can I say?"

"You can say you're gonna drop it. Instead of entertaining revenge."

"It's more like getting even than revenge."

Bobbie looked unimpressed with Ella's rationalization.

"It all sounds nasty to me, regardless of how you word it."

"Look, I'm not gonna have her beaten up or anything like that. It's gonna be subtle. And it's gonna hurt her privately so she won't lose face at school. I won't do to her what she's done to me. In fact, I'm gonna get back at her without even confronting her."

"And how would you do that?"

Ella hadn't had time to think things through, but since Sera had turned on her over Henry when nothing had gone on between them, it would only be logical that taking Henry from Sera would strike a major blow.

"I'm gonna steal that guy from her. Henry."

"I don't think they're together."

"I'm sure she's still interested in him, the way she looks at him. I'll get him interested in me. See what happens."

Bobbie stopped, suddenly upset. "Unless you have feelings for him, you shouldn't even *think* of using him like that. That's . . . ugly."

Bobbie's reaction surprised Ella.

"What? You have a crush on him or something?"

Bobbie made a face.

"No! He's my cousin, and he's a great guy. And with the ugliness you're showing me right now, you're clearly not good enough for him."

What?! *She*, Ella Briggs, was being told that *she* wasn't good enough for a guy? When she had always been quite the prize? As if! How did Bobbie dare say something like this to her?

"I should have known you two were related. Is there anyone around here who's not related to everyone else? In fact, I'm surprised he's not also your uncle and brother!"

It was a nasty, cheap shot. And that did it.

"I don't have to put up with this." Bobbie's voice was quiet but firm. She turned around and left.

Ella watched Bobbie walk away, too stunned and annoyed to react.

LONESOME TONIGHT

ELLA WAS CURSING at Bobbie while making herself a peanut butter sandwich. She was alone, again, and felt even more lonely now that she had fallen out with someone she'd started to view as a friend. And not a superficial, psycho friend either, not to name names. She wanted to blame Bobbie, but the girl was so poised and sensible, it was hard to find fault in her reaction. But Ella had been assaulted and bullied too many times. She felt she was the one who was hurt and needed support.

Why couldn't Bobbie be on her side? Ella needed her. *She* was the victim, here! And why would Bobbie be so sensitive about her cousin Henry? He was a big boy, he could no doubt take care of himself. It's not like Ella was such a big threat. Plus, the guy *was* nice and interesting. She liked him. For real. It wasn't like she would try to hurt him on purpose, or at all. Why would she do that? And why couldn't Bobbie understand that?

Perhaps Bobbie would come around. Ella would give her some time, and then she would for sure, she just knew it.

Ella brought her sandwich into the living room. She would eat it in the dark. She wouldn't even bother turning on the TV. She didn't care to watch yet another ridiculous show about some snotty teenagers backstabbing one another over ridiculous reasons.

Her father would be coming home soon, and he would be tired from his week, but probably happy. She had never seen him so happy as lately. He'd be happy tonight, and his happiness would rain on her parade.

Ella looked out the living room window and noticed Frank was outside, in Inuuja's driveway. Perhaps she should go hug him and say hi to Inuuja. She had promised the old lady she would come over for tea once in a while and felt that she had been neglecting her. The thought made her feel like a fair-weather friend: only there when she could gain something from someone. Was that all she was? Was she using Bobbie too? Well, using one another had been their arrangement, to begin with, so why should she feel bad about anything?

Still, that sucked.

She sucked.

She didn't want to feel like she might be a bad person.

She didn't want to suck.

What if she brought Inuuja something? Some kind of present? That would seem like a good reason to visit and not feel like crap. Or, at least, feel a bit less like crap. She was feeling so bad already, she was willing to make any improvement on this rotten feeling.

Ella stormed to the kitchen and rummaged through the fridge and freezer for food to bring over. Dan usually went grocery shopping on Saturdays, so they were running low on just about everything. They were even out of his homemade spaghetti sauce. That would have been a hit.

Dammit. Nothing?! She very much wanted to go across the street, where she suspected she'd find some comfort, but she couldn't go there empty-handed.

She finally decided to make Inuuja a latte in a travel mug. Who could turn down a homemade latte?

Inuuja was happy to see her young neighbor and accepted the latte gracefully.

"I didn't put any sugar in it," Ella pointed out.

"Very thoughtful. Thank you."

Inuuja took a sip of the foam, and you could tell this was a treat for her.

As Ella had hoped, Inuuja invited her to come in. Frank followed Ella inside, wagging his tail. This rush of fluffy love made a big dent in her somber mood. Things seemed so much better already.

A caribou stew was simmering on the stove top. Ella breathed in deeply to appreciate the wonderful smell.

"What's that?"

"*That* beats peanut butter sandwiches any day of the week, that's what it is," replied Inuuja.

How could she possibly know about Ella's peanut butter sandwiches? Ella ran a finger around her mouth to make sure there were no crusty tidbits of peanut butter stuck there, but her face seemed clean. This was not the first time Inuuja seemed to *know* something about her.

"How did you know?"

Inuuja smiled cryptically. "There are things that I just know." She took another sip of coffee before adding, "This is the first time I've ever had one of these. It's quite good."

Ella wanted to point out that Tim Hortons, the Black Heart Café and other places in Iqaluit had them, and she was frankly amazed Inuuja had never had a latte before. But there was a more pressing issue.

"Do you have, like, *powers?* Like some kind of *sight?*" she couldn't help but ask.

Inuuja put the travel mug down on the kitchen counter and cradled Ella's face in her hands. She looked deeply into her eyes.

"Yes . . . I have sight . . ."

Oh my God, thought Ella, bracing herself. This was at once creepy and exciting. She often wondered if there were "other forces" at play in the world, people with occult abilities and other such paranormal realities. What if Inuuja was indeed some kind of witch after all?

"I can see . . ." Inuuja looked intense. "I can see . . . what's in your recycling bin, my dear."

She burst out laughing.

It took Ella a moment to overcome her surprise and join her —she let out a laugh of relief. Good grief, she could be so gullible!

"You're going through our trash?" Ella asked with puzzlement. She could picture Inuuja doing something like this, perhaps for an art project. But why else?

"Not me. Frank's been fishing your empty jars out of your bin for weeks and bringing them back to play with them. I caught him again two days ago."

"Frank, you gave me away!" Ella started petting him. "You silly pup."

"You and your father go through peanut butter like shit through a goose."

"My father hates the stuff. It's just me."

"Oh, my."

Oh, my was right. It occurred to Ella how poorly she had been eating, lately. But what could she do? She was hungry at dinner time, and by the time Dan came home and got around to cooking, it was often past eight, and there was no way she could wait that long. And anyway, he often was too tired to cook and would end up reheating canned soup. He'd apologize to Ella. Soon, his schedule would be less crazy—he'd say—and he'd be home earlier, and then they'd have more proper meals. But that never seemed to happen. They had been here for a while now, and nothing had changed.

"Actually, lately, it's not all me eating those. Bobbie, too . . ."

Ella often gave peanut butter sandwiches to Bobbie when they hung out at her place. At the thought, Ella's face darkened. What was she going to do about Bobbie?

Inuuja took another sip of coffee. "So, tell me. What's wrong, luv?"

"I'm that obvious?"

"No. You're hiding it pretty well. Just a lucky guess."

Ella sat down at the table and told Inuuja everything that had happened lately, including Sera's recent bullying in the school's bathroom, which was more upsetting than Ella wanted to admit. But here she was, admitting it. And the fact that Sera was now multiplying her attacks upon her, unprovoked, and her falling out with Bobbie. And, once again, Inuuja listened to it all.

Even though the senior barely said anything, as Ella was telling her the facts and how she felt, it became clear to the teen —speaking the facts aloud—that she had been nasty to Bobbie, who had been so good to her. Still, she wanted to be allowed to feel angry, to be allowed to fight back. She used to take care of herself just fine back in Montreal and would never have let it go, back there, had she ended up in this kind of situation. No way. She would have struck first. Like Sera had done.

Like Sera had done . . .

Ella hated the thought of being like Sera. But she used to be like her. She *was* her. And that was upsetting. Sera was a bitch of the highest order. Ella didn't want to be like that. So many things Ella didn't want to be.

What *did* she want to be?

Inuuja poured her some tea—some jasmine tea, this time. Ella thought that perhaps there could be an old Ella and a new Ella. The old one would have had no qualms about taking down Sera. The new one, while still pissed off to high heavens about Sera's treatment of her, was now, at least, entertaining some doubts about retaliating in kind, about her own conduct.

Perhaps there was something in Inuuja's tea that was imparting her with some form of liquid wisdom. Or perhaps the elderly artist did have some kind of psychic power after all and was getting inside Ella's head, subtly guiding her down a better path. Or perhaps Ella was just ready for a change.

"Tell me what you think," said Inuuja.

There was a piping bowl of caribou stew in front of Ella. It looked just like beef stew, with carrots and mushrooms and peas. Something she hadn't had in ages. But this . . . Ella was about to try her very first bite ever of caribou and was not sure she was going to like it.

"Try not to judge before you try."

Ella tried not to judge but was reluctant, nonetheless. She braced herself, took a bite, and was relieved to find that caribou tasted just fine, that she wouldn't have to swallow it fast or find an elegant way not to eat the rest. Inuuja was right: it beat peanut butter sandwiches hands down. She took another bite and started nodding. Appreciating, in fact, that she was eating a nice, hot meal, and also not eating it all by herself in the dark.

"Surely your dad will soon start to come home earlier.

Starting a new job like his, I imagine that's time-consuming. He's lucky to have a daughter like you."

Inuuja always knew what to say. If only Ella could be more like her, she thought to herself. She'd get in trouble less often, for starters. And perhaps she would not have hurt a friend.

"You're a good cook," said Ella.

"Thank you, dear."

"I wish I could cook like that."

"I'd be happy to teach you anytime."

"Cool."

Ella appreciated the offer but wasn't sure it was a good idea. She'd probably end up ruining very expensive ingredients, and she didn't have any more room for guilt. Leaving it to the professionals seemed like a good idea.

"Hey, you know what? I started learning how to sew at school. 'Started' being the key word here."

"How wonderful!" Inuuja's enthusiastic approval made Ella happy.

They shared a moment in silence. Ella ate her bowl of stew faster than she would usually eat. She had to admit it: it was pretty good.

"Glad you like it," said Inuuja.

"Me too. That'll be one more option to consider at the cafeteria." Ella smiled.

A NEVER-ENDING WEEKEND

THE MOMENT ELLA came back home, she sat in the living room's puffy chair—her favorite spot—and texted Bobbie.

Hey. I'm truly sorry. I was a major douche. Pls forgive me.

She hit *Send* and waited.

And waited.

She hated having to wait for an answer, especially a text. Perhaps she should have called instead. But then, she might have said something stupid. Texting was way better in this case.

After seven long minutes of waiting, she added, *Pretty pls?*

Geez, when did she start begging?

Why was Bobbie not answering her? Was she busy or just ignoring her? Would she be answering her at all? She didn't even know if Bobbie was the forgiving kind or one to hold a grudge.

Ella started to feel worse at the thought. What if Bobbie were to give her the cold shoulder from now on and ignore her at school? That would be beyond awful.

Ella's mind raced, looking for solutions. Okay, well, she could still find refuge in the sewing room at lunchtime. On her way to and from school, hopefully, Frank would keep escorting her. And if Sera started bullying her again, she would nip her crap in the bud this time and go tell the school's principal. Or even the police, if she had to, even if Sera's dad was there. Surely, she could talk to someone other than Sera's dad. One way or another, she would find a way to no longer put up with this, a way that didn't involve Henry.

As Ella was thinking and planning for the worst, she moved to the kitchen and started rummaging through the drawers, looking for some sort of weapon to put in her school bag to discourage Sera from attacking her ever again. She looked at the steak knives and her dad's favorite butcher knife . . . but a knife seemed overkill, and the risk was too high. If anyone found out she was carrying one of these in her school bag, a teacher or the principal could confiscate it, and her dad would have a major fit because these were expensive knives.

How about a wooden spoon? A spatula? You could hit someone with a wooden spoon, but they might not take you seriously, and their spatulas all had a silicone top, which would bend upon contact, and perhaps it would be like hitting someone with a tiny pillow.

Ella didn't want to attack anyone. She just wanted to be able to look like she could defend herself if things came to that. She spotted a foldable wine bottle opener with a metal corkscrew. It looked like a Swiss Army knife in its folded state, and it was small enough to conceal in the inner pocket of her backpack. That settled it. She put the corkscrew back in the drawer for now, but she'd grab it at the last minute on Monday morning, in case her dad felt like having some wine over the weekend. She couldn't risk raising suspicion.

Ella checked her phone once again, in case she had not heard an alert, as if that was even possible.

Still nothing. But, at least, Ella felt she had done some preventive crisis management and was feeling slightly better.

She was all set in case of the very unfortunate event that Bobbie wanted to boycott her, too. Which would still be really, really bad. And sad and inconvenient. But mostly sad.

Ugh.

Why wasn't Bobbie replying?

Ella went to bed early that night, especially for a Friday night.

Dan had finally come home. She appreciated his presence for the safety it provided, but now, she had to spend the rest of the evening trying to look and act normal so that he wouldn't ask her what was up. She didn't want to tell him about Sera or Bobbie—who *still* hadn't replied! She was an emotional wreck and felt she could easily start crying if she broached the subject.

So, while waiting for 10 p.m. to come around, she watched a rerun of NCIS with Dan, mostly so that she would not have to talk. She then wished him good night and told him that she was wiped out, and he bought it. It was true anyway.

Ella hoped that she'd feel better in the morning. That Bobbie would have replied by then.

Ella found herself wide awake at the crack of dawn, six-effin'-o'clock. *Ugh.* Even earlier than her alarm would go off had it been a weekday.

As she woke, her fallout with Bobbie bitterly hit her, and she pounced on her cell phone, which was charging on her night table.

Still nothing from Bobbie. *Dammit.*

Ella pulled her arm back underneath the covers and tried to go back to sleep, as if that was an option. She could feel how wide awake she was, and she knew that falling back asleep was not going to happen. She groaned at the thought. What could be worse than not sleeping in on a Saturday morning? Seriously?

Out of the blue, a joyful thought crossed her mind. Perhaps something happened to Bobbie's phone, or there was some sort of rational explanation. Her battery could be dead, and she was charging it overnight. One of her younger siblings (she had four of them!) might have tried to flush it down the toilet. Who knows what kids were capable of these days.

Assuming the dead battery scenario, Bobbie would probably reply to her when she woke up. Whenever that'd be.

When would that be?

Ella hoped Bobbie was an early riser. And given how Bobbie was, that was likely the case. For some odd reason, Ella pictured Bobbie chopping wood in her backyard as the town was still asleep. That'd totally be her style. If she lived somewhere else, where there were trees, that is.

Ella stared at the ceiling for a good ten minutes and then heard noises coming from the kitchen. Could her dad be up already? Or was that an intruder? After Sera's recent antics, Ella hated the thought.

She got herself out of bed very carefully to go take a peek without making noises. Halfway down the hall, she distinctly heard milk being frothed, a noise that answered her question. What intruder in their right mind would make themselves a cappuccino in a house they broke into at six in the morning? Dan was up. Which was a relief.

Ella wanted to join him in the kitchen but hesitated. Would she, once again, have to put in tremendous energy to avoid an emotional breakdown in front of her dad? She noticed she felt quite rested—given the circumstances—and was relatively calm too. No longer on the verge of tears at all. She concluded that a historic meltdown was unlikely to happen . . . at the moment, at least.

"Hey, you're up early," she said to Dan. He looked up from the Nunatsiaq News on his tablet, surprised to see Ella standing in front of him.

"That's my usual time, luv. I should be the one asking you what you're doing up at this hour." Dan gave her a warm smile.

"Right."

"Is everything okay?"

"Everything's dandy."

Ella headed to the coffee machine to avoid having to elaborate and made herself a latte. When she joined Dan at the table, he offered her his tablet. She took it, more to have something to busy herself with than out of wanting to read the news.

The delightful smell of coffee this early in the morning struck her. And her dad being there, things not being rushed, the very atmosphere . . . it reminded her of home back in Montreal. And she was feeling content just taking it all in.

Dan stood up.

"I'm gonna make eggs. Would you like some?"

Eggs! That was even better! They hadn't had eggs for breakfast in ages. Or, rather, Ella hadn't had eggs for breakfast in ages. Was this what her dad was up to on weekends when she was busy sleeping in?

Ella spent a good chunk of the day trying to distract herself. She accompanied Dan to the grocery store, something usually not her thing. But she was so desperate for distractions, she couldn't afford to be choosy.

Once at PolarMart, she caught herself hoping to run into Bobbie. But that didn't happen.

Back home, she helped Dan unpack. Again, another activity that was mostly foreign to her. But it helped nicely to kill some time.

Saturday night turned out just as rotten as the previous night. By then, Ella had exhausted just about every TV show and movie that were merely of interest to her, and everything on social media sucked. Balled up in the living room's puffy chair—which she barely left during the day while at home—she was down to perusing YouTube on her tablet, watching videos of rabbits. They were awfully cute, but how many flops and binkies could you watch in a row before feeling like moving on? Quite a few hours for Ella, it turned out, but eventually, she felt like she had reached the end of the Internet.

For God knows why, an animated video teaching CPR for dummies popped up on YouTube in the recommended videos section. Ella laughed—what a bizarre, yet dead-on suggestion! The video advertised a simple technique based on the disco beat of Stayin' Alive and without mouth-to-mouth. Ella couldn't help clicking and watching it. The video pretty much delivered on its promise, showing how to do cardiac compressions following a disco beat which, Ella learned, amounted to about 100 beats per minute. If only Mr. Moog had been aware of this technique, they could have skipped his entirely boring lecture on CPR in the gym and actually learned something! She had to share this with Sandy. She'd no doubt get a kick over it.

Ella shot her old friend a text. *Yo, sup?* It had been a long time since she touched base with Sandy. It struck her they hadn't interacted in, what . . . weeks?! How could that be? It seemed like distance was finally taking its toll despite Ella and Sandy having sworn to each other that they would not let Ella being away affect their friendship. They had known each other forever, and nothing would ever come between them. Or so they had thought.

Sandy took a while to reply, but she eventually did, as Ella was getting ready to go to bed.

When Ella heard her cell phone chime, her heart skipped a beat. Seeing that it was Sandy replying and not Bobbie, she felt a pinch of disappointment.

Yo. On ski trip. Talk later, k?

Sandy on a ski trip? *Wtf?* Sandy didn't ski. And her idea of sports was shopping for makeup in person as opposed to online. Her friend's phone's auto-correct had to be acting up.

By Sunday morning, there was still no news from Bobbie. Ella was getting discouraged, on top of dreading the worst and feeling ever more lonely. It seemed more and more likely that she might have lost a friend. And she had to admit that Bobbie meant more to her than she would have expected.

Ella noticed that her dad was about to make a batch of spaghetti sauce and she jumped to her feet.

"Can I help?"

Dan looked at her.

"I can chop some vegetables," Ella added.

Dan took a moment to take in Ella's offer. "Are you okay?" He was starting to worry.

"Yeah. Why?" *Oh, God,* thought Ella. She should have kept to herself.

"No reason. Just tell me if you ever need to talk."

"Okay. But I'm good."

Ella felt relieved to have escaped her dad's inquisition.

Though, now, she was facing a bunch of onions to chop. Hopefully, they wouldn't make her cry.

"So . . . Christmas in a few weeks. Ready to go to Montreal?" Dan asked.

Christmas? Montreal? How could Ella have forgotten they were going to Montreal over the holidays? How could she not be obsessing over that? Perhaps she had suppressed the thought, seeing how busy her dad was all the time and with all the crap happening with Sera. Her subconscious must have stopped believing a trip would happen at all. Another reason to get hurt if it fell through. But now, the very thought of being in Montreal, back to her old life, instantly elevated Ella's spirits.

"Yeah. That'll be great!"

"Have you thought about what you want to ask Santa?" Dan winked at her. This was a tradition for them. Ever since Ella had figured out Santa wasn't real, whenever they talked about him, Dan would wink at her and pretend Ella still believed in him. She would play along, simply to keep the spirit of Christmas alive. Ella was now the one to leave a plate of baby carrots on the table for Rudolph before heading off to bed every Christmas Eve. For cuteness alone. It was one of her favorite moments of the holiday season.

Ella would usually start thinking about her Christmas present list pretty early in the fall—in fact, the moment the stores switched from Halloween decorations to holiday ones.

But this year was different. The thought of presents and the holidays had barely crossed Ella's mind. Now that she was being asked what she wanted, she nearly blurted out "I just want my friend back." Instead, she replied, "I'll have to think about it."

"Alright. Keep me in the loop."

As she chopped vegetables, Ella pondered what she really wanted for Christmas. For as long as she could remember, she would normally ask mostly for clothes. This year, she could get a new wardrobe guaranteed to drive Sera even crazier. But she wasn't sure about clothes right now. She hadn't shopped in ages, mainly because clothing stores in Iqaluit were sparse and expensive, and online shopping had astronomical shipping fees, which wasn't really an option. But for Christmas—and being in Montreal—she could do all the shopping she wanted. Except . . . weird: the prospect didn't bring much excitement, nor even joy, to Ella.

For the rest of the day, Ella's mind went back and forth between the agonizing wait to hear from Bobbie and wondering what she should get for Christmas. Her mind eventually put the two together: she should ask to bring Bobbie to Montreal with her for Christmas. That would be a dream for Bobbie, a golden opportunity to get a hands-on taste of city life like she would so love to experience. An offer she surely couldn't refuse.

This would be the best present ever. She would run the idea by Dan.

"Do you have any idea how expensive plane tickets are for Montreal?!"

Fudge. If a pack of cheese could easily be twenty dollars, Ella could imagine she was asking for the moon. She was truly miffed.

"How about I chip in with my own money?"

Dan could see this meant a lot to Ella. After some thought, he volunteered, "How about I look into it?"

Ella's face brightened. "Could you? Please?"

Dan got on his laptop and started looking.

Pls gimme a 2nd chance. I'd like to bring u to Mtl with me at Xmas, Ella texted Bobbie after dinner.

Dan had managed to find a reasonable trip arrangement for Bobbie to tag along. He did, however, make it clear to Ella that this was a little over-the-top, busting their budget big time, so that she clearly understood this was a very expensive, one-time deal.

But Dan also told her that she had made several sacrifices since their arrival and many efforts to adapt. He was proud of her. Ella was happy to hear that from him—and so excited, too, by the thought of bringing Bobbie to Montreal! This would be so much fun! Probably a little weird, but mostly fun.

Now, if only Bobbie would forgive her and give her a sign. Better even: accept her proposition. It would be such a shame if she didn't.

But what if she didn't?

Come Monday morning, Bobbie had still not replied. Ella felt devastated and barely ate anything for breakfast, too busy wondering what she would do when she saw her at school. Should she avoid her? Give her space? She thought she should at least *try* to plead with her. And she would do so as soon as she saw her at school.

Ella remembered she used to have a talent for pleading and negotiating, but she felt rusty and might have to brush up on her skills. For the time being, she would be honest and try her very best.

Just as she was packing the corkscrew into her backpack, the doorbell rang. She gasped and raced to the door, corkscrew in hand for good measure.

She flung the door open . . .

And was floored to see Bobbie!

"I'm not here 'cause of your bribe. Just so we're clear."

"It wasn't a bribe—okay, understood."

Ella was giving Bobbie a big smile of relief. Bobbie herself was fighting back a grin.

"All set?" Bobbie asked before noticing the corkscrew. "A bit early to be drinking . . . ?"

"You don't want to know." Ella gave Bobbie a cryptic smile and went to fetch her backpack. She quickly put on her boots and jacket and joined her friend outside. She felt at once nervous and happily relieved.

They started their walk to school. Frank came running up to join them and ran a few circles of pure happy puppy joy around the two girls.

"I'm sorry. I spoke out of anger," said Ella.

"I know."

"This is hard for me, but I'll try to let it go with Sera. Or, at least, not be nasty about it."

"Alright."

"Why didn't you answer my texts?"

"My battery was dead. I got them this morning. I thought I'd reply in person."

You spent an entire weekend without a phone?! Ella kept this outrageous thought to herself—now was no time for criticism.

Still . . . "You know, you nearly gave me a heart attack! Several heart attacks. I thought you were ignoring me."

"Sorry. I didn't mean to freak you out. My mom was working double shifts at the hospital, and the twins are sick."

"Oh."

It dawned on Ella that Bobbie might have had an even worse weekend than she did. If she did, she didn't let it show. And could she blame Bobbie for holding back, after how she treated her?

"So, you're coming to Montreal with us?"

"Yeah, about that. Is that really . . . for real?" Bobbie couldn't help looking skeptical.

"Yeah! Of course! I would never joke about something like that!"

"Okay. Good."

"Okay . . . So . . . ?"

"I'll think about it."

She'll think about it. Really? What is there to think about?! Ella wanted to scream.

"Okay. But I really hope you—"

Bobbie gave Ella a look that warned her not to rush her.

"Okay. Take your time. But not too much. My dad has to buy the tickets."

Ella gave Bobbie another big smile. Bobbie softened.

"It would be a wonderful trip," Bobbie recognized.

And suddenly, everything wrong was right again. Ella couldn't believe how pleasant and reasonable Bobbie was being about all this. She was definitely one of the most mature people she knew. Perhaps Bobbie would rub off on her in that department.

And now, once again, she couldn't wait for Bobbie's answer. And Christmas!

This year had the potential to be the best Christmas ever!

GOING SOUTH IN A GOOD WAY

Landing at Trudeau Airport would be such a contrast with the departure from Iqaluit Airport. Bobbie had her face glued to the plane's window for most of the four-hour flight, but even more so from the moment they started seeing lights from civilization below.

"Is this Montreal?"

Ella looked. They seemed to be flying over a countryside community.

"Oh, my, no! This is nothing. You'll see."

The lights soon became more numerous and brighter. The suburbs became denser, followed by urban neighborhoods. And then, there it was: a majestic view of Montreal, with the Mount Royal mountain at its center, the old Olympic stadium, the skyscrapers of the downtown core. This was Ella's favorite part, when the plane made its approach from the northeast and had to fly over the city to do so.

"Isn't that cool?"

Bobbie was busy taking everything in. This foreign, dense landscape of lights and buildings.

This was beyond cool.

This was also almost too much to process.

Ella, Bobbie, and Dan took an electric cab from the airport. Ella was enthused to see a Tesla show up. The car would no doubt impress Bobbie.

"They have free Wi-Fi," Ella whispered to her friend.

"Who has free Wi-Fi?"

"The car. In the car!"

"What?! No way!"

"Yes way!"

The notion impressed Bobbie, but she was not so much interested in browsing the Internet at the moment. She could do that at home. Once again, she was excited to look out the window. It was snowing lightly outside, which helped make the otherwise ugly and grey journey from Trudeau Airport to the Notre-Dame-de-Grâce neighborhood look better. The cab slowed down as it entered a construction zone filled with orange cones—a staple of Montreal life—near the Turcot yards.

"Don't worry, it's not all concrete and depressing like this. This part is just . . . I dunno, I guess it's to give tourists very low expectations so that they're bowled over when they finally get into town."

Ella was joking, but it seemed like a logical explanation for the abomination that Highway 20 was in that part of the island of Montreal.

Ella's words turned out to be spot-on. They soon started seeing downtown skyscrapers ahead, some decorated with colorful holiday lights. Approaching the residential streets of Notre-Dame-de-Grâce, with its older, red brick houses and duplexes with large and inviting front porches, and all the holiday decorations, was even more of a treat.

"This is like in the movies!" said Bobbie, who could barely believe her eyes.

Ella had never looked at it this way. But now that her friend was mentioning it, she was seeing the grand old houses of her neighborhood with different eyes. They were beautiful. And she couldn't wait to show Bobbie her home.

Bobbie couldn't believe how much stuff Ella had in her room. And Ella was almost as shocked, after spending weeks with the bare minimum.

"Oh my God, this looks like an episode of Hoarders!" Ella recognized.

"Now I understand why you act like a spoiled brat," Bobbie teased.

"Now even *I* understand why I act like a spoiled brat," retorted Ella. She grinned and added, "We should go shopping!" She was half-joking, half-serious. As if she needed any more stuff! They were also pretty beat from the plane ride, but the evening was young, and Ella was eager to show Bobbie around the city and get her to finally soak in, firsthand, a true city atmosphere.

At the bottom of the hill of Grey Avenue, they hopped on the 24 bus on Sherbrooke Street. Ella had considered them taking the metro, as the Vendôme station was nearby, but she figured the bus would be a more impressive way to get downtown.

The bus drove by the quaint shops of the Lower Westmount neighborhood, followed by the grand old architecture of a residential strip. As they neared Atwater Avenue, taller buildings appeared. Ella pointed at Dawson College, where she would be applying in the spring, in case she and her father moved back to Montreal in time for next fall.

A few blocks later, they got off next to the Museum of Fine Arts, walked down Bishop Street all the way to St. Catherine Street, and headed east to see Ogilvy's famous holiday window display. But the anticipated dancing animatronic bunnies and forest critters were nowhere to be seen.

"That's bizarre," Ella mumbled to herself as she whipped out her cell phone and started googling. "They've had the same holiday display since, I dunno, like the 1940s or something. And it was crazy cute. And my dad used to bring me to see it every year when I was a kid. But now . . . Ah, crap!"

Ella was bummed to learn from her Internet search that the store had chosen to no longer continue their well-loved display. The little guys were tired and had found a new home at the McCord Museum for a well-deserved retirement. Ella couldn't hide her disappointment.

"You would have loved this!" she said to Bobbie. "I'm sorry you won't get to see it. Unless we find time to go to the museum."

Bobbie was too dazed to follow what Ella was going on and on about to share her friend's disappointment. She looked like a deer caught in the headlights. She was trying to get accustomed to the overpowering sights and sounds around her, the particular whooshing sound of so many cars driving by them, the pedestrians crowding the sidewalks, some of them not caring if they walked right into you while buried in their cell phones.

Ella grabbed Bobbie by the arm and pulled her away.

"Come on! The shops close in a few hours!"

As they were about to cross Drummond Street, Ella had to grab Bobbie once more, but this time, to hold her back from crossing on a red light.

"Red light, girl!"

"Where?!"

There were lights everywhere! Everything was melting into one giant blur of colors and movement. It took Bobbie a moment to even spot the street light across the street.

"Okay, listen. City living rule #1: if you're gonna jaywalk, you at least have to be aware that you're jaywalking. You could get killed or get a fine."

As Ella was explaining this, a trio of partying college students started crossing on red, barely paying attention.

"I guess they didn't get the memo," Bobbie pointed out.

"Yeah. Not everyone's a role model."

"Got it."

The light finally turned green, and they crossed the street, engulfed in a wave of pedestrians that had accumulated behind them on the sidewalk.

They headed to the Cours Mont-Royal building, which offered an access to the underground city, a string of shopping malls all connected to one another indoors, below street level.

The crowded Place Montreal Trust mall—with its noisy seas of shoppers, Christmas music blaring, an infinite number of lights, and the pervasive smell of popcorn from a specialty shop—was giving Bobbie a major sensory overload. She followed Ella like a nervous lapdog, too dazzled to truly see any of the things her friend was showing her. She was getting hot, too, in her parka, and this was making her even more tired. She couldn't believe the sheer number of people all in one place.

"So, this is where the entire city shops?"

Ella looked around.

"Oh no! This is a slow night. In a few days, right before Christmas, it's gonna be crazy!"

"Oh, joy."

Ella dragged Bobbie into a clothing store, proposed various cute outfits to her, attracting her attention to the price tags —"Bargains, Bobbie!" But all Bobbie was interested in were jeans and T-shirts.

"Do you think we could come back later? Like tomorrow?" pleaded Bobbie.

"Alright. Let's get out of here."

They took several escalators down. Bobbie didn't look down to avoid vertigo. She couldn't help but wonder how deep below street level they were getting.

"Does any of this ever cave in?" she inquired.

"What do you mean?"

"This is, like, a major hole in the ground. We're under buildings—skyscrapers—and streets and . . . Is this safe?"

Ella never really gave this any thought. It was true that, in the past, the city's aging underground water pipes had caused some major issues here and there, the occasional street pavement caving in. Shit did happen. But this was obviously not the best time to mention this to Bobbie.

"Of course it's safe."

"Okay."

Bobbie didn't seem entirely convinced. Perhaps it was tiredness that was making her worry more than necessary. She followed Ella, who led the way towards the McGill metro station entrance.

As they reached the metro's platform, the doors of a metro train on the opposite track shut all of its doors at the same time. Some of its cars seemed filled to the brim, like cans of sardines.

"How can people breathe in there?" asked Bobbie, concerned. She was starting to be aware of her own breathing.

The place was warm and crowded, and overwhelming. Mostly overwhelming. A brief melody was heard as the train started moving and quickly picked up speed, disappearing into a dark tunnel down the track. Bobbie took a few cautious steps towards the edge of the platform to see where the train had disappeared. She felt a tug at her sleeve from Ella.

"See the line here?" Ella was pointing at the canary-yellow band bordering the edge of the platform, forming a line right underneath Bobbie's boots. "You want to stay on this side of it. You don't want to fall on the tracks. 'Cause you could get electrocuted. And perhaps get hit by a metro train, too, if one was coming."

Ella didn't know she was not helping—*really* not helping. Bobbie's breathing was becoming uncomfortable.

"Is there anything around here that might not result in sudden death?" asked Bobbie. She was trying to joke, but a quiet panic was overtaking her.

Their metro train emerged from the tunnel, approaching fast. Bobbie was beginning to hyperventilate. Her ears were ringing, her vision was blurring. She headed back to the escalator. She had to get out of there and get some air. Ella followed her.

Rushing out of the nearest exit, Bobbie found herself on De Maisonneuve Boulevard.

"Come on," said Ella, seeing that her friend was no longer her usual calm self. She guided Bobbie to the front lawn of McGill University, where the peaceful surroundings made the air feel fresher and more breathable. Bobbie was gasping for air.

"Your brain is trying to trick you. You're getting enough air, but you think you're not. Try not to take in so much of it. Try to slow your breathing down."

Bobbie gave Ella an inquisitive look—how did she know all this? Ella was far from medically proficient.

"Are you sure?"

"Oh, yeah. There was nothing on TV the other night except this reality show following paramedics. And there was a guy doing what you're doing."

She didn't specify this happened during that awful weekend when she was desperately waiting to hear back from Bobbie.

"Yay again for reality TV," Bobbie managed to crack.

"We can go get you a paper bag if it doesn't get any better."

"I don't think I need to throw up."

"No, it's for the breathing."

"Oh."

Ella pointed to a bench. Bobbie nodded. They sat on it. It was freezing cold, but it would be okay for a short time. Bobbie's breathing started to come back to normal.

"Well, that bodes well for my city-dwelling future," she said, feeling discouraged.

"That doesn't mean anything. You're tired. And this is a lot to take in."

"What if I'm hopeless? What if I can't adapt?"

"What if you're trying to psych yourself?"

Bobbie took a moment, but she could feel a few tears coming.

"I find all of this so exciting and beautiful—well, most of it. But . . . it's like I'm already feeling homesick. How lame is that?"

"It's not lame at all! It's normal. I, myself, I'm still adapting to Iqaluit. You have to give yourself a chance. And time . . . How about you try not to think about it right now? Try not to judge yourself. Or judge anything, for that matter."

Bobbie nodded. Ella could see her friend was taking in what she said. Ella felt good to help. It was like she was channeling Inuuja, and that made her smile.

❄

The next day started out mellow with the girls sleeping in.

Later, Dan brought them to a swanky café on Monkland Avenue for brunch. Bobbie didn't know eating eggs could be such a fancy affair. They then headed to a grocery store the size of PolarMart to do a little shopping. Bobbie had the shock of her life when she saw the prices.

"A brick of cheese for $2.99 . . . that's a typo, right? Please tell me it's a typo!"

Every single price seemed to be a typo. This made Bobbie somewhat sad. It was hitting her hard: not only how high a rate of poverty her community was clearly locked in, but how they had been paying through the nose all these years for the same products the rich city folks got for so much cheaper. How could one manage *not* to be poor in these inequitable circumstances? The deck was so stacked against them!

"I understand it's because of shipping and everything that we're getting shafted up North. But, man, I can't help feeling like this is a little unfair."

Ella and Dan nodded sympathetically.

"How about we stock up on a few otherwise expensive items for you and your family before we go back? Our treat," offered Dan.

This offer made Bobbie hugely happy and Ella proud of her dad for suggesting this.

Later on that afternoon, Ella brought Bobbie to Pi Café, the cozy coffee shop to which she had planned to bring Ryan for coffee and math tutoring, months earlier.

"If you feel like it's too crowded or if you want to go home, we can just split. Does that work?" Ella asked Bobbie.

Bobbie agreed. And she became glad that she did because

the place had a warm, laid-back atmosphere and a few students working on laptops. This was how Bobbie had pictured coffee shops near a college campus to be, and now she was seeing it with her own eyes. She loved the plush sofas and comfy chairs. She was charmed.

"Can you picture yourself hanging out in a place like this?" asked Ella.

Bobbie nodded enthusiastically.

"Can you picture yourself studying in a place like this?"

Bobbie nodded a definite yes.

"No matter how crazy a big city seems to be, you can always find a little oasis like this one. Keep that in mind."

Right. Bobbie would keep that in mind.

After dinner, the girls spent some time vegging in Ella's room, with Bobbie going through her friend's stuff. They would soon have to get ready to go to the holiday party Sandy was throwing at her house. Ella was at once looking forward to going, to see her old friend, but also a bit apprehensive. How would Sandy react to Bobbie? Would she feel like Ella had a new best friend? What would they talk about?

Ella had been gone for only a few months, but she had gone through so much in so little time that it felt like she had been gone forever. Plus, she and Sandy hadn't had a real talk in ages.

Thinking about it, Ella couldn't even remember the last time they had any kind of a real talk. Ella had survived hell, she felt, and pretty well, if she did say so herself. She assumed she'd come off to Sandy like a wholly different person. But surely, though, not much could have changed in Sandy's life.

Could it?

SOUR PUNCH

"You guys don't have basements?!" Sandy was stunned to hear this fact.

"Most houses don't anyway," Bobbie added. "They're built on stilts. The ground's frozen year-round."

"Where do you guys store all your junk?"

"Usually in shipping containers, next to the house. Or in the backyard," replied Bobbie.

"Or they don't have junk to store in the first place. Everything there is soooo unbelievably expensive," Ella added.

"Wow. That sounds crazy. The whole thing. So, where do you throw parties when your parents are out?"

"When their parents are out, two dozen siblings and a handful of cousins are still over at the house," Ella teased Bobbie.

"What?!"

Sandy looked truly interested in hearing all about life up North. And this made Ella so happy, that things were going great. Bobbie seemed at ease despite them being in a basement stuck in the 1970s and filled with a dozen strangers. Sandy was being the genuinely nice person she always was. Things were better than Ella imagined they'd be.

"It's not that bad! Okay, it's not *always* that bad," added Bobbie. "For parties, there's always the community center. And, of course, the school gym."

"Ah, yes, the infamous school gym parties." Sandy shot a look at Ella. "I heard about those."

"What about those?"

A voice coming from behind Ella made her turn. It was Ryan. Her stomach flipped. She had no idea he would be showing up—why would he be showing up? At Sandy's house, no less! They must have somehow stayed in touch, but the notion felt strange to Ella. Sandy was always so scared of boys.

Ella smiled. She *was* happy to see Ryan, but her feelings about his impromptu presence also felt strange. She didn't understand how she felt right now, seeing him again. But God, did he ever look good!

"Welcome back, Ella," Ryan said as he greeted her with a kiss on both cheeks. This, too, was fully unexpected. Ryan turned to Bobbie, extending a hand. "Hey, I'm Ryan."

Bobbie shook his hand. "Bobbie."

"Welcome to Montreal, Bobbie." Ryan gave her a warm smile before turning to Sandy.

"Hey, babe," she said to him.

And then, they kissed.

Full on the lips.

Ella gaped.

She was thrown aback. What the hell just happened?! What the hell was going on here? Her heart sank. Sandy noticed and became uneasy.

"Would you guys like more punch?" she asked Ella and Bobbie.

"Yes, please." Bobbie offered Sandy her empty plastic cup, on which she had scribbled her name with a Sharpie.

"Alright. Ryan, dear, would you mind?"

"That's why I'm here, your majesty."

"Punch bowl is on the table by the stairs. Thanks!" Sandy gave him a little girly smile.

Ryan walked away, and the second he was out of earshot, Sandy started whispering to Ella. "I should have told you. So many times, I . . . I'm so sorry I didn't." Sandy looked quietly panicked, as if bracing herself for a massive reaction from Ella. "I thought it would be . . . a surprise?"

Judging by Ella's sour expression, it was.

And now that she was looking at her friend, Ella saw how much Sandy had changed. How confident she seemed to have become. Ella almost felt jealous that Sandy had grown so much, without her help. Or perhaps, even worse, had grown *because* of her absence.

"I'm sorry, I thought you were over him," added Sandy. Ella knew she meant it and tried to fake an authentic smile to avoid giving her old friend any more of a guilt trip.

"Oh, yes, completely. I mean, there was no future for us, you knew that."

Sandy nodded and let out a relieved smile.

"That's what you said, I remember."

Yup, that's what Ella had said. Though now she wasn't sure she ever really meant it.

"You two seem to go well together. You . . ." Ella didn't know how to finish that sentence. *You're both good at math?* That would sound weird. "You seem happy," she managed to add. And she meant it, too.

Ryan came back, and they talked some more about Iqaluit. He, too, had so many questions for Bobbie, and he, too, was just as sincerely interested in what she had to say.

It struck Ella that Sandy and Ryan had this in common: they were both two people genuinely interested in others. *Whereas, I'm a selfish, navel-gazing bitch. On a good day,* she thought to herself.

The evening felt like it went on forever. For the most part, Ella forced herself to smile and show how much of a good time she was having, when she was, in fact, feeling so very miserable. And when an old acquaintance named Clara pointed out how quiet she was, and how unlike her that was to be so quiet, Ella blamed it on being tired.

By midnight, Ella was exhausted from pretending. She was so ready to go home. Bobbie was just about done as well—she had spent most of the evening patiently debunking clichés about "Eskimo life." No, she didn't live in an igloo. No, she didn't ride to school in a dog sled. No, she didn't eat only seal. Yes, she knew what vegetables were—and ranch dip—and yes, they did have cake at home. Right now, she was answering for the fifth time that, no, they didn't have a hundred synonyms for the word "snow" in Inuktitut, per se—that'd be overkill. It was more that they had different words to describe various types of snow, like falling snow, or snow that's on the ground, or wet snow, or a blizzard.

Ella tugged on Bobbie's sleeve, and Bobbie acknowledged her silent signal. They made a quick round to wish everyone goodnight and a Merry Christmas.

Ella hugged Sandy at the door. She felt like this was more than a simple good night. It felt more like a goodbye.

HEADING BACK AND BACKWARDS

Bobbie, too, was kind of saying goodbye.

Goodbye to her dream of ever going to college down South. A dream she had had since she was young, when she first witnessed an older girl leave the community to study and become a rights activist for First Nations.

Bobbie, too, wanted to help and give back to her community. Whether it was becoming a doctor to help people or a scientist to fight off climate change. To achieve this, she would have to go to college elsewhere since the college options interesting her were not available in Iqaluit at the moment.

Bobbie was bright and studious, and she had the marks at school and the perseverance to succeed and make a difference. For as long as she could remember, she pictured herself on the campus of a majestic, centuries-old college to learn from the best and bring the knowledge back to Iqaluit.

However, while she was having a great time in Montreal and would cherish the memories made, she missed her family like crazy. She missed the North. The open spaces and the quiet. The sometimes-deafening silence. The impression that the land went on forever.

A big city like Montreal was beautiful in its own right and definitely exciting, but there was so much of . . . everything! A bit like Ella's room. So much stuff, and buildings, and cars, and people. Bobbie felt at times like she could barely hear herself think. It was all too much for her. She couldn't help but wonder how much worse this would be if she went to an even bigger city like Toronto, all by herself. Her odds of survival, she thought, of her plan succeeding, seemed less and less realistic.

It didn't dawn on her that she could always try and return to Iqaluit if she "failed," that it didn't have to be all or nothing. There was a pride in Bobbie that made her commit the whole way and see through whatever she started because she just wouldn't give up. Giving up was never an option, and it never had to be, until now. She would always carefully, meticulously plan the crap out of everything in order to take any potential failure out of the equation from the get-go. Even down to befriending some self-centered ditz from Montreal, in case there was anything she could learn from her.

To her surprise, she had grown truly fond of Ella and had developed a veritable friendship with her since they started hanging out together. She could honestly say she had gained much more than mere knowledge from this relationship. And the trip to Montreal was just an incredible bonus, for which she was truly grateful. Never in her wildest dreams would she have dared imagine being offered such an opportunity!

But never in her wildest nightmares would she have imagined herself hyperventilating on the McGill campus, her closest brush with her scholarly fantasy. Instead of soaking in the grandeur of the campus and feeling that she belonged there, she'd panicked and felt like she wasn't up to the task. At all.

Be careful what you wish for . . .

She had failed before she even began.

Game over.

This hurt deeply.
Way to go, girl.
Bobbie was so mad at herself.
It was all so disheartening.

On Christmas Eve, Ella had brought Bobbie to the Westmount lookout on the mountain, thinking the bright lights and vastness of the city landscape would impress her friend, just like the northern lights had bowled her over. But it turned out to be the last nail in the coffin as far as Bobbie was concerned. Taking in the sheer size of the city sprawled before her was the final, over-powering sensation of alienation that convinced the Inuit girl that there was no way in hell she could possibly do this.

"Imagine this: Toronto's even bigger!" Ella exclaimed with excitement.

Bobbie forced herself to smile. But the smile came out more like a cringe.

Christmas Day turned out bittersweet. It was a lovely, quiet day spent indoors with hot cocoa and various old board games played in front of the crackling fireplace. Christmas music was sweetly emanating from Ella's tablet. And the two girls were afflicted with a melancholy they were both trying to hide from each other.

Bobbie didn't want to risk looking ungrateful, so she kept her emotions in check and didn't say anything about her decision to alter her college plans, nor the debilitating panic slowly filling her that she no longer had a bright future.

Ella was confused and didn't know how to express how she

was feeling—about Ryan and being back home—and she didn't want to ruin Bobbie's trip with her self-absorption anyway. So, she kept everything down inside as well.

Dean Martin began crooning about being home for the holidays, but not for real—he could only be there in his dreams—and the song hit both girls hard. Ella and Bobbie both fought back silent tears as they played Monopoly.

Ella rolled a seven and landed in jail. *What else is new?* she thought and stood up. "Washroom. I'll be back." Her voice cracked.

Bobbie nodded, relieved to be able to blow her nose and regain her composure away from her friend's gaze.

Meanwhile, Ella allowed herself to weep quietly in the bathroom.

The day after Christmas, Ella, Bobbie, and Dan flew back to Iqaluit. It was Ella's turn to have the window seat. She was staring outside in the distance.

"Do you still have a thing for that guy?" Bobbie inquired softly out of the blue.

"What guy?" Ella replied, feigning ignorance.

"Ryan."

"What makes you say I might still have a thing for Ryan?"

"I'm becoming fluent in Ella."

Ella snorted.

"Right."

Ella didn't know what to say. She didn't want to talk about Ryan, but she also wanted to talk about Ryan. Or, more specifically, about how she felt betrayed over finding out that a) her old best friend had somewhat stolen a guy she had been interested in—even though she thought she was over him, but seeing him again, perhaps it stirred something up, and she wasn't sure anymore—how could her friend do that to her? And b) how this same (perhaps former) best friend managed to get a guy without her help, let alone *the* guy *she*, Ella, had been interested in. *Had been*, but still.

This was blowing her mind, her heart and surely a few other organs because her whole body had been taken over by a dull ache since that evening at Sandy's. Paradoxically, there was also the fact that Ella had truly stopped giving a rat's ass about Ryan the moment she decided to leave him behind, so why the hell did she care so much about any of this? Why did she hurt so much?

"I dunno. Everything feels so weird right now." That was all Ella managed to express out loud.

Bobbie nodded.

Ella had no idea at what exactly her friend was nodding, but she could use her support—any support!—so that was good. She added, "It feels like . . . It feels like everything changed while I was in Iqaluit, and I have nothing to return to when we move back to Montreal. It's like I'm stuck in an alternate reality. Another dimension. You know? Like my old life no longer exists. Or, at least, like I can never quite go back to it."

Bobbie felt Ella's pain more than Ella realized. She wondered to herself: what if she went to Toronto and her own hometown, her old life, was no longer there for her when she went back? That was such a scary, unbearable thought. No, there was no way she'd leave Iqaluit now!

Bobbie's silence prompted Ella to go on, "Sorry, I don't make any sense. But once again, as I said earlier, I had made it clear to Sandy when I left that I was no longer interested in Ryan. She didn't go behind my back or anything like that. But somehow, seeing him again . . . with her . . . I dunno, it stirred up something."

Saying this out loud made Ella feel better. Seeing Bobbie listening so intently to what she was trying to verbalize, that, too, helped a good deal. It also helped Ella reach a conclusion she might not have reached otherwise, or even admitted to herself.

"Perhaps I'm just jealous."

Upon saying this, Ella's pain became clearer to her. Her, jealous? How did that ever happen?! Other people had often been jealous of *her*, but never the other way around.

"It would be understandable, given the circumstances," said Bobbie.

"Perhaps. But I don't want to feel jealous. Especially not of two people who are good people, really."

"At least, you're mature about it. That beats just about every other kind of jealousy out there if you ask me."

That made Ella smile. She could see how Bobbie was making her a better person.

"I'm glad you came."

Mike's taxi dropped Bobbie home first, then headed to Ella's house. It was only early afternoon, but the sun had already set, and it was dark outside.

Ella noticed there was no light on at Inuuja's house and thought that was bizarre. As they went up their front steps, Ella surprised herself thinking *Home, sweet home.*

There was a note on their front door for her.

Dear Ella. Inuuja wants you to know that she fell and is at Qikiqtani General. Don't worry about her, she will be fine. Frank is at her sister's.

This bothered Ella, learning that the senior had an accident. What if she was not doing as well as the note was claiming? What if the note was several days old and things had gotten worse?

"Dad, could you please give me a lift to the hospital?"

Inuuja was in good spirits despite being sore. She was being monitored here, at the hospital, for the concussion she suffered when she fell in her bathroom, banging her head against the edge of the bathtub. Frank had helped her come back to consciousness by nudging her and licking her face. He had also managed to fetch her the cordless phone from the kitchen counter so that she could call for help.

"I wish you had been there. You would have been so proud of him."

"For sure! He totally floors me! But if I had been there, I would've jumped on the phone myself to get help the moment you slipped. He wouldn't have needed to bring you the phone."

Inuuja laughed. She reached to grab Ella's hands and squeezed them.

"A concussion. That sounds pretty serious. What did they say?" asked Ella, who vaguely remembered once again that paramedics show, the episode in which a cyclist without a helmet had been hit by a car.

"My balance might be affected for a while. Or forever. It's too early to tell."

"Will you still be able to dance?"

"How do you know that I dance?"

"There are things I just *know*." Ella stuck her tongue out at Inuuja.

Inuuja laughed again. She was so happy to have a visitor. And her visitor was so happy to be spreading some joy.

"So, tell me all about Montreal. Did you have a good time?"

Ella told Inuuja all about the good things that happened during the trip, leaving the depressing parts out. And that was just as well. It lifted the elderly woman's spirits as well as her own.

❄

On her way out, Ella found a nurse to inquire about Inuuja's health.

"Is she going to be okay? I was only gone a week. She was so full of energy before I left. Now, she looks so frail."

"Well, it's hard to recover from this kind of fall at her age. And it's also hard to tell how her health will be from now on," replied the nurse.

"So . . . she might not be herself again?"

"Knowing Inuuja, I expect she'll always be herself. I'm sure she'll find a way to keep living life to the fullest, even if that means making some adjustments."

Life to the fullest. Always herself. The words echoed in Ella's mind that night as she looked outside. Inuuja's blue house was still in the dark. The sky was also dark, devoid of northern lights.

Ella felt blue.

Ella celebrated part of New Year's Eve at the hospital. With the help of Bobbie's mom, Ella and Bobbie were able to bring Frank to visit Inuuja in her hospital room. That made things feel a little less blue. She loved that dog, and making Inuuja happy was priceless. It felt good, too.

In the evening, Ella and Dan joined Bobbie's family at their house to celebrate New Year's Eve. They had a fun time meeting everyone and hanging out in the kitchen, sharing food and anecdotes.

Later that night, they all headed out to see the fireworks near the Road to Nowhere and attended a snowmobile parade on Frobisher Bay. This was far at the other end of the spectrum of all of Ella's past New Year's Eve celebrations, mostly spent in posh living rooms, eating fancy hors d'oeuvres and stealing sips of champagne. Ella was not wearing a glitzy dress for the occasion. She was, in fact, bundled up in her snowsuit, a scarf covering most of her face. It was all so odd and unglamorous, and yet, the contagious, lively spirit of everyone gathered outside in the freezing cold made Ella feel like she was a part of something amazing and so much bigger than herself.

Ella waved goodbye to a year that had given her one hell of a bumpy ride and that kicked her around more times than she could count.

She waved goodbye to all that and braced herself for the New Year.

NOTHING LIKE A GOOD CHALLENGE

GOING BACK to school after the holidays proved particularly hard. Both Ella's and Bobbie's spirits were out lying in a ditch somewhere.

Ella felt like her life lacked purpose. Now that Bobbie had learned pretty much everything there was that she could learn from her while in Montreal, Ella felt she had nothing more to offer her friend in that department—or in any other department, for that matter. What if, like Sandy, Bobbie didn't need her anymore? The thought made her stressed and sad. What if they drifted apart and she lost another friend?

Ella tried to chase out these crippling thoughts, but the new ones that popped up were equally distressing. What did she want to study after graduating high school? What did she want to do with her life? She had no idea. She felt like she was adrift on an ice floe.

On the upside, she had been making progress on her parka at the sewing club and felt she could learn to sew pretty well if she kept at it, which would give her a creative outlet in line with her passion for fashion. But even there, despite being impressed with herself, her heart wasn't really in it these days. Not as much as she would have liked anyway. It still felt like something was missing.

Perhaps she should start looking at boys again, to find someone to go out with once in a while, even if it was more just to hang out with someone new than actually be in a serious relationship. Perhaps this would help her forget how crappy her life was.

But whenever she thought about boyfriend material, her mind always went back to Henry—the one guy Bobbie had deemed too good for her (and probably rightly so) and still the biggest landmine as far as keeping some kind of "peace" with Sera was concerned. In a way, thinking about Henry inevitably made Ella feel like shit. So, she tried to move on from that thought, too.

When Inuuja got out of the hospital, hopefully, she would be back to her old self. Perhaps she would teach Ella to make caribou stew and give her some advice on how to cope better with life.

Bobbie, too, seemed blue. She was zombie-marching through school and seemed self-absorbed, so unlike her usual caring self. She still excelled in her classes, because she didn't know how to be a bad student. But what Ella couldn't know was that, now that Bobbie had decided to not pursue her studies down South anymore, it seemed to her like there was not much point to anything, really.

If the two girls had shared their thoughts with each other, they would have realized how much they had in common at this very moment in their troubled lives. On the surface, they just kept hanging out, chatting about nothing over lattes and hot chocolates, doing homework side by side, hanging on to forms of routine for a sense of comfort. They knew deep down they had each other's backs, and that was, at least, a kind of balm to their separate pain. But a layer of melancholy—and another of secrecy—still remained underneath the balm.

It had been a pretty bland Thursday morning when Sera shook things up, breaking the status quo at recess. Since the return from holiday break, she had quickly noticed Ella looking down in the dumps. And was there ever a better time to kick someone than when they were down?

Sera was still clinging to the fact that her backstabbing of Ella at the party in the school's gym had failed and backfired on her. Not only had she not succeeded in beating Ella's spirits to a pulp, more importantly, Henry seemed to have been keeping a polite distance from her ever since. They still went running together on occasion, but she felt like she had somehow disappointed him. And despite her trying to recover from this unfortunate perception in his eyes, no matter how nice she tried to be, it didn't seem to make a dent. It felt like whatever mistake she'd made could not be unmade.

So, on this drab January morning, Sera noticed on the cork board an announcement for a new winter games event for the students. The weather had been unusually mild for this time of year, and the school had decided to organize impromptu outdoors activities to take advantage of it. The event was loosely inspired— mostly in spirit—by the popular Toonik Tyme Festival, which had occurred every spring for more than fifty years and which featured traditional Inuit games and activities for the whole community. The school administration thought it'd be a good idea to host friendly competitions for the students, to liven up their winter doldrums.

On top of being a good athlete and despite her royal attitude, Sera had learned several skills in survival and other related fields, and she could see herself doing extremely well in this type of event. More importantly, perhaps she could impress Henry, too.

Just as she was thinking these thoughts, Ella and Bobbie passed by. Seeing Ella at the same time as she was actually thinking about Henry was too much of a temptation.

"It's too bad they don't have a nail polish competition!" Sera couldn't help yelling at Ella's receding form. Ella whipped around.

This was the first time Sera had addressed her since their unpleasant encounter in the girls' washroom. Ella wasn't even sure she had heard right, but Sera was staring at her with an arrogant expression, and that was enough to engage her.

"You talking to me?" Ella barked.

Sera scoffed and gave her a taunting smile. "It's too bad you're so useless. It'd be fun to beat you."

"Don't," Bobbie said to Ella, but it was too late: the gloves were off. Ella now felt like she had nothing to lose and had no intention of letting Sera further ridicule her. Enough was enough.

Ella glanced at the poster quickly to see what the hell Sera was talking about. In big letters, it announced a winter games event. Memories of the winter carnivals they used to have at St. Mary's flashed through Ella's mind: skating, dodgeball in the snow, chess tournaments in the cafeteria. *Right. Whatev.*

"I bet you'd excel in the backstabbing event," she quipped back at Sera.

Sera scoffed. "It's too bad you wouldn't dare sign up. I'd love to see you embarrass yourself all over again. You're so good at it —I'll give you that."

"Who said I won't sign up?"

Sera made a face of disbelief. "Alright."

"Alright yourself."

"It's on, bitch!"

Bobbie grabbed Ella by the arm and dragged her away from Sera—this was not the day to be mopping up blood from the aisles.

"Are you insane?" she almost yelled at Ella.

Ella shrugged. "What? For standing up to her?"

"You have no idea what you just got yourself into, do you?"

"Did you see her face?"

"That was soooo impulsive. You let her get to you. And now . . . now, you're screwed!"

"Hardly! I finally have a way to get back at her! And fair and square, like you wanted."

"How is getting crushed in front of the whole community getting back at her!?!"

"I can beat her at chess."

"What the hell are you talking about?"

"The winter thingy, there, on the cork board."

Bobbie sighed. "I don't think chess is up there . . ."

"Look, I stood up to her. All I know is that makes me happy."

Ella meant it. Though now, she couldn't help wondering *what* she had gotten herself into. She headed to the cork board to actually read the details. "I know how to skate," she mumbled to herself.

Bobbie followed her. "Ella, you don't know how to do 99% of this stuff!"

Ella was getting the dreadful feeling that Bobbie was right, but she didn't want to admit that she acted impulsively. It felt good not to let Sera walk all over her for once! And she would pay the consequences if need be.

The poster listed a snowmobile race, igloo building, bannock making, a snowshoe biathlon, and an ice fishing competition. Each item made Ella's jaw drop a little lower as the reality sank in.

Oh. Crap.

But retreating now was not an option. Not after that confrontation with her dreaded enemy.

"Well . . . I've been looking for a challenge anyway, okay?" Ella tried to convince Bobbie and herself.

"How are you going to learn how to do all this?"

"With your invaluable help, of course," Ella replied with a hesitant smile.

THE "WHAT NOW?" STRATEGY

"Oh, God. Why did you let me?"

Sitting at her kitchen table, Ella buried her face in her hands.

"Yeah, why did *I* let you?" Bobbie rolled her eyes.

The two girls were going over the list of events and skills they would have to cover for Ella to compete in the winter games without killing herself, or anyone else for that matter.

"Alright, let's not panic. Yet. Let's just break this down." Bobbie studied the list for a moment. "Ice fishing. I could help you with that."

"Awesome!" said Ella. She uncovered her face and craned her neck to look at the list. "If only Inuuja were feeling better, she could teach me how to make bannock bread. D'you know how to make it?"

"I'm kinda rusty with baking . . . But it's pretty simple. I'm sure YouTube would work just fine for that."

"Okay."

Bobbie wrote "YT" next to bannock making.

"What about snowmobile racing? Can't you help with that?"

"Not really. But you already drive your dad's car like a maniac, so there's hope you'll pick up that one fast."

Bobbie grinned teasingly at Ella. But her expression changed as she considered something.

"What is it?" Ella asked.

Bobbie seemed reluctant to answer. "I know an expert who could actually coach you in that department," she finally replied. "And with the snowshoe biathlon."

"Who?"

"My cousin."

"Which one?" Ella guessed Bobbie's answer, and her heart skipped a beat.

"Henry."

They both knew how awkward this was to even mention Henry. But the situation called for desperate measures.

"I'm sure he'd be happy to help," said Bobbie to reassure Ella.

"Can't *you* help me with the snowshoeing?"

"The snowshoeing, yes, but not the rifle shooting part."

"The rifle? What!? You mean, like, a gun?"

"Not *like* a gun. It *is* a gun."

In reaction to Ella panicking, Bobbie added, "You have nothing to worry about. It's just a BB gun, and Henry's a great guy."

"I'm not sure this is gonna work . . . with Henry."

"Why not?"

"The last time I was seen with him . . . I'm still paying for it, remember?"

"You're already at war with Sera. What difference would it make at this point?"

"Then, what about the fact I'm not good enough for him?" Ella tried to joke, but there was an obvious sting in her voice.

An uncomfortable silence ensued. Bobbie broke it.

"Like you, it was the anger talking," Bobbie apologized.

"Perhaps. But you were right."

"No, I wasn't."

"Yes, you were. I was being ugly, and you called me out on it."

Bobbie smiled at Ella. "Are you still being ugly?"

"I don't know. Trying not to be. But you tell me."

"I think we can hit the reset button on what I said. And then you can be the judge of your own intentions."

"Right. 'Cause no pressure."

"No pressure."

They smiled at each other.

"Speaking of pressure, please don't shoot the messenger, but your college application is due soon," said Ella.

Bobbie's smile vanished, and she withdrew. Her reaction took Ella by surprise. When did this become a touchy subject?

"I can help you fill it out and mail it if you'd like," she ventured.

"That won't be necessary."

"Of course, I didn't mean to imply that you'd need help with that. It's just to make sure you won't procrastinate. Like me. I don't even know what I want to do."

"Look, I decided not to go for it, okay?"

"What?! What do you mean?"

"I'm staying here. I'm gonna go to Nunavut Arctic. Case closed."

"But . . ."

Bobbie started waving the winter games list in the air.

"You want me to help you with this insanity? Yes? Then, quit it with the college thing. I changed my mind."

Ella wished they could keep discussing this, but she had never seen her friend this upset and sensed it was best to drop it. For the time being, at least.

TRAINING DAYS

THE FOLLOWING weeks were beyond busy. Ella was on a count-down to learn as much as she could, as fast as possible, from whoever was kind enough to teach her.

First, Bobbie showed Ella how to use a hand auger to make a hole in the ice for the ice fishing event. Ella observed Bobbie put in a lot of effort to make the hole. After the demonstration, Bobbie handed her the hefty metal tool.

"Here. Go for it. Just be super careful with the blades."

Ella contemplated the auger but didn't take it.

"Go for what? You want me to use this *now?*"

"What do you think we're here for?"

"I think I got it. The way you showed me, that was pretty clear."

"Seeing how it's done and actually doing it are two different things."

Bobbie looked puzzled as to why Ella seemed so determined not to touch the instrument.

"Okay, what's the problem? What are you afraid of?"

Ella looked embarrassed.

"Well . . . I might . . . chip a nail?"

Bobbie shook her head. That took the cake! And they had just started! She took in a deep breath to not lose patience. Helping raise her younger siblings was finally paying off.

"Go home, clip your nails. We'll reconvene."

"But I just manicured!"

Bobbie glared. There was definitely no room in the equation for a manicure—or anything girly for that matter—Ella realized as she watched Bobbie take another deep breath.

"OK, look. The day's young, we'll deal with your nails later. I'm gonna call Henry and see if he'd have time to give you a snowmobile crash course."

"Now?!" Ella panicked.

"Yes, now."

But I look like crap! I don't even have lipstick on!

"Is this at all compatible with your fashion sense, your highness?" Bobbie asked. She was running out of patience.

Ella nodded. She guessed so. Though she could feel her heart pounding like crazy at the mention of Henry.

Henry showed up ten minutes later. He seemed happy to help Ella. Or perhaps just happy to be of help. Ella wondered at times if he was awarded some kind of Boy Scout badge from a secret entity every time he did something good. And where did all of his cheerful motivation to help other people come from? In this case, perhaps he was helping her out of pity, having witnessed firsthand Sera's trick on her at the party in the gym. What kind of badge was there for "pity"? How many celestial points would he get for this one?

Ella forced herself to stop this line of thinking. Surely, all this self-beating-up would do little more than seriously cramp her carefree projection.

Ever since that last conversation with Bobbie—when her friend told her she could hit the reset button and, by the same token, gave her her implicit blessing to pursue Henry—Ella had been thinking of doing exactly that. Giving it a go, an honest go. And she would make sure to be more than good enough for him —not just for Bobbie's benefit, but for his and her own. She really liked and respected this guy. He would be worth all the effort.

From that moment on, he was all she could think about. Looking forward to every weekday to catch a glimpse of him at school. Going around town on the weekends in hopes of running into him. The old Ella would have cut straight to the chase and made a play for him. But she was no longer that girl. Why was that? Had she lost her confidence? Perhaps it was more a kind of arrogance that used to drive her, that she had since lost.

Maybe it wasn't such a bad thing to have lost a bit of this self-entitled, blind faith in herself. An attitude that had, at times, allowed her to act in insensitive ways. However, this also complicated matters. She wished she could simply go for him without a fuss. She could be kissing him right here and right now, and whenever she felt like it, instead of feeling insecure and paralyzed.

Minutes before Henry showed up, Bobbie unexpectedly had to go—her sister Megan had called, needing her help with something at home. Ella had said nothing to Bobbie about her new intentions towards Henry, but it was as if Bobbie had guessed anyway. Perhaps it was Ella's sudden squirming and blushing at the mention of Henry's name that had given her away. In any case, Bobbie had patted her on the shoulder just before leaving.

"Just be yourself," she told her. "You'll do great."

Ella appreciated the support, but then she wondered what

her friend meant. Be yourself. *Be myself.* Easier said than done. Especially these days. *Who am I anyway?* She wasn't sure, and if anyone knew and could tell her, she'd love to know.

Henry's snowmobile turned the corner of the road ahead and headed her way. While she was alone on this deserted stretch of road, she still felt the need to wave her arms in the air so that he wouldn't drive past her. She had been dreaming about this very moment, when she would get to be alone with him. And here it was. Here *he* was. She wondered how she should behave and what to say, and her mind went blank. Except for the part that allowed her to recognize she must look like a total moron, waving her arms wildly for nothing. She stopped, feeling like a turkey, which was *not* helpful.

Henry cut the engine of his snowmobile and got off.

"Hey!" he said.

"Hey!"

"Sorry for the wait." Henry made a face. A cute one at that.

"Are you kidding? I'm so very grateful that you're taking time to do this!" Ella meant it, and it showed.

"Don't mention it. It's my pleasure."

"You're saying that now, but wait until you find out how hopeless I am."

Henry laughed.

"If that's the case, then, I'm not afraid of a good challenge."

He handed her a helmet and patted the seat of the snowmobile, inviting her to sit on the driver's spot.

"After you."

"What? Already? Just like that!?"

"Were you expecting a twenty-hour class with videos and a written test?" he joked.

"Well, that'd be a start!" Ella was taking in the snowmobile and feeling a little intimidated.

"Just hop on. You'll be fine. I'll be right behind you."

Oh, God. How am I supposed to be fine with you right behind me? So darn close . . . Because he would be so darn close to her. And that would be . . . *Oh, God.*

Ella sat down on the snowmobile, stiffly. Henry got on right behind her. He leaned forward to show her the controls, pressing himself against her back to do so.

"On the right handle, right here, is the throttle. To make it go," he said, guiding her right hand to rest over the throttle. "On the left is the brake lever." He guided her left hand to the left handle.

"Let me guess: that one's to go *faster?*" Ella quipped with a grin.

"You're a fast study," Henry replied, matching her grin.

He pointed to the control panel. "And here, we have . . ."

The fabric of their snowsuits was rubbing against one another. His chin was resting on her shoulder as he spoke. Ella could feel his face oh so very near hers. Her thoughts were racing. It was hard to listen to Henry explain the controls and how the snowmobile would react on various terrains and types of snow while thinking how sexy this all was and wondering whether she had brushed her teeth recently enough. Crap, the coffee she had with Bobbie earlier!

Ella started to hold her breath to avoid expelling a cloud of bad breath towards his face. She considered putting on her helmet to trap any undesirable odor, but that would look like a weird move, and he might ask her if there was a problem. She didn't want him to think she had a problem.

On his end, Henry seemed enthusiastic and totally at ease about the whole thing. How the hell could he be so laid back? Surely, he had absolutely zero interest in her. That would explain it all. Ella's face darkened.

"Are you okay?" asked Henry. "Is there a problem?"

Ack!

"No. NO! No problem. I'm low maintenance, believe me. It's all good. I'm good!" Ella rambled frantically. *Okay, you can shut up now, you dork!*

"Alright. Then, let's go."

"Okay."

"I'll let you start the engine."

The engine. Ella started freaking out. Why didn't she listen better to what he had said!?

"Remember . . . Turn the key and release the choke when you hear the engine."

Henry guided her hands, and before Ella knew it, she was driving a snowmobile for the first time in her life.

The ride started a little choppy, especially with Ella struggling between paying attention to the road, learning to feel the way the vehicle handled the curves and her burning desire not to miss any second of Henry's presence. The way he moved. The way he was.

Accelerating on an open, endless stretch of white land turned out to be an exhilarating experience. Ella wished the moment would never end. Later on, as she reminisced about every second, she'd kick herself for being such a good student and learning so fast the various maneuvers Henry taught her. She might still be with him, right now, if she had played a little dumb. Then again, playing dumb was never her strong suit. Instead, perhaps she would eventually manage to impress him by exceeding expectations.

At the end of their first riding lesson, Henry dropped Ella off at her house. Dan's car was not there—he must be running an errand. There was obviously no one home. Ella came close to inviting Henry inside to hang out a bit, but she caught herself and refrained from doing so. On the one hand, she feared he might politely reject the offer. And that would kill her. On the other hand, things seemed to be going pretty well. They made each other laugh several times. They seemed to be connecting. So why spoil a perfectly good moment?

But dammit . . .

With the help of Bobbie and Henry, Ella made leaps and bounds as far as her participation in the games was concerned. She also felt she was making progress with Henry on the personal front. At the very least, it felt like they were bonding, becoming pals. Would this ever evolve into a romantic relationship? Ella had absolutely no idea, though she ardently wished so. But for the time being, she was savoring every bit of attention Henry gave her, every little gesture. She also felt proud of her accomplishments. It took some time, but a healthy sense of self-confidence started growing in her.

Ella cut her nails short and got rid of her precious manicure —or rather, the manicure that was making her act precious—and Bobbie showed her once again how to drill a hole in the ice with the hand auger. This time, Ella picked up the tool and proceeded to drill, at first with all her might, but she tired pretty fast and slowed down.

"I don't think you should drill sideways," teased Bobbie.

"I'm not that bad!" Ella rolled her eyes.

It took a while, but she managed to drill her first proper hole and got all excited at her success. The girls gave each other a high-five.

"I just dug a hole, and I feel so proud of myself . . . 'cause I dug a hole. Is that normal?" Ella scoffed.

"Well, it's consistent. You always seemed like an over-achiever to me."

"Yeah, it must be that."

The two girls often found each other amusing, in a way Ella had never felt with Sandy, who took everything so literally. Bobbie was on the opposite end of the spectrum, a lover of the absurd and the humor that came with it. She, too, enjoyed these silly interactions with Ella. For one thing, they made her forget to obsess over her "failed" future and made her feel less blue.

"Isn't it a thing of beauty, though?" Ella was goofing around, admiring the hole she made in an exaggerated manner.

"A work of art." Bobbie took out her cell phone. "How about you bring your face close to your masterpiece and I'll take a picture of the two of you. Then, you can have it framed."

"Are you kidding? It's totally going on the fridge door!"

Bobbie snapped a few shots of Ella and entered the frame herself to be in one of the pictures.

"We should take pictures together more often," Ella suggested. Bobbie agreed.

"Alright, it's hot chocolate o'clock!" Ella declared. If it were up to her, whenever she was outside, it would always be the right time for hot chocolate.

"Not so fast!"

Bobbie fished a can of worms from her backpack. A literal can of worms.

"What's that?" Ella asked apprehensively.

Bobbie opened the canister and showed its squirming contents to Ella.

"Oh, God, gross!"

"So, first, we fish, with these little guys. Then we go for hot chocolate . . . with the remaining little guys *and* the fish we're gonna catch."

"Ugh! Never mind the hot chocolate, then! You're just trying to gross me out!"

"I'm not trying. It's working."

What Bobbie said ended up being true—they would indeed, later on, end up at the Tim Hortons with worms and fish in a backpack. But in the hour preceding the fish-and-donuts excursion, Bobbie patiently taught Ella how to hook worms on a fishing line—preferably without making a face, because that looked way more professional—and they fished for a while. And they did catch a few fish, which made Ella ecstatic.

"What's wrong with me? First, I freak out over making a silly hole. And now, it's getting a handle on this whole slimy worm-and-fish thing that's floating my boat. I must have a fever or something."

"You're hooked. And before you know it, you'll be begging me to show you how to gut these yourself and cook them."

"Let's not push it. You can have the fish."

Ella was not ready to bring any fish home. They would probably go to waste with her dad still coming home late, and the freezer was full. But the sole thought of gaining these weird skills—however impractical for city life—made her smile. Not many kids at her old school could boast about being able to do that. And perhaps she could ask Henry to teach her how to gut and cook fish someday. Wouldn't that be romantic?

The next skill Bobbie taught Ella was a snow block carving technique to build an igloo. She was pretty good at it and made it look easy, slicing through hardened snow with a *pana*, a dagger-like snow knife, like she was slicing through butter.

"This reminds me of when we used to build forts when we

were younger. Did you guys build snow forts or igloos back then?" Ella asked.

Bobbie scoffed. "Are you kidding me? Forts are soooo colonial! We used to build modern skyscrapers with multiple floors, glass windows, and elevators. Of course."

"Of course. What was I thinking?"

"Exactly."

"I stand corrected."

With its techniques and snow blocks needing to be carved the right way, igloo building turned out more of a craft than anticipated and frustrated Ella to no end. She couldn't believe how crooked and wrong her blocks kept turning out. Too big, she'd shave them off until they were too small, or they had the wrong angles—or both. An across-the-board disaster. She needed to master the right angles to build towards the dome part of the igloo successfully, which was most of the structure. Her mittens were getting wet, and she felt she'd made zero progress. The wind was getting colder, and she could hear the very distinct call of the wild hot chocolate . . . with whipped cream . . . and sprinkles, dammit!

It also seemed to her that she used to be much better at this as a kid and, therefore, refused to fail. Later on, she practiced on the snowbank in front of her house to get it right or, at the very least, get better at it. Still no luck. She looked so dejected that Frank crossed the street to hang out with her and cheer her up. At least that part worked.

The last thing Bobbie coached Ella on was how to walk with traditional snowshoes. Made from wood and rawhide lacings, these were much wider and harder to walk with than their modern counterpart.

From then on, every weekday morning, Bobbie showed up early to pick Ella up, and they trudged to school in snowshoes. It would take them longer than usual as Ella seemed hell-bent on walking like a penguin, but they kept at it despite the slowness of it all.

As much as Ella thoroughly enjoyed her time training with Bobbie, sarcasm and all, she looked forward even more to being mentored by Henry. At times, Sera would see them together. And while she maintained composure, Ella always noticed a glimmer of jealousy in her eyes. While she no longer cared to goad her nemesis on purpose, deep down, Ella had to admit she still got a kick out of seeing Sera annoyed and envious.

Ella quickly became a pro at driving Henry's snowmobile, and they went on a few longer rides. He'd hold on to her, and they would glide at great speed across the vast, snow-covered land.

On one such outing, Henry handed Ella a shotgun-like BB gun. They had stopped in the middle of nowhere to admire the landscape, and he thought it was a perfect spot for her to learn how to shoot blanks. It was unlikely she would hit an animal or anyone.

Ella took the gun timidly.

"Now, don't shoot your eye out," Henry said, holding back a grin.

At first, Ella seemed concerned.

"Oh, God, do I have to worry about—"

She stopped herself in mid-sentence as she noticed the words "Red Ryder" branded on the wooden stock of the gun. *Red Ryder*, like the BB gun Ralphie so desperately wanted in *A Christmas Story*, a quirky comedy she had watched with Sandy years ago. Ella smiled, finally getting Henry's joke. "That was a weird film."

"We watch it every year!" Henry seemed thrilled she got the reference.

Ella pictured herself watching the movie with Henry, nestled next to him under a blanket. A fire roaring in the fireplace, of course. Big snowflakes falling outside. He would laugh as hard as the first time he had seen the movie, and his laugh would be contagious, and she, too, would laugh to tears. How wonderful that would be . . .

Henry started rummaging through his backpack, yanking Ella out of her reverie. She inspected the BB gun with a newfound fascination.

"So . . . this is what he wanted, the kid in the movie? Wow. I never thought I'd ever hold one of these in my hands. They let kids have these?"

"Yeah. Well, around here anyway, a lot of kids learn to hunt. Though I wouldn't recommend hunting with one of these. They're mostly to learn. But still, they should be handled as carefully as a real gun and treated as such."

"Right."

A feeling of apprehension came back in Ella. This gun still felt dangerous, far from a natural thing to her. But then again, neither had fishing before she learned, and now she was getting used to that, too.

Henry sensed the gun was making Ella tense. "Keep in mind that you'll be shooting targets," he said, "not hunting down killers and whatnots."

Ella nodded. That was a good point. "Hear that, whatnots? You get to live!"

"And you'll be shooting these—BBs."

Henry showed her a small clear bottle filled with tiny metal balls.

"Let me show you how to load it."

She happily handed him back the gun and watched him. He explained the process as he poured some BBs into the load door. This looked somewhat manageable, even for her.

Henry brought the gun up in front of his face.

"One trick to aim well is to restrain your breathing."

"Okay."

"I'll fire a wild shot, so you can get used to the noise. Alright? Ready?"

Ella nodded.

"Okay, in three . . . two . . . one . . ."

Henry fired the gun—CRACK! Ella jumped, but much less than anticipated. The noise echoed a bit, but overall, it wasn't even that loud.

Henry handed Ella the Red Ryder. Without him saying anything, she raised it in front of her face, trying her best to mimic his previous movements.

"Like this?"

"Pretty much."

He guided her hand a bit, and she was good to go.

"You feel comfortable trying?"

Ella moved her head in several directions, suggesting that she was mostly there. Seeing how confident Henry was in her brought her the rest of the way there. It helped that where they were was so remote, there was no one at risk of getting shot in case she didn't aim right. In fact, there was nothing to aim at, at all. Which made for much less stress.

Ella took a deep breath, making a face, and braced herself for the noise and the impact. She fired—CRACK!

"You did it!"

"I did it!" Ella repeated, as if she didn't quite believe it.

Henry was smiling at her, and this gave her wings.

"How about you take a few more shots, and then we'll see how good your aim is?"

"Alright."

While Ella fired a few practice shots, Henry lined up a bunch of empty tin cans on a small snowbank behind her.

"Here." Henry's voice made Ella pivot. "Try hitting these."

Ella began shooting at the cans, and her aim turned out to be all over the place. A few lucky hits and a lot of misses.

"There goes my career as a sniper."

"Unless you're prepared to offer some serious discounts . . . and have good insurance."

Ella laughed. Henry was as funny as Bobbie. *That must be a family thing,* she thought. Ella liked that in him and her friend. That and their shared kindness.

"I love how you always seem to find a silver lining in things," said Ella.

"Do I?"

"I think so."

She was looking at him admiringly. He was looking back at her, and there was something in the way he, too, was looking at her. Ella could feel her heart beating a little faster.

The sun was starting to set.

"We should probably wrap up and head back," he finally said.

"I guess so."

Ella made a big effort to hide her disappointment and look casual. Now was not the time for her to betray herself and declare her crush.

A GIRL LIKE HER

THE WINTER GAMES event was just around the corner, on the upcoming Saturday. And it was already Wednesday. Tick-tock.

After school, Ella was browsing the cork board while waiting for Bobbie. She came across a sign-up sheet for the prom party at the end of the school year. Her eyes lit up—the thought of a prom party, here, in Iqaluit, had not even crossed her mind. And despite the debacle at the only party she briefly attended here, this was graduation! Something entirely different. At the very least, she would be much better informed this time around.

Staring at the sheet, she felt a strong desire to sign up. She looked to see who was already on board, and there it was, of course, the name of the devil herself. *Ugh.* Sera had beat her to it, claiming the territory as hers. This was heartbreaking.

"Don't worry, I've got it covered. And I'll have a great time doing it too."

That was Sera, with impeccable timing, approaching her.

"I don't remember summoning you. You're worse than a cockroach," Ella told her with a smile.

Unfazed by the insult, Sera added, "Just so you know, he could never go for a girl like you. So, nice try, loser."

"What are you talking about?!"

"He's only helping you to be nice. To be polite. Nothing more."

On that fine little dose of venom, Sera flitted away.

A girl like me? What the hell did she mean by that? What could Sera possibly know? She hardly looked like Henry's confidante. If anything, it was to *her* that he seemed polite and nothing more.

Ella knew better than to believe the hateful words of someone intent on hurting her, but this still stung. A lot. Why couldn't Sera just let it go and let her be?

What if there was some truth to what she was saying? What if Henry was indeed only being his usual nice, helpful self? Like she herself has suspected before?

Bobbie finally showed up, and Ella forced a smile. On their way home, she was quiet but tried to chat just enough so Bobbie wouldn't guess how heavy her heart was. She didn't want to talk about this. And even if she did, what could she possibly say?

Is it true that your cousin could never care for a girl like me?

For the rest of the day, Ella felt crushed and discouraged. That night, she even picked up her cell phone and brought up Sandy's number . . . which now showed an avatar of her and Ryan posing cheek to cheek.

Ella turned her phone off. She bundled herself under a blanket on the living room's comfy chair and stared at the wall right above the TV set. Despite her dad being home with her, watching television next to her, she felt pretty alone.

WAY BACK WHEN

The next day—Thursday, tick-tock—after school, Ella met with Henry to practice her aim by shooting more cans on a vacant lot on the outskirts of town. The sun had long since set, but the lot was well lit up by nearby street lights.

Henry was being his usual very pleasant self. He didn't look like the type of person who could dismiss anyone based on . . . based on what, exactly? Sera's surely unfounded declaration was just cruelty and didn't make any sense. Deep down, Ella knew this was Sera playing with her emotions to destabilize her, but a pernicious seed of doubt had been planted in her mind, and Ella couldn't shake off the resulting torturous, damaging thoughts.

So, she spent the whole time with Henry overanalyzing his every move, word, facial expression, and body language. This proved at once tiring and maddening. Not to mention completely distracting. On the outside, she was doing downright terribly at shooting cans—or rather, at *not* shooting any of them. On the inside, she couldn't help but feel upset and awkward, and a burden to Henry. The need to act distant to protect herself from further getting hurt was taking precedence.

"Don't worry about hitting them, eh? I assure you, they won't feel a thing. And they're heading for recycling anyway, so they don't care," he teased her with a smile.

"Right." Ella forced herself to smile back.

"You seem a little out of sorts, today."

"You could say that."

Yeah, it was better to say that than tell him she had barely slept the night before, too busy agonizing over him and most probably a lie spread by her worst foe. She felt like an idiot. And now, she didn't know how to act around him nor how to make the awful feelings go away.

"Would you like to take a break?" he offered.

Ella knew she'd keep being a total waste of time at the moment, so they might as well do more than just take a break and, instead, call it quits for the day. Even though this was more than likely her very last chance to practice shooting before the games. The pressure was on for her to get better at it, but this was just too much to ask of herself right now. Ella simply couldn't deal with this. She'd have to do her best in the biathlon event, and her best would have to do.

"Yeah . . . You know what? I don't think I'm gonna be able to concentrate today . . . I'm so sorry."

"Oh. Okay. Why is that?"

Ella scrambled for a reply. She *could not* go there.

"I'm worried about a friend who's at the hospital. I should probably go visit her."

This wasn't entirely true, but at least it wasn't a total lie either. She had been thinking about Inuuja, who was back at the hospital due to balance issues.

"I'm really sorry I wasted your time today," she added.

"You didn't. I didn't have anything else to do, and it got me out of the house. That's all good."

"I'll help you pick up the cans."

"Thanks. And I'll give you a lift to the hospital."

Henry's offer took Ella by surprise. Thank God she didn't lie.

"Oh, but, no, I—"

"You know I won't take no for an answer. It's on the way back anyway."

It's on the way back if you make one hell of a detour . . .

Why was he fibbing?

Why was she overanalyzing everything?!

Stop it!

Ella capitulated and accepted the ride. Giving in would help expedite things and make him go away sooner.

Or so she thought.

Henry parked the snowmobile near the entrance of the hospital. Sitting behind him, Ella jumped off the snowmobile as if her life depended on it. She handed him the helmet.

"Thanks a lot for the ride and for your time. I'll see you tomorrow!"

Henry got off the snowmobile.

"How about you go in and visit, and I'll bring you home after?"

Ugh! Why couldn't he just leave and give her the time and space to sort herself out? She *so* wanted to be with him, but right now, it hurt so much to deal with him, to feel like she was hiding something from him—which she was. And why did he have to be so goddamn wonderful?!

"Henry, that's very generous, but I'll be just fine."

"Not in the dark."

"My dad can pick me up."

"I'm already here."

Ella tried not to squirm. The way he was looking at her, like he was trying to read her and find out why she was acting like this with him.

"Look, the real reason I'm here . . ." he said, as if he was about to make a confession. Ella's heart started to beat fast again. *Oh my God!* Was he about to say what she hoped he would say?

Henry went on, "I need to catch up on celebrity gossip. Please don't tell!" He winked at her. "I'll be in the gift shop. So, you take all the time you need."

He gave Ella a charming smile and headed inside the hospital, leaving her without much choice.

Ella wanted to scream.

Ella poked her head inside Inuuja's hospital room and was surprised to see her awake and looking much better than the last time.

"Hey! I wasn't expecting a visit!" Inuuja was beaming.

That makes two of us.

"How are you doing?" inquired the senior.

"Shouldn't I be the one asking that question?"

"I'm doing as great as I can. How about you?"

"Oh, I'm alright."

But Inuuja could tell, once again, that was not truly the case.

"What's eating you, dear?"

Ella hesitated to say.

"Don't you know? There's always something eating me. Like there's a tapeworm in my soul. And I'm always unloading on you. You should be resting. Not dealing with my silly crap."

"Tell me whatever it is. That'll make me forget my own silly crap."

"I . . . I'm not sure."

Ella had no idea what was going on with her anymore, past the obvious facts that Henry was driving her crazy and Sera was also playing with her head. Ella had played with other people's heads before. She knew the drill. The games. She should know how to handle this better and not be such an emotional wreck. But, on top of this, ever since the trip to Montreal, many little things also didn't feel right anymore, contributing to a lingering sense of uneasiness in Ella.

"It's like I feel lost and alone," she blurted out. "Like I don't belong anywhere."

Inuuja nodded. She understood.

"And . . . no matter what I do, it's the wrong thing. And . . . and . . . well, the list goes on. How long do you plan on being here?"

Inuuja let out a big laugh and looked at Ella endearingly.

"Everything feels shitty, and you want the world to stop so you can get off? Is that it?"

"In medical terms, yes, that's probably it."

Inuuja looked at Ella for a while and turned serious.

"Did you still want to know about Marvin and me?"

"Yes! Absolutely."

Inuuja patted the edge of the bed for Ella to sit down, which she did.

"I was in your shoes once. Living in a strange land, feeling like an outsider. And to be with Marvin, I felt I couldn't come back to Iqaluit. I had to stay in Montreal, or I'd lose him. Feeling like I had no choice made me feel . . . resentful."

There was a tinge of regret in her voice, but also acceptance.

"Marvin—the love of my life . . . I drove him away by refusing to adapt to his big city. *Your* big city. I was so stubborn. And selfish. I gave him so much hell."

"Couldn't he have come here if you didn't like it over there?"

"Oh, he did offer to move here . . . But I refused."

"Why?"

"I was too afraid of what people and my family might think of us. Of me, living with a black man . . ."

Inuuja took a moment. All these memories coming back to the surface, it wasn't easy for her to deal with them.

"I felt horrible inside, and I was horrible to him. As if lashing out would make me feel better. Get the pain out. I was seriously impossible. He finally had enough of my antics and left me. I came back here, and the most bizarre thing happened. Coming back was the biggest culture shock I ever felt, can you believe it? Coming back home, but no longer home—feeling like a stranger in my own land. It's as if all of Iqaluit had changed while I was away, and I no longer belonged here."

Ella took the senior's hands into hers. She felt for her. She could understand what she must have gone through.

"I didn't have a husband or kids of my own, and I felt I was getting too old to start a family. I was so lovesick, missing Marvin so terribly and longing for a life that no longer existed."

Inuuja stopped talking for a moment.

"Did you talk to anyone about this?" Ella asked.

"I eventually told my father. He was old and ill. Soon after, as fate would have it, he died of a heart attack, and I blamed his death on the shock I gave him."

"Way to give yourself a guilt trip!"

Inuuja nodded.

"You've been hiding so much pain . . . But you seem like such a happy person! I'm so sorry, I didn't—" Ella added.

Inuuja let out another one of her typically hearty laughs.

"Oh, dear girl, I've been doing much better for decades, thank God! It did take me years of grieving and isolation, but one day, I realized it was not my relationship with Marvin that had broken my father's heart, but rather, seeing me, his beloved daughter, so determined to feel miserable and rejected. When it was up to me to take my place. Regardless of geography."

Inuuja paused and said something in Inuktitut, before adding, "Or as they say in English: Home is where the heart is."

"Oh my God, is that an old Inuit saying?! Is that where it came from?"

Inuuja looked at Ella with a sparkle of mischief in her eye.

"No. I saw that embroidered on a hand towel at PolarMart, in a discount bin."

Ella laughed. Inuuja loved to pull her leg, and she always fell for it.

"You know what else would look great on a hand towel?" asked Inuuja.

"*Home, sweet home?*"

Inuuja shook her head.

"*Life is too short? If you give a man a fish?*"

Ella racked her brain. She was running out of ideas. One last try. "*I'm with stupid?*"

"How about *Don't give a crap and just do what you gotta do and be who you gotta be?*"

"Or *Give a crap only when you feel like giving a crap?*"

"That's right. About the things that matter to you. The rest is just noise. The rest shouldn't matter."

Ella understood. Perhaps she would try and start giving a crap only about what mattered to her and tune out the noise. This sounded like a good idea.

THE LOVELIEST RIDE

"So, she's an artist, eh?" inquired Henry as he and Ella walked down the long hospital corridor on their way back to the parking lot.

"Yes. Yes, she is. And she's great. Have you seen her stuff?"

"Hmmm, I don't think so."

"Ah." *Weird.* "How d'you know she's an artist?"

"My aunt told me. I ran into her."

"Ah. Bobbie's mom?"

"Yeah."

Why did he ask his aunt about Inuuja? Was he spying on them? On her?

Stop it.

Stop overthinking everything.

Ella was feeling awkward again in Henry's presence. But at least, now, with Inuuja's advice, she gave herself permission to stop feeling so damn tortured. To give herself a break and just let it go.

"Is she doing better?" Henry added.

"Yeah. She might be getting out soon. I look forward to her being home again. With Frank. Frank's her dog. He's a love."

"Cool. You like dogs?"

"Yeah. I do. Especially dogs like Frank. He's a husky with an old soul. I swear, he understands everything. I think he even understands me better than I understand myself." *Not that it's such a great feat*, she thought. *Right now, a clam might have a better understanding of me than myself.* "What about you? You like dogs?"

"Very much! We have three of them. They're total nut jobs. Not exactly old soul material."

That made Ella laugh. Henry felt the need to add, "I didn't mean that in a bad way. They're just big goofs. They're so funny and sweet. They're pretty grand."

They reached Henry's snowmobile. He hopped on the vehicle and started the engine.

"You should come over and meet them one of these days." His words got lost under the noise of the motor.

"WHAT D'YOU SAY?"

"I SAID, YOU SHOULD COME MEET MY DOGS ONE DAY!"

"AH! OKAY!"

And off they went, on a motorcycle ride heading home. For Ella, it was also an emotional roller-coaster ride. So much inner turmoil and conflicting feelings. Henry's dogs were not the only total nut jobs around.

Ella was elated that Henry would invite her over to his house to meet his dogs. That had to be a good sign. Unless he didn't really mean it. Did he mean it? Surely, he wouldn't have said it if he didn't mean it. And he wouldn't have said it only to fill the silence since the snowmobile's engine was already taking care of that.

GOD! Could she stop overthinking and rehashing everything already?! Like, seriously?! She'd end up with an ulcer. Or a rash. Which would be ugly and inconvenient. She couldn't handle a rash right now. They'd be taking pictures at the winter games, and even though she would no doubt look like a mummy with her scarf wrapped around her head, a rash would still be annoying.

The snowmobile took a sharp turn into a street, prompting Ella to hold on to Henry a little tighter and bringing her back to reality, to an awareness of where she was. What was she doing right now? In essence: hugging Henry. So why the heck was she worrying over a stupid hypothetical rash right now instead of savoring this moment?

Ella forced herself to be in the present. She focused on feeling her arms wrapped around Henry. And hugging him tightly.

It had just started to snow, and snowflakes were landing on her visor. Despite the cold and the whipping wind, she was feeling warm, blissful, and safe with Henry.

She wished the ride would never end.

The snowmobile came to a halt in front of Ella's house. This time, she slowly got off, trying to make this sweet and precious moment linger. She fiddled with the helmet to take it off. In the meantime, Henry had also gotten off the snowmobile. Ella was surprised to see him standing tall, right there in front of her. She handed him the helmet.

"Thanks again for the ride."

"Don't mention it."

They just stood there for a moment. He was looking at her

intently. What was he expecting of her? Was she forgetting something?

"I . . . I'll see you at school tomorrow," she said.

"Yeah. See you at school."

OK, so, what now? Ella wasn't sure whether she should go, or . . .

"Bye," she tried.

" . . . Bye."

The way he was still looking at her, something intense dancing in his beautiful eyes.

A lovely gaze.

A loving gaze?

Getting weak in the knees and convinced her imagination was playing a trick on her, Ella gave him a little wave and headed to her house.

She took extra care not to slip on the icy walkway and the front steps, too—she had forgotten to pour salt like her dad had asked and came close to taking an embarrassing plunge as the steps rivaled the best skating rinks. She grabbed hold of the front door's handle and steadied herself. She unlocked the door, and as she opened it, she saw out of the corner of her eye that Henry was still there, standing still, looking her way. No doubt making sure she got in safe. She couldn't help turning her head to face him.

He awkwardly waved to her, got on the snowmobile and drove off.

THE HOME STRETCH

THURSDAY NIGHT. Tick-tock.

The way Henry had looked at her when he had dropped her off moments earlier was etched into Ella's memory and giving her a major boost.

She wondered what Inuuja might say if she told her about him and her crippling doubts, and what had been going through her mind. She could picture her neighbor telling her that if she truly believed she wasn't worthy of Henry, she should stop moping, give herself a good kick in the ass and work her hardest to become worthy. Nothing in the world prevented her from bettering herself, from becoming a better person. *At least, give it a damn shot*, Inuuja would surely say.

Yeah, she would totally say that! Ella was convinced of it. And she liked this imaginary advice very much.

Ella sat down at the kitchen table with a decaf latte—at this time of the evening, she didn't want to risk staying up all night—and the list of events she had to master to avoid coming across as a total twit in front of everyone at the games. The big day was coming fast, and she was running out of time. Still, she was determined to make the most of the remaining time she had, to be Zen about it all—shutting out the noise, her self-doubts, and her fluctuating moods over Henry, Sera and anything else driving her up the walls. She needed to be kind to herself right now.

Ella went through her list, pondering each item.

1. *Ice fishing*

She knew how to drill the hole. Check.

The one concern was the worms. The goddang worms. *Ugh.* She was still not completely comfortable with the worms—they grossed her out so much. And now that she was thinking about them, a shiver of dread went through her. Why did they have to be so gross?

She'd just have to force herself to get a grip.

The rest of what came of it—whether a fish liked her chosen worm or gave her the finger—was up to chance. No use losing sleep over this.

And worms didn't have fingers. So, plus one right there.

2. *Igloo building*

Hmmm. She'd have just to do her best. And that would be that.

3. *Snowshoeing biathlon*

She would no doubt waddle her way through the snowshoeing part. Everyone would stare at her and laugh, and her performance might very well end up on social media. For posterity. To be ridiculed for all times to come.

Oh, well. Tough shit. She'd have to get over herself.

Now, the shooting part of the biathlon. Starting from zero, her aim had improved, but there was still much room to do better. Perhaps she could borrow someone's pellet gun tomorrow after school and . . . and what? Shoot at stuff in her tiny backyard? The neighbors probably wouldn't like that. And who could blame them? She herself still considered herself a menace.

Fudge. What could she do? Practice her aim using darts? That might be a way. She'd have to see if some café or the recreation center had darts. Of course, it would be so much simpler to just ask Henry for one last practice session or Bobbie to help her find a place that had darts. But Bobbie would ask Henry for help, and Ella didn't want Henry in the equation right now. Her emotions were hard enough to manage as they were. There was no room for another layer of challenge.

4. *Snowmobile race*

That part was mastered. Totally. Yessssss!

5. *Bannock making*

Crap. She had forgotten about this one. And she hadn't done anything about it yet. *Crap. Crap. Crap.* This could be her downfall. Well, that and all the other events at which she was already failing miserably.

Much like the worm-related shiver of dread that had passed through her, a similar wave of discouragement now washed over her. But this latest feeling lingered. How could she possibly learn to make bannock on such short notice? She would totally fail, she could feel it.

She thought about Henry. He would no longer look intensely at her when he found out that she didn't even bother learning that baking skill, when he invested so much of his time teaching her stuff for the games. What a negligent ding-dong she was!

Ugh! I'm such an idiot!

Don't go there.

Back up.

Think happy thoughts.

Ella reminisced once more about the knee-weakening look Henry had delivered her, and she longed to get that look from him again. She'd do anything to get a look like that from him again. What girl wouldn't? It was probably the look that drove

Sera to hate her when she thought it might have shifted her way. The look that made Sera do all those horrible things to her all the time. Sera, the whole reason she was even *doing* these games. Who probably knew all about bannock bread and could bake one that would make Henry's mouth water. *She* should be making Henry's mouth water, not Sera! *Dammit!*

Ella flung open her laptop and hit YouTube.

Bannock bread recipe.

There.

Make his mouth water over your bannock bread, I'll show you . . .

On the counter, Ella lined up enough ingredients to open a bakery shop. There was a new resolve in her. She rolled up her sleeves, cracked her knuckles, and pictured herself as a contestant on a bake-off reality show. The thought amused her. It was nearly 8 p.m., and she was ready to start.

Over the following hours, Ella measured ingredients, melted butter, stirred and kneaded until her arms were ready to fall off. She fried little circles of dough in a pan. Tasted the results and threw them in the trash.

Measure.

Stir.

Fry.

Yuck.

In the trash can it went.

Repeat.

Measure.

Stir.

Fry.

Blech.

Trash.

New recipe.

Measure.

Mix.

Bake.

Gross!

Trash.

Repeat.

Here and there, despite the repeated failures, Ella danced in place a little, like she had seen Inuuja do in the past—out of fun and an overflow of frustrated energy, but also on the off chance this would channel some of the old lady's feisty spirit into the dough. Nothing stopped her, not even Dan coming home, asking if she wanted a hand, asking her about her day. Ella mumbled something incoherent and distracted. He could see how busy she was and didn't insist. He wished her a good night and headed off to bed.

Ella was in the zone now. Contemplating her latest batch, she thought self-deprecatingly that a handful of wriggly worms might actually improve it. She tossed it into the trash and pushed doggedly on to the next one.

"Oh my God, it's edible! It's actually edible!"

At 2 a.m., Dan got yanked out of a deep sleep by Ella proudly screaming. He came shuffling into the kitchen, still unsure what Ella was up to.

"That sounds great, Ella. But why don't you go to bed? You have school tomorrow."

School shmool. This was one of the biggest successes of her life!

Dan turned around and headed back to bed. Ella was too high on her breakthrough to care about sleep.

In the middle of the night, a selfie of Ella smiling wide and showing off her majestic bannock went up on her Instagram account. It was the very first item she had posted there in a long time.

Hours later, the image would puzzle Sandy and Ella's other followers.

SCREW THE NAYSAYERS

THE NEXT MORNING—FRIDAY, tick-tock—as they were walking to school, Ella insisted on Bobbie sampling her bannock.

Bobbie was unsure about putting into her mouth something that Ella had baked, but she tried a bite anyway with an open mind. And she was pleasantly surprised.

"I thought you said you've never baked before!"

"That's right! This is my first time. What d'ya think?"

Bobbie's expression hesitated between suspicious and impressed. She settled on impressed. This made Ella so proud of herself. She beamed, grinning like a Cheshire cat.

"I did tell you you had potential, didn't I?!" Bobbie pointed out.

"And so do you! If *I*—of all people—can master bannock bread and risk losing whatever's left of my dignity in this crazy competition, then *you*, Bobbie, my dear, can manage college with your eyes closed."

Bobbie's face changed.

"You *had* to ruin the moment."

"It's *my* moment! I can ruin it if I want to!"

"Do we have to do this right now?"

"It's just that it occurred to me, while I was waiting for the bread to bake, how completely crazy I'm being. And yet, I committed to doing this, and seeing how I finally had this little success . . . Long story short, I really don't understand what your deal is—"

"And you don't have to!"

"—but why don't you apply for college anyway? You can always change your mind later, right? No one has to know you're applying."

Bobbie groaned. She knew that Ella's suggestion was sensible, but she clearly didn't want to have this conversation.

"Have I ever rubbed your nose in *your* failures?" Bobbie's tone was edgy.

"Who's talking about failure?"

Ella couldn't wrap her head around her friend's change of attitude towards her own dream. What the hell was going on with her?

"Look . . ." Bobbie said. "Just get the damn message, and let me be, okay?"

"Fine." Ella was dealing with enough as it was, she might as well let Bobbie be.

But *ugh*, stubborn people could be such a pain.

At lunchtime, Justine offered for Ella to stay with her after school so that Ella could finish her parka on time to wear it the next day for the games.

Justine's offer touched Ella. It was very generous of her. The idea of wearing her parka—no matter how imperfect it was—to the games made Ella very happy. And it gave her a sense of strength.

She also couldn't wait to show it to Inuuja.

At afternoon recess, Ella spotted Sera down the hall. Her nemesis had spotted her, too, and was, in fact, staring her down. As tempting as it was to hold her gaze, Ella decided she didn't care right now. She was too busy savoring the things that were exciting her, like her bannock bread victory and the artsily embroidered finishing touches she could put on her parka with Justine's help.

Oh, and Henry. Henry's phenomenal gaze. She'd bet now he never looked at Sera that way. The thought gave her a little smirk as she walked confidently right past Sera.

Of course, Sera had to goad her. "I hope you're ready to crash and burn."

Ella looked over her shoulder. Not aggressively. Just casually.

"Oh, very much. It's gonna be great fun," she replied calmly.

Not the answer Sera was expecting. She frowned a *wtf?* at Ella.

"You know what, Sera? Life's too short. Come with me," Ella added.

Puzzled and suspicious, Sera didn't follow her.

"Come on," Ella insisted as she headed to the cork board with the prom sign-up sheet. She searched for a pen in her pencil case. "D'you have a pen?" she asked Sera cheekily.

Sera's whole demeanor visibly darkened when it finally dawned on her what Ella was doing.

"Oh, never mind. Found one!" Ella brought her pen to the sign-up sheet.

"Hey! You are *not* welcome to join!"

"Says who? You? Tough shit!"

Ella proudly added her name to the sign-up sheet and left

with her head held high, smiling to herself. She could just imagine Sera, behind her, repressing a violent urge to scream.

That evening, Ella visited Inuuja, back home from the hospital. As Ella had hoped, with Justine's help, she was able to finish her parka after school, and she couldn't wait to show it off, especially the little blue-eyed huskies she had embroidered along the bottom trim: they were a series of miniature Franks, put there so she could be surrounded by her furry guardian angel, wherever she went.

She also wanted Inuuja to try her bannock. Before crossing the street, Ella made one last batch to make sure she had memorized the process and still had her newly acquired touch. It turned out pretty good again, which was really encouraging.

Inuuja and Frank were both happy to see her. The spry senior admired Ella's craftsmanship evident in her parka at great length, and she also thought the bannock was very tasty, very fine work indeed. Ella could see her neighbor was proud of her.

"I'm so relieved the bannock works! I'm only doing okay in two events, and my time's up." Ella grimaced. "I'm so gonna go down in flames. But who cares, right?"

"That's the spirit!" Inuuja laughed.

"Yeah . . . but, I dunno. I'm really trying hard not to care about what people will think after I humiliate myself big time tomorrow . . . again."

"It's normal, luv. I think you're being incredibly courageous to keep your engagement. So many people would have just given up."

Ella nodded. But as much as she pretended to Inuuja, the wise old woman could sense the fear and the desire to excel fighting for dominance within Ella.

"Mind you, it's also okay if you decide to stay home tomorrow. It's not worth torturing yourself over, and you gained so much from the experience already." Inuuja waved a piece of bannock around as she spoke. "So, do as you wish! There's no wrong answer." She took another bite of bread.

Ella understood what Inuuja was saying to her. It put things in a needed perspective. And realizing that she had options relieved some of the pressure.

Inuuja gave her a sympathetic smile. "But, if you must proceed and you go down in flames, go down in style. And have a blast! Don't ever forget to have a blast, whatever you do. That's the most important part."

Right! Ella might as well go big and bold and embrace her fall, and do it with her own brand of style.

But having fun doing it? That remained to be seen.

"Inuuja, can one wish upon the northern lights, like you do on a star? You know, for good measure?"

"Whatever inspires you, dear!"

THE BIG DAY

ON THE MORNING of the games, the doorbell rang. Ella was fiddling with a piece of toast—she wasn't really hungry—while watching YouTube videos on how to better your aim when shooting a BB gun. Dan answered the door and came back with a beautiful bouquet of mixed color roses.

"These are for you," he said, handing the flowers to Ella. This was unexpected and mysterious. She put the bouquet down on the table and struggled with the little white envelope—on which her first name was written in fancy calligraphy—to extract the card. She was already so nervous, now was not the time to test her nerves even more. She finally managed to take the card out.

Wishing you a great time at the games. Don't forget to enjoy yourself. You're already a winner!

That was it.

Dammit! The card wasn't signed!

She looked at her dad.

"So, who's the fan?" he asked.

"They're not from you?"

Dan shook his head. "No."

Ella pondered a moment. "They must be from Bobbie or Inuuja." Her greatest cheerleaders. It dawned on Ella how lucky she was to have these two friends in her life.

Dan fished an empty carton of orange juice out of the recycling bin and opened up the top. He filled the carton with water and put the stunning flowers in it.

"We should get going soon. Are you almost ready?" he asked Ella.

"You're coming to the games?"

"Of course." Dan nodded, and Ella almost fell off her chair. It hadn't occurred to her that Dan might come to the games. Even on weekends, when it wasn't food shopping or cooking a batch of something, he'd be busy catching up on his work. She hadn't mentally prepared herself for him seeing her make a fool of herself. The whole town? Sure. But her dad? Ella's expression became one of dread.

"Oh, sweet . . . Do you have to?"

The weather was quite cooperative for this late February Saturday. There was a light breeze, but it wasn't too cold—a perfect day to be outside. And a perfect day for Ella to wear (and show off!) her handmade parka. It reminded her that even if she bombed big time today in the games, she already had this one little victory, of having made leaps and bounds in the sewing category. And for her, that was far from nothing. Plus, she thought she looked really cute in her beautiful garment, especially with the hood on.

The site of the games was bustling with people and activity, and there was much joy in the air. The event went way beyond the student community of Agloolik High. A good portion of the town had seized the opportunity to come out, mingle, cheer on the participants, and have some fun.

Upon their arrival, Ella and Dan were greeted by Bobbie and Henry. Ella was surprised to see Henry there. She figured he was hanging out with Bobbie to keep her company until she arrived, and he'd soon be on his merry way, to wherever that merry way was. He was kindly lending her his snowmobile for the race, but since he lived a few blocks away, he wouldn't be stranded at the games.

Bobbie was holding a sheet of paper on which she had printed the details of each competition, and the first event for Ella was bannock making. Bobbie steered the group towards the bannock station. As they headed there, Ella asked Bobbie, "Should I say thank you?"

Bobbie didn't understand the question. "Thank you for . . . ?"

"The flowers."

"What flowers?"

"Oh, never mind then. It must be Inuuja since she couldn't make it here to see me."

"She sent you flowers?"

"Yeah, an enormous, gorgeous bouquet of roses."

"How nice!"

"I know!"

Ella was beaming at the thought of the flowers.

As they neared the bannock station, they spotted Sera, already on the premises and ready to kick everyone's ass. She, too, spotted Ella, and her jaw dropped. Clearly, she didn't think Ella would have the gall to show up, and—equally clearly—she was all the more annoyed to see Henry by her side, looking to be quite supportive on top of it.

"Looks like your number-one fan is there to greet you,"

Bobbie whispered to Ella. "Maybe *she's* the one who sent you the flowers."

Ella couldn't help but snort out a very loud, weird laugh, something halfway between a human chuckle and a piglet's oink.

"What was that?!" Henry asked, amused.

"It's just my nerves." Ella giggled. "Just nerves. I'm in so much trouble."

"That's one word for it," added Bobbie. This made Ella snort a second time. Bobbie, Dan, and Henry couldn't help letting out a laugh too. The four of them were clearly in a great mood.

There were twelve contestants in all at the bannock station, all of them from Ella's grade. A volunteer guided Ella to a small table on which there were ingredients and cooking utensils. This workstation was right next to shrimpy Tim's, who greeted Ella with a friendly, comforting smile.

"Hey, El! I wish you the best of luck!"

"Thanks, Tim! You too! Though I suspect I'll need luck much more than you."

On the ground next to her, Ella noticed some kind of fire pit filled with wood, and there was a box of matches next to the flour bin on her table. It struck her that they would not be using an oven, but rather, bake the bannock over an open fire.

Oh God! She was completely unprepared for that! How could she have been so dumb as to think they'd be using ovens? Outside? In the middle of winter?

Ack!

"Tim, who's gonna start my fire?"

Ella was trying not to look panicked. But judging by the sympathetic smile on Tim's face, she could tell she was doing a bad job at it.

"You are."

Ella's heart sank. *Dammit!* She had managed to learn to make bannock and was supposed to shine at this event! But now, she was going to fail before she even started.

Fudge!

Dammit!

DAMMIT!

FUUUUUUUUUUU—

"Everyone ready?" a female volunteer holding an air horn asked the group of contestants. But it clearly wasn't a real question—ready or not, she was about to give them the starting signal.

Ella looked at the other participants. Like her neighbor Tim, most seemed eager to get started and determined to have fun. And then there was Sera, who looked so focused and hell-bent on winning, her face consumed by a deep, constipated frown.

Among the small crowd of onlookers, Ella spotted Bobbie and Dan, standing in the closest possible spot to her. And there was Henry. Why was he still there? Their gazes crossed, and he mouthed something to her.

Damn, what did he say?

Ella was a big zero when it came to lip-reading, and she was so stressed right now that there was no way she could decipher what he was saying. She made a frowning face at him so he'd understand she didn't get what he said. He replied with two thumbs up as the starting signal wailed from the air horn.

The ear-piercing noise startled Ella, and her mind went blank. She looked at the ingredients without really seeing them, as if reality was now happening in slow motion. What was going on? What was she supposed to do?

"Breathe, Ella!" That was Bobbie. Ella heard her friend's voice, looked up, and saw Bobbie making gestures to remind her to breathe. "One thing at a time! You can do it!"

One thing at a time. Right. Ella looked at the ingredients and tried to remember how she had done it before. She pictured herself back in her kitchen. It was coming back to her. The flour. Measuring the flour, two cups. Then, the other dry ingredients . . . Ella let her hands do the work. They seemed to know what to do better than she did.

Before long, Ella was multitasking, mixing the dough while fretting about her fire. She had never started a campfire—that's not something you usually did as an urban teen in Montreal!—and she had rarely struck matches before. Why would she need to? At least, she *had* matches and wouldn't have to rub two sticks together to start a fire. That was at least that. Still, Ella couldn't help feeling and looking dejected.

"Ella!" That was Henry. "You're a quick study!" he said while gesturing that she should look around her.

Right.

Ella stole a few looks around her to see if anyone else was already tackling their fire. Sure enough, about half of the contestants were already at it, including Sera and Tim. Ella tried to keep calm and took to observing Tim's technique. He was lighting up balled-up newspaper bits underneath pieces of kindling wood.

Okay, that seemed straightforward enough.

Ella took a match from the box. There was a first time for everything, she reminded herself. Although, whenever possible, she'd rather have first experiences away from the scrutiny of a hundred pairs of eyes, thank you very much. But hey, you don't always get to choose circumstances.

Ella grabbed sheets of newspaper and bunched them up into balls—so far so good. She tucked them underneath the kindling and tried to light the match. It didn't light. She struck it against the pad again. And again, it failed to ignite.

"Don't pet the pad, Ella. Be firmer!" That was Dan.

Alright, firmer.

Ella struck the match firmer against the pad, and it felt right. Except that the match broke. *Aaaaaargh!*

Deep breath.

She could do this. She could totally do this.

This time around, the second match worked on the first strike. Ella let out a little shriek of surprise. And pride. YES!

"Woohoo!" That was Henry. His excessive cheer made Ella laugh and encouraged her. She proceeded to light up the little balls of newspaper, the fire quickly spread—it worked!

YESSSSS!

Now that she had her fire going, Ella saw that Tim was holding a long stick above the fire, tempering it. She imitated him and concluded it was to prepare the stick, to reheat it perhaps?

Tim moved on to wrapping his dough, which he had modeled into a long snake, around the stick. Ella imitated him again. As she was handling the dough, it all started to make sense to her. She could now see how the bread would bake.

She continued taking her cues from Tim and baked the bread a few inches from the flame, turning it occasionally so that the dough would bake evenly.

The crowd was starting to cheer—Ella looked up and saw that all attention was aimed at Sera, whose bannock was already off the fire, a rich golden brown. She handed her stick to a judge —dammit, she was already done! And the first one at that!

Ella tried to keep her bannock stick steady over the fire while keeping an eye on the judge's reaction. Sera's bannock was perfect, and since she also finished first, she was declared the winner on the spot. Ella noticed part of her bannock was charred. *Dang it!*

"Alright, chefs! Take a step back and surrender your bread!" a volunteer yelled.

The judge went around, evaluating every bannock. Ella

noticed Sera staring at her with a major smirk across her face. She even brought her fingers to her forehead to form the letter "L" for "loser" . . .

But just then, before Ella's anger could even develop, Bobbie joined her and gave her a side hug. She was followed by Dan and Henry, both patting Ella on the back. Ella had some satisfaction, after all, seeing Sera's victorious smile suddenly turn sour.

"As long as you don't poison the judge, you're pretty much ahead," Bobbie teased Ella.

"You're right. And that should be my new mantra to live by," Ella retorted.

The judge gave Tim a big thumbs-up, and he approached Ella next. She handed him her stick, bracing herself for the terrible comments sure to come.

Perhaps the judge was lenient on her, for whatever reason, or perhaps she *did* deserve some praise? In any case, she received kudos: her bannock was fully cooked and, apparently, tasted very good. The judge looked amused to see Ella's shocked expression. He gave her back her stick and invited her to taste her own bread. She did and was elated to find that it tasted even better baked over an open flame than her most successful tests at home!

Ella shared her bannock with Bobbie, Henry, and Dan, who all agreed this was fine bread indeed. That victory—winning over her friends and family—was probably the best thing yet. Who knew she'd feel that way after all?

But when the judge gave her 5 points (for the taste), Ella's mind went back to racing, and her feelings became mixed. On the one hand, she was stoked to have gained any points at all. On the other, if only she had known how to start a proper fire, she could have finished faster and gotten a better score. She could have gotten closer to beating Sera . . . A spiral of disappointment was beginning to swirl within her.

"Hey, you're doing great!" Bobbie told her.

"But I could have done better," Ella replied.

"And you could have done worse," Bobbie countered.

"Gee, thanks!"

"You know what I mean. Don't take any of this too seriously, alright?" Bobbie looked in Sera's direction. "You made her lose her smirk. You're way, way ahead."

Bobbie had a point, and Ella relaxed a bit. Still, she wanted to go through the games without giving Sera the satisfaction of ever calling her a loser again.

The next event was ice fishing. Unsurprisingly, it took Ella longer than her fellow contestants to drill her hole, but she still managed to do it in a reasonable amount of time. She then struggled to get a worm out of the can, making faces of disgust while doing so.

"Come on, Ella, one worm is all it takes!" cheered Bobbie.

"They're no worse than the slimy cheese curds on your beloved poutine!" That was Henry, who was still along for the ride.

Ella noticed cab driver Mike and two strangers had joined with Bobbie, Henry and Dan to cheer *her*, Ella, on. How bizarre. And they didn't seem to be there to watch her fail, either.

"You used to play with worms as a kid. You might even have eaten a few, too!" added Dan with a smirk. Ella pretended to gag at her dad's remark.

"You're so not helping, Dad!"

Ella gave herself a mental kick and faced the worms sternly.

"Alright, guys. Gimme a hand, here, will you?"

She took a worm with the tip of her fingers and hooked it. This was instantly met by a loud cheer from "team Ella." This over-the-top show of support made her laugh.

"You guys are being so silly!" she said.

More cheering was heard, but from a different crowd a few feet away. Ella turned around and saw Sera, showing off an impressive catch. *Dammit!*

Ella threw her line down the hole, and before she knew it, there was a bite! YES!

"It's biting!" Ella couldn't help yelling at her support team.

With great excitement, she pulled out . . . probably the tiniest fish of the entire bay. Her face dropped.

Ugh! Was some force of nature conspiring against her today?

"Ella, you caught the cutest little fish!" Tim told her.

Tim was right: this was the cutest little fish.

Dan came over to take a picture of Ella with her fish. Bobbie and Henry joined Ella to be in the picture, too.

"I'm not sure this one counts," Ella pointed out.

"Is it a fish?" asked Bobbie.

"I think so."

"Then it's a fish!"

Bobbie grabbed Ella's arm and lifted it in the air.

"We got a fish, here!" she said to one of the volunteers.

The volunteer agreed. "You get 10 points for catching the second fish. Probably no points for size, but well done."

"10 points? Wow! Yay!"

Ella could live with this. Because, once again, this was so much better than she expected.

"You should have it stuffed and put it on your mantel," joked Henry, which made Ella smile.

"Hey! Don't make fun of my fish! I'm proud of my fish!"

Ella realized she really was starting to enjoy herself. Heck, if she couldn't win, at the very least, as Inuuja told her, she should have some fun along the way.

Ella jumped into the igloo building event with gusto. She worked harder and faster even though she was still unable to make a proper dome with the blocks she carved. Her efforts looked like she was going for a cylindrical building.

"Don't forget the roof!" Bobbie yelled at her. "Igloos usually have a roof!"

"Who said anything about an igloo? I'm making a medieval castle tower!" Ella declared self-deprecatingly.

A few feet away, Sera was putting the finishing touches on an architecturally perfect igloo, but barely anyone was paying attention to her. A good part of the crowd was watching what Ella was doing and cheering her on. And the more cheers they gave her, the more people came to see why they were cheering.

Ella never thought, in her wildest dreams, that she would, someday, be an underdog.

"Okay . . . Picture this: at the finish line, there's a rack of clothes on sale, and you have to get to it before all the other girls do."

That was Bobbie's silly last-minute advice to Ella for the snowshoeing part of the biathlon. Ella laughed.

"You know I can barely walk in these, let alone run."

"Then, imagine that it's just like running in high heels. Just there, you're overqualified," Bobbie retorted.

"High heels. Got it! Worth a try."

"On your mark. Get set," yelled a volunteer. "Go!"

The air horn blared, and all the participants, including Ella, took off like race horses. For shits and giggles, she adjusted her running gait . . . and started picking up speed. In fact, she was doing not bad at all!

"It's like running in high heels? Really?" Henry asked Bobbie.

"How the hell would I know?" She shrugged. "But looking at the way she's going . . ."

Ella was gaining ground on the participants ahead of her.

"Go, Ella!" Bobbie screamed.

Still picking up speed, Ella started passing Tim and two others.

"Go, Ella! Go, Ella!" Henry, Dan and a handful of other spectators chanted.

Ella ran past another teen . . . and another . . . until she actually passed Sera! Ella couldn't believe her eyes, but she was taking the lead!

"WOOHOO!" screamed Bobbie and Henry in unison.

Ella reached the shooting area before everyone else, while her crowd of supporters went wild. Still dumbfounded, Bobbie and Henry nevertheless high-fived each other and ran to the shooting area to watch Ella perform.

Ella loaded the BB gun with a steady hand, fast and efficient. She dropped to the ground and, lying down on her stomach, readied herself to shoot. Sera landed next to her within seconds, BB gun in hand.

Ella aimed, pulled the trigger . . . and missed the target. She and Sera shot seconds apart—Ella missed, but Sera hit.

The two girls shot the next rounds almost at the same time, Ella missing all of them—and Sera getting a perfect score.

Sera shot Ella a look of superiority and stood up, victorious. Ella was still high on getting to the finish line before everyone else and loading the gun quickly without dropping even one BB.

She didn't even care that she missed the target, nor that Sera got a perfect score.

Ignoring Sera—who was waiting for her reaction—Ella quickly stood up, brushed the snow off her pretty parka, and headed towards her posse, yelling at Henry, "Did you see how fast I loaded it?"

"And how fast you got rid of all your BBs!" teased Henry.

Ella laughed and started jumping up and down like she won the lottery. Henry and Bobbie joined in, and before long, they were jumping up and down in each other's arms.

Dismayed and irritated beyond words, Sera just rolled her eyes at them in disbelief.

BY A THREAD

Lastly came the snowmobile race.

In her group, Ella was ranking tenth place out of twelve. While there was no hope of her beating Sera, who reigned in first place, for Ella, not being the very last was already a very big deal. She was also relieved not to have come across as a *total* lost cause. Her plan now was to do her very best in the snowmobile race and to keep her tenth position, at least, if not slightly better it. If she could accomplish just that, Ella reasoned to herself, she'd be happy to call it a great day.

At the starting line, Henry did one last check on his snowmobile to make sure that everything was still A-OK before Ella raced.

"Last one, Ella! Hang in there and remember to go easy on the curves. I know you know the trail, but I want to see you arrive in one piece at the finish line, okay?" he told her.

Ella nodded.

"And one last thing . . ."

Henry leaned in and dropped his voice. "Whatever happens, don't forget . . . *you're already a winner.*" He winked at her and quickly left to join Bobbie and Dan on the sideline.

It took a moment before it hit Ella: Henry was the one who had sent her the flowers?! *Oh my God! Could that be?*

She was so giddy and confused and couldn't process this wonderful piece of information. She shouldn't get too happy too fast, though. What if his choice of words was just a coincidence? What if . . . ? Ella had better check with Inuuja first. The odds were still good that she was the one who had sent her the flowers.

But Henry . . . *Oh, God, if only they really were from him!*

He had winked at her . . .

"On your mark!" a volunteer yelled.

Ella was feeling so wonderfully fuzzy inside, she was barely aware the race was about to start.

"Get set!"

He winked at me!

Next to Ella, Sera was staring at her. The fury in her eyes was palpable through the visor of her helmet, but Ella didn't even know she was getting murderous looks. There was a chance that Henry had sent her a beautiful bouquet of roses, and right now, that was pretty much all that mattered in the world to her.

The air horn wailed the start signal.

The snowmobiles roared and were off to a spectacular start —including Ella, who snapped out of it just in time.

Sera quickly moved her snowmobile in front of Ella, zigzagging to prevent her from getting ahead. Trying to evade her, Ella nearly clipped another racer. The near collision freaked her out —she slowed down to better assess the situation. This feud was so not worth it to get into an accident.

Ella quickly was able to accelerate again and started catching up to Sera, who was busy dealing with another racer. Ella zoomed past Sera on the left, surprising her.

Sera roared after Ella and ended up parallel to her, pacing

her, and aiming her snowmobile dangerously close to Ella's. For a single moment, their eyes met, and the modest determination in Ella's gaze met the raw fury in Sera's.

Maybe that was all it took to kick Sera into overdrive. In a nasty maneuver, she reached for Ella's parka and grabbed onto it, destabilizing Ella. Ella nearly fell off but was able to push Sera away with her right foot.

Ella let go of the gas and slowed down considerably to prevent Sera from playing the same dirty trick against the long curve Ella knew was coming up ahead.

Accelerating to a dangerous speed, Sera glanced furiously at her rival over her shoulder. She didn't get her eyes back on the trail ahead of her fast enough to notice the sudden uneven terrain.

Sera's snowmobile hit an icy patch at an unforgiving angle. Without ever slowing down, the vehicle propelled itself up over a snowbank at considerable speed and vanished from view over the other side.

It all happened so fast in front of Ella—one moment, Sera was speeding like a maniac in front of her, and the next, she and her snowmobile went flying over a snowbank. Thankfully, Ella was far enough behind that she had time to see it happen and react by pulling over safely. Other snowmobile racers, coming from the long curve behind them and having seen nothing, whooshed right past her as she ran to see if Sera was okay.

Over the edge of the snowbank, a steep hill of a dozen feet or so led down to a frozen river. On impact, Sera's snowmobile had cracked the ice, and the teen had landed near her vehicle, lying face down in a puddle of water from the river, that was gushing to the surface from the cracks.

Ella turned around to flag someone, waving her arms frantically in the air and screaming for help inside her helmet. She quickly realized everyone had already zoomed by. She took her helmet off and headed down the hill.

"Help! Help! Someone, help!"

Ella kept screaming for help as she cautiously made her way down the hill. She let go of her helmet and patted her parka to find her cell phone.

Where the hell was it?!

With horror, she remembered she had left it at home because she didn't want to risk damaging it in the games. The *one* time she didn't have it on her!

Dammit!

"HEEELLLLLLLLLLLLLLLPPP!"

Ella reached the river. Sera was a few feet away.

"Sera! Sera, are you okay?!"

Sera was not responding. Not even a muscle twitch. Was she dead? How could this be happening?

Ella swiftly took in the situation. Not knowing how deep the river was, she dropped to the ground and crawled to the inert girl. Carefully, she removed Sera's helmet. As she feared, the girl was unconscious. Thankfully, water had not seeped into her helmet.

"HEEEEEEEEEEELLLLLLLLLLLLLPPPPP!"

Help was not coming.

"Sera, it's me! Wake up!"

Ella's mind raced.

"Sera! You hate me! Tell me how much you hate me! I'm right here! Talk to me! Insult me!"

Still no reaction from Sera.

"HEEEEEEEEEEEEEEELLLLLLLLLLLLLPPPPPPPPPPP! SOMEONE!"

What was Ella to do? If only she had listened to Mr. Moog's CPR presentation, this wouldn't be happening. This had to be the cruelest cosmic joke in the history of the universe.

Sera couldn't just be dead! Not just like that! That'd be utterly senseless. She had to be alive, and Ella would have to make sure she stayed that way.

"Don't die, Sera! Please don't die! Please stay alive!"

Stay alive . . . Staying alive . . .

The YouTube video! The disco song CPR. She had watched it a few times, and it seemed legit. Surely no one would be deranged enough to make an expensive video on a bogus technique for a matter of life and death. How did this go again?

Focus. One step at a time. You can do this.

An eerie calm took over Ella, as if she was having an out-of-body experience. The video asserted that the layperson had only to focus on the victim's breathing, the most important part.

Ella checked to see if Sera was breathing, bringing her ear close to the girl's face. It crossed her mind that Sera might come to and jump up at her, like in some horror film. Because this whole ordeal was already utterly horrifying and surreal as it was. Ella shook off her grim reverie and listened for Sera's breathing.

She could not hear anything.

She didn't want to take any chances.

She carefully rolled Sera onto her back, while supporting her neck, and unzipped her parka. It was apparent that the unconscious girl wasn't breathing. Her chest was completely still.

Okay, Ella, you can do this.

The song.

How did it go?

Ella's mind drew a blank for a moment, but she decided to start doing compressions regardless. Time was of the essence, and surely some slightly off-the-mark compressions were better than no compressions at all.

Disco beat . . .

Disco beat . . .

Come on, what are you?

Dis. Co. Dis. Co.

You will survive.

Yes!

You will surviiiiiiiive.

Shit, wrong song!

But that's a disco beat. Disco's all the same. Good enough.

You will survive!

Was she doing this properly? Was this a good rhythm?

You will survive!

How did the rest go? Ella didn't know the lyrics. *Ack!*

Focus!

Disco beat. That's all that matters.

She started humming the melody out loud to herself so that she could keep the proper beat.

"La-la-la-la. La-la-la-laaaaaaa . . ."

"Get the defibrillator and a stretcher!" shouted a male voice from the top of the hill. It was Henry, who was running down the slope towards Ella and Sera.

Like Ella had done, Henry crawled over the ice to reach them.

"She's unconscious?"

Ella nodded while keeping the compressions steady.

Sera suddenly regained consciousness and gasped for air. Ella exhaled an explosive sigh of relief. As if both girls were breathing again for the first time.

"Don't move, Sera. Don't move," said Henry with a collected voice.

Two paramedics were making their way down the hill now, with two hard plastic cases and a stretcher.

"Are you dizzy?" Henry asked Sera. "If you can't speak, blink once for yes and twice for no."

Sera was barely conscious and fought hard to blink one long blink. She tried moving her head and winced.

"Okay, try not to move your neck," he went on.

Sera's eyes kept closing.

"Stay with us, Sera!" Henry added.

"Stay with us," Ella heard herself mumble.

Hearing the paramedics behind him, Henry turned. "She might have a concussion, and God knows what else."

He moved out of the way to give them the room they needed to work on Sera and helped Ella move aside.

"Are you okay?" Henry asked Ella.

"I'm not hurt." Ella's voice broke. She was not hurt, but she was far from okay. The rush of fear and adrenaline that had overcome her was now subsiding and making way for a new cocktail of strong emotions: a sudden understanding of what she had just done and the dreadful reality that someone could have died right in front of her today and totally out of the blue. The newfound, firsthand knowledge of how fragile and unforgiving life can be.

All of this hit Ella at once, and she started shaking.

"You did great, Ella. You did so amazingly great. You're terrific!" Henry said to her softly and gave her a look so penetrating, so admiring . . .

Ella lost it. Her eyes welled with tears, and she began to sob uncontrollably. Henry hugged her and held her tight.

Henry helped the paramedics haul the stretcher Sera was strapped to back up the hill. Ella followed them despite being in a total daze herself.

The snowmobile trail was wide enough for the ambulance to have made its way to the scene. Sera's state was stable, but the ambulance still departed as fast as possible, with its lights flashing. Henry drifted aside, on his cell to inform Sera's parents of the bad news.

Bobbie and Dan came up to Ella, who moved like a zombie. Her face was puffy from crying.

"Are you okay?" Bobbie asked.

Ella answered with a distracted nod. Bobbie hugged her, and Ella started bawling her eyes out again.

"I can't stop!" Ella managed to say between two sobs.

"It's okay. Shhhhhhhhh."

"I just can't stop crying!"

"Don't worry. You'll eventually dehydrate yourself, and the crying will have no choice *but* to stop," Bobbie joked.

Ella choked out a small laugh and looked at her, then her dad. "She always knows the right things to say," Ella joked back, as she sniffed to prevent her nose from running.

"Yeah, it's a real talent." Bobbie fished a pack of tissues from her pocket and handed them to Ella. "You really need to start carrying these."

Ella took the tissues from her and started a new round of sobbing. Dan rubbed her back consolingly.

"You did great, Ella," Dan said. "You did great. You saved that girl's life."

This made Ella cry even harder.

"Will you stop crying if I tell you I'm gonna apply to that damn college after all?" Bobbie asked Ella.

Ella started to laugh and snort while still crying.

"You're just saying that to make me stop!"

"No. I'm not." Bobbie smiled. "I figure if *you* can do all this crazy stuff, willing to look like a fool . . . a *damn brave* fool—"

Ella interrupted her friend with a huge bear hug.

ELLA WAS so tired and overwhelmed from the day's events that she was in bed by seven and slept until ten the next morning.

When she woke up, she felt like she had just emerged from a cocoon. Everything felt different, a little off-kilter, but mostly in a good way. The fact this was a long weekend for the students didn't hurt either.

Dan made an egg brunch for Ella. She asked him if she could have some money to invite Bobbie out to a restaurant to thank her. Dan said yes, and Ella texted her friend.

She wished she also dared to invite Henry to the restaurant, but she was still so raw, she felt she needed to recover before entertaining any bold steps involving him. One thing she quickly did was cross the street—still in pajamas under her parka—to ask Inuuja if the flowers were from her.

As Ella had hoped, they weren't.

Over the course of the day, she learned on social media that Sera was going to be fine. The girl had a concussion and several broken bones that would take a while to heal, and she would be staying at the hospital for a while, but she was no longer in critical condition. While Ella still felt hurt by all that Sera had done to her, she was relieved to know that she was out of danger. She was also touched to read several kudos addressed to her from various fellow students and members of the community for saving Sera's life. Ella still couldn't quite believe what had happened and what she had done.

In mid-afternoon of that glorious Sunday, Ella received a text from Henry asking if she'd like to come over to his place the next day to meet his dogs.

Would she ever!

For the rest of the day, Ella lounged in her bedroom, doing nothing but replaying in her head the dizzying day of the games, especially the moments when Sera had gasped for air and when Ella was crying on Henry's shoulder. She kept reminiscing about the way he had looked at her when she saved Sera, but also throughout the day as she progressed through the events on her own terms.

And then those splendid roses, which could only have come from him.

On Monday morning, Ella was so excited to be meeting with Henry that she woke up at the same time as Dan and got to eat breakfast with him before he headed out to work. She then found herself with not much to do, other than kill time until she could head out to Henry's place after lunch.

In mid-morning, the doorbell rang. Ella thought it might be Inuuja—she couldn't imagine who else it could be. As she neared the front door, she caught a glimpse of an RCMP cruiser parked in front of the house. That was bizarre. She opened the door and found herself in front of a very tall RCMP officer.

"Ms. Briggs?" he asked with a deep voice.

If she said yes, was that a good thing or a bad thing?

"Yeah?"

"I'm Officer Kalluk. Sera's dad. Would you mind coming with me?"

Holy crap! What did Sera say to him? Did she make him believe that Ella had caused her accident? Was she under arrest? What was she supposed to say or do to not incriminate herself? What was it they said on TV?

"I have the right to a phone call!" she blurted out, panicked.

Sera's dad looked at her, confused for a moment, then smiled.

"You're not under arrest, Ella. Sera would just like to see you. We're all very grateful for what you did."

Ella couldn't remember the last time she felt *this* relieved. Okay, perhaps the day before, when Sera turned out not to be dead. But this was a close second.

Sera's dad escorted Ella to his daughter's hospital room. "I'll come back in a bit to bring you home," he said before leaving.

Ella was surprised to see all the machines attached to her old nemesis, and Sera's left arm and leg covered in a thick cast. Sera's eyes were open. She looked weak and small, which was also surprising considering how strong she always came across. At least she was conscious.

With her good hand, Sera invited Ella to come closer to her.

Seeing how kindly Sera was looking at her, Ella couldn't help wondering if this was yet another trap. What if Sera just wanted to spit more verbal venom in her face?

Chasing the thought, Ella carefully approached the bed.

As Ella got closer, Sera's eyes started to fill with tears. She mumbled, "Thank you."

Ella came close to replying, "It's nothing. You would have

done the same," but she wasn't sure if this was true. Had the roles been reversed, would Sera have done the same? This was a horrifying question to ask oneself. Ella would like to think that Sera would have helped her. But—even worse—what if she had wanted to help her, but hadn't known what to do, just like Ella herself came very close to not knowing what to do?

Ella had gotten lucky. Just so very lucky. She should not forget that. She had no business acting holier than anyone else.

"I'm sorry, Ella," Sera went on.

Sera seemed truly sorry. Ella was moved and speechless.

"In case you're wondering, it's not the morphine talking," Sera added with a weak, contrite smile.

Ella let out a laugh of relief. "I appreciate you saying that."

"This is not easy for me to say."

"I know. I can imagine."

Sera laboriously turned her head towards a bedside table. There was a little gift box on it.

"Take it. Open it."

Ella took the box and opened it. Inside was a stunning, handcrafted necklace with an Arctic snow fox pendant on a white gold chain.

"I asked my mom to find you something beautiful and elegant."

Ella didn't know what to think. She understood that Sera felt grateful to her for not dying and all, but she had been so conditioned to expect the worst from her, this immense change of attitude was jarring.

"I'm not trying to screw with you," Sera added in response to Ella's skeptical glance. "It's truly meant as a 'thank you.' I hope you like it."

"It's gorgeous."

"I don't know if it'll make any sense to you, but to me, this feels like going full circle."

Sera brought her fingers to her neck to show Ella that she was wearing the friendship velvet choker Ella had given her back when they were actually friends.

"To me," she went on, "this feels like a fresh start. But I'll understand if you're not comfortable with this. I'll respect that."

Ella could see where Sera was coming from. And the idea of a fresh start sounded appealing to her. Or, at least, the absence of conflict did.

"The necklace has no strings attached." Sera paused for a moment before adding, "The eyes are real sapphires, by the way. Blue looks good on you."

The blue sapphires made the beautiful piece of jewelry even prettier. Ella felt conflicted. On the one hand, strings or no strings, accepting this gift meant that she forgave Sera for all the crap she had given her and made her go through. On the other hand, perhaps it wasn't such a bad thing to forgive her. In her previous life, she would have been too proud and stubborn to forgive someone so easily. But right now, the thought brought her some much-desired peace. Moving on sounded really good, like a tremendous relief. It's not like they had to be best friends again or anything like that. Just being civilized to one another would be a great start. There was nothing serious they *had to* fight about. After all, what had sparked this wretched feud was nothing but a silly misunderstanding. Nothing worth dying over.

That was when it hit Ella. It hit her that Sera could have died for the stupidest reason, a silly misunderstanding, which Ella had not even tried to clarify on her part. Someone could have died because she had chosen to let things escalate. Was it her being secretly malicious or a passive desire for revenge? Either way—or even if neither—she couldn't deny she had played a part in this.

Ella's expression saddened. She put the gift box down on the side table. "I can't accept this," she mumbled.

A look of disappointment appeared on Sera's face. "Believe me, I'm truly sorry."

"Sera, you could have died over . . . over me not lifting a finger! I'm the one who should be sorry. In fact, I apologize."

"What do you mean? You did lift a finger! Several fingers, in fact. You performed life-saving CPR on me . . ."

"No, what I mean is . . . That picture you saw of me with Henry . . . It was stupidly cold that day, and he *insisted* on giving me a lift because he's a nice guy and he thought I was an underdressed twit—which I totally was. There was nothing going on between us, and I swear, I tried turning him down. And I shouldn't have accepted the damn lift. But more importantly, I should have told you it was a misunderstanding. Even if you were livid. Your friendship meant a lot to me. Believe me, I never tried to go behind your back."

Ella's honesty was obvious. She went on.

"I should have told you all this. I'm sorry I didn't. I'm not sure why I didn't bother telling you."

"You didn't tell me because you knew I wouldn't have believed you," Sera replied.

"But perhaps you would have. I still should have made an effort to clear the air."

Sera considered Ella's words for a moment and shook her head.

"Nah. I would still have believed what I wanted to believe. And we'd still be here having this conversation."

The two girls looked at each other. A knowing glance.

"Please accept the necklace, Ella. That would make me feel less shitty."

Ella reached for the box but stopped herself. She was about to see Henry. Would that set Sera off again when she'd find out?

And should she and Henry become close? Not that there were any guarantees of that ever happening, but what if it did? As much as Ella would love—loooooooove—to take the stunning necklace with real sapphires, she wanted even more to have Sera off her back for good.

If she wanted to say something, now was the time.

But was mentioning Henry, right now, a good thing?

Ella surveyed all the medical equipment attached to Sera. How was her pulse? Her heart? Would Ella be triggering alarms and color codes by mentioning Henry? Would a team of nurses and doctors come rushing into the room? Would she get escorted out of the hospital with people glaring at her? Would she end up in the back seat of Sera's dad's cruiser for recklessly giving his recovering daughter a heart attack?

Stop it with the worst-case scenarios!

Still. Even if she was trying to reason with herself, the tension Ella felt was worse than a high-stakes round of Jenga.

Just do it, dammit.

Ella cleared her throat.

"Okay, full disclosure: I'm meeting Henry at his house this afternoon," Ella blurted out.

The words made Sera flinch.

Sera's flinching made Ella flinch.

Sera's face darkened.

Oh, God. Wrong move. Here we go . . .

But Sera didn't react. And her absence of reaction seemed to go on forever.

Ella started wishing Sera would react. That she'd say something. Anything.

When she finally did, her response was different from any of the ones Ella was expecting. There was a tinge of resignation in her voice. "I can't force him to like me . . . Please take the necklace, Ella."

Ella tried not to show how relieved she was. She just nodded and said, "Okay," softly.

She picked up the box.

She couldn't help but smile as she handled the pretty necklace. What an amazing piece of jewelry!

"How about you put it on?" Sera suggested. She looked eager to see how it would look on Ella.

With nervous fingers, Ella put on the necklace. She imagined how amazing it must look on her. Sera seemed to think it did, judging by her expression.

The two girls exchanged a timid smile.

A VERY FINE DAY

Ella's heart was beating faster and faster with every step that brought her closer to Henry's house. Before heading to his front door, she double-checked the address she had noted on her phone—twice. She felt considerably light-headed and wanted to avoid the embarrassment of ringing some stranger's doorbell. She was feeling so self-conscious, and her mouth was so dry, she only hoped to God she wouldn't make a complete fool of herself.

She rang the doorbell, and the chime provoked a symphony of barks, with a howl thrown into the mix. *Must be the right place.*

The impromptu canine concert came to a halt. Henry opened the door.

"Hey! Come in," he said with a welcoming smile. "Meet my posse!" He waved his hand towards three dogs of various sizes, obediently sitting next to each other and waiting for his next command.

"I'm impressed," Ella said as she struggled to take off her boots. "They're all so well-behaved for a bunch of nuts."

She tiptoed around the puddle of wet snow she'd made on the entrance carpet, her socks all bunched up around her toes.

"You need help?" Henry asked her with a laugh.

"I'll manage." Ella grinned as she adjusted her socks. She looked up at the pooches. "Aren't you gonna introduce us?"

"Of course. This one is Steve."

Steve was the biggest dog of the three. He had the markings of a husky, but his face had a different shape, and if he was a husky, his hair was on the shorter side.

"Is he a mix?"

"We think so. Lab and husky, maybe? Not to be mistaken with the Labrador husky breed. Steve's a pure mix. I've read about that weird term for it, a *labsky*."

"Sounds like a dog engineered in a Russian lab."

Henry chuckled. "It does, doesn't it?"

He turned to the dog. "Steve. Shake."

The dog lifted his right paw. Ella bent down to shake it. "Nice to meet you, Steve."

Steve responded by giving her a good lick on the cheek.

"Whoa! That was wet! You're a little sneak, aren't you?"

Steve's kiss surprised Ella, but she didn't mind his innocent canine forwardness. She gave him a good scratch behind the ears.

"I've been telling them about you. They're very happy to finally meet you," said Henry.

Ella laughed. "You guys are charming." While she said this to the dogs, she hoped that Henry would feel as included as he was in her comment.

"This is Anachim." The second dog, also large, was a stunning grey-and-brown shepherd mix.

"Anachim, like in Star Wars?"

"Oh, no. It means *lake* in Inuktitut."

"Oh. Sorry. Nice to meet you . . . *Lake* Skywalker." Ella grinned.

Henry laughed.

"Okay, that was bad. I'm such a dork. Sorry, Anachim."

Ella brought her hand in front of the dog, and he gave her his paw to shake. She shook it and gave him a petting.

"As you can see, he's more inhibited than Steve."

"That's alright. I'm good."

"And this little one is Paisley."

Paisley was a feisty little whitish-grey terrier, with hair as fluffy as cotton candy.

"Little in size, but big in personality. She loves to get picked up."

Sure enough, as Ella bent down to say hi to her, Paisley pushed herself upwards to help Ella pick her up. Ella got the message and indulged her. Paisley gave her a kiss under the chin and tried to kiss her again and again.

"My, she's an affectionate little one!"

Ella giggled as she moved her head up and down and left and right to avoid getting drenched. But the energetic ball of fluff was determined to show her how happy she was.

A young girl of about six years of age peeked her head in from the kitchen. Ella caught sight of her.

"And who might this be?" Ella asked with a wide smile, despite the fact she had secretly hoped to be alone with Henry today.

"That's my sister Anya," said Henry. "Who makes the very best cookies. Right, Anya?"

"We made cookies! Would you like some?" the girl asked Ella proudly.

"I'd love some," said Ella.

❄

Ella and Henry ate cookies and drank coffee at the kitchen table, with Steve and Anachim lying down at their feet and Paisley on Ella's lap.

They first had a clumsy talk about the weather, followed by some general tidbits about school, the cookie recipe, and then Henry mentioned Bobbie raving about Ella's killer latte, which gave Ella an opening to invite Henry to come taste one for himself. While the conversation was rather on the surface, neither of them cared, too happy to be together and take in one another's flirty body language. They could have been in a fancy restaurant with a candlelight dinner, their interaction couldn't have been any more enjoyable or intimate.

Little Anya hung out for a while, then got bored and disappeared to go play in her room. The moment she was out of earshot, Henry moved closer to Ella.

"Did you like the flowers?"

He seemed eager to broach the subject. Ella was elated to finally have that confirmation, that the roses had indeed come from him.

"Very much! Thank you! They really lifted my spirits when I needed that and—"

She stopped herself. *And what? I was so happy to think that perhaps, just perhaps, you were interested in me?* Instead, she sent the ball back into his court to avoid going out on a limb.

"Were these meant to be, like, as a coach to his athlete . . . or . . . ?"

Henry let out a shy laugh.

"They were meant as several things. From a coach . . . a friend . . ."

Not the "f" word, dammit!

" . . . Perhaps more than a friend, if you'd like?"

He said this in an inquisitive manner, searching for the hint of a clue in her reaction. Judging by the look on Ella's face, "more" was clearly the desired option.

This encouraged him to add, "But since I've already taught you all that—"

"You could teach me how to make cookies!"

Ella would be happy to learn anything if it meant spending more time with Henry, and she made it obvious to him.

"Or how to do an oil change on a car . . ." she added playfully.

"How to do an oil change on a car?" Henry was amused.

"Yeah. That's an old dream of mine."

"I bet it is."

"Seems utterly fascinating!"

"It is. Across the board. What else would you like to learn?"

"Um . . . everything?"

Henry chuckled. That was the best answer he could have hoped for.

"Everything. You're on."

The front door of the house burst open, and in came Henry's mom with grocery bags, followed by two rambunctious tween boys.

Henry stood up. "Gimme a minute. I better go give a hand."

Ella stood up, too. "I'll help."

Ella got to meet Henry's mom and have more of a blast unpacking groceries than she ever had unpacking groceries in her life.

"There's something I want to show you," Ella said to Henry after he killed the motor of the snowmobile. Henry's mom had invited Ella to stay for dinner. It was now early evening, and since it was dark outside, Henry had given Ella a ride home.

"Sure," Henry replied.

"Great. Follow me."

Ella's dad was not home yet, and the house was in the dark, both inside as well as the exterior. Ella led Henry around the house, to its bare backyard.

"What is it?"

Henry was intrigued. There seemed to be nothing to see in the darkened space. Ella was tempted to reply, "A quiet spot where the neighbors can't see." Instead, she led him up a snowbank, and a killer view of the illuminated city, down below, appeared before them.

"They say the best things in life are free," she said.

Like kissing . . .

As if to add the perfect touch to an already perfect moment, some colorful northern lights began dancing in the sky.

"Amazing!" Henry seemed to love what he was seeing.

"This is the view I have from my window. It never gets old."

"I'd say! I've watched these countless times in my life, but with the town's lights, here, it's just . . ."

"Breathtaking?"

"Breathtaking, yeah."

You know what else would be breathtaking?

It had been such an amazing day already, and Ella didn't want to push her luck. But giving it a little nudge . . . why not? Judging by their interactions, the way he had been looking at her, Ella thought the odds were in her favor.

"You really impressed me at the games," he said.

"With Sera? That was dumb luck, believe me."

"With Sera, yeah, but the way you were determined to compete in the games, no matter what, and you got so good at several things in such a short period of time. When you put your mind to something, Ella, nothing stops you. That's inspiring."

Inspiring?! Wow. Ella had not seen that one coming.

"Thanks. But it's funny you'd say that. I always thought that *you* were the inspiring one. I mean, all that patience you had with me, for starters. I was such a lost cause."

Henry chuckled. "We all feel like a lost cause, at times. But your potential was always there. Ella Briggs, you're a force of nature."

Henry leaned towards Ella to kiss her, just slowly enough to give her a chance to move away should she not feel the same as he did.

Instead, she pushed herself towards Henry to accelerate their kiss. They locked lips, and it was wonderful.

Ella cupped her hands around his face.

Henry put his arms around her.

Time stood still for a while.

And then, Ella felt a pressure against her leg. This was a little odd. It was accompanied by a panting noise . . .

"Ella . . . ?" Henry's tone suggested that he, too, was wondering what was going on.

They both looked down.

Frank was there. Happy to say hi and wanting merrily to be petted.

"Frank! You noodle head!"

Ugh! Way to break the magic!

But it was funny too, and Ella couldn't help but laugh.

Ella and Henry both crouched to pet Frank at the same time. And then, being so close to one another again, they couldn't help having another kiss . . .

That is, until Frank decided to join in.

"Okay! No! Frank! I love you, man, but I've had my share of slobber for the day!" Ella said.

"I wasn't slobbering that much," Henry couldn't help teasing.

"Not you, silly." Ella gave him another kiss. "You slobber in just the right amounts."

"Ewwww! Good to know."

A car pulled up in the driveway, its headlights throwing beams of light against the nearby snowbank. It was Dan, finally arriving home from work.

"And we're busted." Henry looked at Frank. "For a second time."

"At least, we're off to a good start."

"I couldn't agree more."

Henry grabbed Ella's hand, and they headed out of the backyard, with Frank trotting enthusiastically between them.

ROAD TO SOMEWHERE

At school, of course, and on the weekends, spending every bit of free time together. And when Henry was working at the arena, Ella would usually pop by—bringing him a latte in a travel mug during his break—and watch him teach skating and hockey to young players.

They also cooked together. Ella's new main hobby, besides perfecting her sewing techniques, became searching the web for new recipes to expand her repertoire beyond lattes and bannock and sharing them with Henry. With time, she gained skills and confidence and became a pretty good cook.

Ella and Henry's relationship developed into something serious. Ella had never felt this strongly towards anyone else she had dated before. This felt beyond dating, more like a truly deep connection, and she was savoring every moment. But it was at once incredible and heart-wrenching. She and her dad would be moving back to Montreal at the end of the summer, in time for the next school year, and now the thought of separating from Henry freaked her out to no end.

At first, she tried not to think about the moment they'd have to separate, with the impending move still a few months away. But still, the thought was always there, at the back of her mind. Until she received her acceptance letter from Dawson College, a bittersweet moment. On the one hand, Ella was relieved to have been accepted in Social Science, her program of choice, but the looming separation ahead suddenly felt more concrete, irreversible in fact. It seemed time itself was somehow accelerating, which, to Ella, was beyond awful.

As she was holding her acceptance letter in her hand, the doorbell rang. It was Bobbie and Henry, both all smiles. But when they saw how grim Ella looked, their great mood passed over to concern.

"You didn't get in?" Bobbie asked Ella.

"What do you mean?"

"Dawson," Henry replied.

Ella showed them the letter with a heavy heart.

"You *did* get in!" Bobbie and Henry replied at once, with enthusiasm.

Why are they so happy to see me leave?

To Ella's surprise, Bobbie and Henry both whipped out a sheet of paper each. They were letters like hers—they both had been accepted to Dawson as well!

"What?!" Ella couldn't believe her eyes. "Henry, aren't you going to Nunavut Arctic?!"

"Well, Bobbie's been yakking non-stop about her trip to Montreal. I figured I should see for myself what all the fuss is about . . . Oh, yeah, and the fact you're gonna be there doesn't hurt," Henry replied with a grin.

Ella smiled wide. She couldn't believe this wonderful turn of events.

"Bobbie, what happened to Toronto?" Ella asked.

"I did get in Toronto as well. But I think Montreal would be a better fit. I don't know why." Bobbie was beaming.

"Oh my God! Why didn't you guys tell me about this before?! I've been fretting so much over this! I . . ."

Tears of joy appeared in Ella's eyes.

"I didn't want to disappoint you if I didn't get in," Henry replied. "And I didn't want to get my hopes up either."

"Same," said Bobbie.

"Guys, I'm so happy!" Ella jumped into Henry's arms, kissed him and hugged him tightly. She then invited Bobbie to join them for a group hug.

After a moment, Henry said, "You know what's missing?"

He turned towards Inuuja's house. He whistled and called, "Frank! Boy! Come here!"

Henry winked at Ella, and she started laughing. Frank heard the invite and came bolting. He began to prance around the trio, and they all petted him.

Ella felt like a tremendous weight had been lifted from her shoulders. She couldn't believe this. Such wonderful news! Not only would she not have to say goodbye to Henry and Bobbie at the end of summer, but they could all keep seeing each other! Ella couldn't believe her good fortune.

The rest of the school year also turned out quite well for Ella. The fact that she no longer had to watch her back, as far as Sera was concerned, made all the difference in the world. Sera had returned to school a changed girl. Sure, she still had style and attitude, and a strong temperament, but she also made sure to let her fellow students know how grateful she was to Ella.

On top of her physical health, Sera had serious wounds to lick, about Henry being with Ella, and how she had treated Ella in the past. While she kept a polite distance from Ella to leave her be, she also made efforts to make her feel comfortable on the prom dance committee, on which both of them were.

On her end, Ella often wore the snow fox necklace Sera had given her, because she loved it, but also as a show of good faith.

The two girls managed to have the occasional respectful conversation and learned to work rather well together, putting past animosities behind them and uniting their strengths instead of tearing each other apart. By the end of the school year, they both felt very proud of the work they did on the committee and with each other. They had come a long way.

One thing that helped Sera heal and get over Henry was the arrival of a bright, funny and—of course—gorgeous Swede to their school. Sera and Tore instantly hit it off, and they turned out to be a great fit for each other.

The school year culminated with graduation, at which Bobbie was valedictorian and, of course, the much-anticipated prom, which turned out to be even better than what Ella had hoped for. The theme was "Northern Lights" and the night was "magically indescribable" as Ella put it on her Instagram account, underneath a selfie of herself with Henry, Bobbie, Justine, and Henry's friend Wallace—all having a blast.

Ella, Henry, and Bobbie all moved to Montreal in August. Henry and Bobbie rented a small apartment within walking distance of Ella's home.

Ella renewed her friendship with Sandy, and it felt like they were at once reconnecting and starting something new. They both had palpably changed when they were apart, but both were happy and relieved to see how compatible they still were with each other. Ella was also very glad that Henry, Bobbie, and Sandy hit it off, and Ryan was a nice addition to the group as well. Ella now saw him in a different light than when she had briefly seen him at Christmas the year before. She realized he had been a sweet crush, but the way she had felt towards him was nothing compared to the way Henry was making her feel. As she had suspected, Ryan was indeed a good guy—and a great boyfriend for Sandy—and Ella now considered him a friend, but nothing more.

All in all, it felt good to be a part of a small, solid group of friends who were there for one another.

The funniest thing happened when Sandy finally got to meet Henry. Ella and Henry were set to go on a double date at the movies with Sandy and Ryan. When Sandy showed up, and Ella pointed to Henry—who was buying them drinks and popcorn at the concession stand—Sandy could barely hold it together.

"No way! He's the guy from the website!"

"Huh?" Ella had no idea what Sandy was talking about.

"You know, the cute guy I showed you before you left for Iqaluit. On the web. I told you to look for him."

"What? Nooooo . . ."

This now rang a bell for Ella, but it would be way too bizarre a coincidence if that were the case.

During the previews, Sandy gave Ella one of her typical jabs and showed her the picture of the cute guy on her cell. Sure enough, it *was* Henry.

"That's him! Don't tell me that's not him!" whispered Sandy.

Ella studied the picture and was stunned. How could that be? What were the odds of that?

"No way . . ."

"Yes way! That has to be him."

Ella nodded. "Yeah . . . Wow."

She couldn't take her eyes off the picture. How funny was this?

It dawned on her that everything in the world had been feeling very right since the winter games, since she and Henry had gotten together. Was it fate?

Had this been fate all along?

Fate or coincidence, after so much chaos, right now—to Ella —life sure felt like it was the way it was meant to be.

A THOUSAND THANKS

To you, the reader, for picking up Igloo High and taking the time to read it. I hope you had as much fun reading this book as I had writing it. If you enjoyed Igloo High, please consider leaving a review on the site where you purchased the novel or on a site like Goodreads–I'd love to know what you think and it could help another reader like you find the book.

To Lynn and Marie Betts, Jennifer Shelby, Melissa Ruthman and Karine Dessureault for giving me their thoughts on an early version of Igloo High.

To Craig A. Schwartz for going above and beyond in his line edit.

To Michael Hodgson and Irene S. (Red Adept Editing) for combing through the final version to hunt down typos.

To my fellow writers who helped me shape the concept very early on and, more recently, gave me a hand with the blurb.

To Christopher Lockhart for bringing my writing to a whole new level.

To my husband for believing in me and pushing me to make the jump into novels, and to my parents, family and friends for all your love and support. You guys rock!

ABOUT THE AUTHOR

Jacinthe Dessureault writes paranormal mysteries and humorous fiction. She is also a big fan of lemon meringue pie and of the silly antics of Boonie and Jackson, her family's two adorable lop buns. She lives in Montreal, Canada with her husband and daughter.

Jacinthe is currently working on the Elenora Bello mysteries, a paranormal mystery series for adults. For updates on this new series (and rabbit pictures!), join her newsletter: www.jacinthedessureault.com/newsletter-signup/

facebook.com/jacinthewrites

instagram.com/jacinthedesert

bookbub.com/authors/jacinthe-dessureault

goodreads.com/jacinthedesert